THE
COVE

THE DEVIL'S COVE TRILOGY: BOOK ONE

Malcolm
Richards

BOOKS BY MALCOLM RICHARDS

The Devil's Cove Trilogy
The Cove
Desperation Point
The Devil's Gate

PI Blake Hollow
Circle Of Bones

The Emily Swanson Series
Wish Me Dead (Prequel)
Next To Disappear
Mind For Murder
Trail Of Poison
Watch You Sleep
Kill For Love

Standalone Novels
The Hiding House

For Xander

PROLOGUE

MARGARET TELFORD'S bones creaked as she closed the front door of her cottage and ambled to the garden gate. At her heels, a white West Highland Terrier named Alfie trotted excitedly, his slathering pink tongue lolling from the side of his mouth.

It was precisely six o'clock on a Saturday morning in early September. Children had returned to school the week before, bringing the holiday season to an abrupt end. Not that the town had seen an influx of tourists this summer, which was a good thing in Margaret's mind. But it wasn't a good thing for the town. No tourists meant no money. Now, most of the small businesses would be closing until spring with their pockets half empty.

No doubt about it—it would be a hard winter in more ways than one.

Reaching the gate, Margaret stooped to fix Alfie's leash to his harness. A bolt of arthritic pain shot up her left leg. She winced.

"We're certainly not getting any younger, are we, Alfie?" she said, rubbing her thigh. Alfie looked up with round, dark eyes and whined a little.

Porth an Jowl was a small cove tucked away between two

granite cliffs like a secret. Margaret had lived at the very top for most of her seventy-six years. Standing here, as she did every morning, she had a fine view of the cove. On a clear day like today, with blue skies and little cloud, she could see all the way to the ocean's horizon. As she began her journey downhill, she smiled to herself. No matter how many times she saw this view, it always managed to bewitch her.

Below, the town spread out in a half circle. Beyond it, lay a brushstroke of golden sand. The ocean was blue-green and flat. The sun, bouncing off its waves, made it shimmer and dazzle.

Teetering on the left cliff, the Mermaid Hotel, once resplendent and gleaming, was slowly crumbling into the ocean brick by brick. On the right cliff, Briar Wood was beginning to turn the colour of rust, contrasting with the old lighthouse that stood on the edge in desperate need of a fresh coat of paint.

The beach looked empty. This pleased Margaret. Having to make conversation with people these days felt like a chore. And now she was retired, chores were for other people.

As she and her companion reached the bottom of the hill, the view slipped away. The town was made up of a few wide streets with a square at its centre. Shops selling surfboards and wetsuits, and buckets and spades for building sandcastles, all had bright banners filling their windows declaring SUMMER SALE—70% OFF! LAST WEEK BEFORE CLOSING—BUY ONE GET ONE FREE!

Alfie came to a halt outside the post office and promptly urinated on the bright red post box.

"Oh, Alfie!" Margaret said, even though the dog made a point of marking his territory in the same places each morning. The post office hadn't opened yet, but Margaret knew that Mabel Stevens was somewhere inside, sorting out today's mail. She also knew that Mabel Stevens would turn as red as the post box if she knew what Alfie got up to each morning. The thought made her smile.

Once the dog had finished his business, Margaret gave a soft tug on the leash and they moved on. The only sounds were the soft thump of her feet on the pavement and the clack and click of Alfie's claws. It was like walking through a ghost town; just how Margaret liked it.

Reaching the beach didn't take long. She left the town square via a short alleyway and emerged on Cove Road, which circled Porth an Jowl like a noose, providing the only way in and out.

On the other side of the road lay the promenade, and the beach beyond. The taste of sea salt on Margaret's tongue grew stronger. She stopped at the edge of the road, eyeing the row of terraced cottages behind her. As much as she loved her home and the view that came with it, living at the top of the town was becoming increasingly punishing for her knees. At some point soon, these early morning walks would have to stop. And then what would she do?

Alfie was old but not old enough to be confined to the garden. And what about her own needs? These morning walks gave her purpose. Tugging on Alfie's leash, she made her way across Cove Road and stepped onto the promenade. One of those seafront cottages would suit her and Alfie nicely. He would still get his walks and she would still have purpose. But living right on the seafront would, for half of the year, place her dead centre of the town's tourist hotspot. She couldn't think of anything more hellish.

Alfie had begun to yap and strain against his leash. He gazed longingly at the sand below.

"All right, all right!" Margaret said, half laughing.

Gripping the railings, she took the stone steps one at a time. Together, they reached the beach and their feet sank into the soft sand. Margaret shielded her eyes and stared out across the beach. Low tide had been at three this morning. She could see the ocean in the distance. It would be a long walk, but the joy she would feel watching Alfie bounce through the surf would make it worthwhile.

With Alfie straining on his leash in front of her, she got going. Up ahead on the right, The Shack was dark and silent, its metal tables and chairs stacked up against the wall. Sometimes on summer nights, when the air was still, she could hear music blaring from the bar, all the way up to her bedroom window. That was another good thing about the season coming to an end; she might actually get some sleep at night.

Alfie was now choking himself, no longer able to restrain his excitement. Bending down on creaking knees, Margaret fumbled with the catch and took a moment to free him. Before she could stand up again, Alfie raced ahead like a bullet, yapping and bounding in the direction of the ocean.

Chuckling, Margaret followed him. That stupid dog never failed to amuse her. It took just thirty seconds for Alfie to become a dot on the horizon. Margaret squinted. It was only when she saw a flurry of wings burst up from the tide that she knew he had reached his destination.

Pausing for a moment to catch her breath, Margaret glanced back at the town, taking in the tiered rows of two-hundred-year-old cottages that climbed all the way to the top. She turned back to the beach. A large, rocky arch protruded from the lower half of the left cliff and planted itself in the water. Locals called it The Devil's Gate. There was a legend behind it; one she thought was utter nonsense.

She pushed on, heading towards the ocean tide. Now that she was closer, she could see Alfie happily bounding in between the waves and chasing after the gulls, who were already growing tired of his games. Margaret called out to him but was ignored. She quickened her pace and was rewarded with aches and pains.

Those damn seagulls were a nuisance. Of course, their abhorrent behaviour was thanks to the tourists. Each summer, hordes of them descended upon the beach with their ice cream cones and Cornish pasties and home-baked goods, and they would throw their scraps to the birds, ignoring the signs all over Porth an Jowl that blatantly commanded: Do Not Feed The Seagulls! And of course, the gulls grew bigger and more aggressive.

Then came the news reports of young children being attacked, ice cream cones snatched from their hands. But still the tourists fed the birds and laughed as the creatures swooped over their heads. At the end of each season, the tourists would go home. But the gulls remained, fat and growing more dangerous with each passing season.

She knew Alfie could handle himself, mostly. But there had been a story last summer about a small terrier who had been torn to pieces by a flock of gulls right in front of its owner.

Her legs aching, Margaret hurried towards the shore. Alfie was oblivious, splashing and barking, the sea birds flapping around his head. But then he froze. Forgetting the birds, he pointed his nose into the air and sniffed. Margaret came closer. Alfie suddenly turned and dashed through the flotsam, racing along the edge of the beach.

Margaret followed with her eyes. He had come to a halt and was barking loudly. Turning direction, she attempted to catch up with him. As she came closer, she finally saw the cause of his excitement.

There was something on the beach. Lying at the edge of the tide. Something that looked like an animal.

At first, she thought it was a seal, washed up on the shore. It wasn't unheard of to find seals splashing in the waters of Porth an Jowl. Upon occasion, even dolphins could be seen.

But as she drew nearer, as her ageing eyesight pulled into focus, she saw that it was no seal.

It was a body.

It lay face down on the beach, half in the water, as Alfie continued to bark and growl.

Margaret drew nearer, her skin slick and clammy beneath the early morning sun. The tide rushed back in, suddenly animating the body, making its arms and legs sway up and down like a marionette.

"Dear God," Margaret whispered.

It was a boy. He was naked except for a pair of torn shorts. Purple and yellow bruises covered his limbs and back. The tide drew away again and the boy grew still. Alfie's barking grew to an unbearable pitch.

Margaret tore her eyes away and stared into the water. Where had he come from? She could see no boats on the horizon. No ships. She stared up at the scorched exterior of the Mermaid Hotel towering above, then glanced across to the lighthouse on the opposite cliff. That particular coastal stretch had become infamous within the county due to its popularity as a suicide hotspot, earning itself the name Desperation Point.

As Margaret returned her gaze to the boy's battered body, a question forced its way into her mind.

Was this the Pengelly boy?

She glanced back at the town. It was at a time like this where owning a mobile phone would have been a good idea. Her eyes found their way back to the body, drawn to it against her will. She knew of the family, although she'd never paid much attention to the children. The missing boy's mother owned the flower shop, which had been owned by the Pengellys for generations. Until recently, her tear-streaked face had made frequent appearances on Margaret's television screen.

Was this the Pengelly boy lying at her feet, his face half covered by sand, the rest hidden by a wet mop of dark hair? It had to be. But Margaret was sure the boy whose face had been repeatedly shown on the news was younger.

A wave of nausea rushed over Margaret. Alfie continued to yap. Stooping down, she reattached the dog to his leash.

"Quiet," she said in a hoarse voice. But Alfie would not be quiet.

Margaret thought about what to do. The cove's police station had been closed since last year. Budget cuts—it was happening all over Cornwall, leaving whole areas under the care of stations several miles away. Fat lot of help that was on a day like today, Margaret thought. She would make her way back to the town. There was a phone booth next to the bakery. She would call the emergency services from there. It would take her at least ten minutes.

But the tide was already making its way back in. By the time the emergency services arrived, the boy would be halfway out to sea.

Margaret cursed under her breath. Stooping down once more, she reached out with trembling fingers and prodded the boy's shoulder, feeling the bones underneath. He was painfully thin, as if he hadn't eaten a scrap in the two months he'd been missing. She could not leave him to be swept away. The last thing she needed was the inhabitants of Porth an Jowl whispering behind her back.

Letting go of Alfie's leash, she gently turned the body over. The boy's head lolled on his neck, his mass of dark hair concealing his features. Being careful to avoid the bruises, Margaret grasped his arms. She began to pull, dragging him away from the tide.

There was no weight to his body. Alfie probably weighed more. What a terrible thing, she thought. She dragged him for several more metres, until her hands began to ache with arthritis and the boy's body had made long, winding tracks in the sand. Satisfied he would now be safe from the tide until the emergency services arrived, Margaret set him down.

She stared at her hands. They felt dirty. Wiping them against her skirt, she glanced at Alfie, who had ceased barking and now stood with his tail tucked between his legs. He nudged up against Margaret's calf and let out a low whimper.

She would have to explain to the police why she had moved him, but the family would be grateful that she had not let him float away. A thought passed through her mind: at least there would be a lovely floral arrangement at his funeral.

She stared down at the boy once more, who now lay on his side, those bruises reaching around his ribs and torso. The hair that had been covering his features had slipped away a little. The more Margaret stared at him, the more she grew uncertain that this was the Pengelly boy. And now, as she stared at the child's deathly pale face, a memory surfaced in her mind and she was overwhelmed by a nauseating sense of familiarity.

"But it can't be . . ." she gasped. Her elderly mind was playing tricks on her. Tightening her grip on Alfie's leash, Margaret turned away from the boy. Alfie wouldn't move.

"Come on now," she said.

The dog continued to whimper and stare at the boy. Margaret gave him a sharp tug and Alfie began to growl. She watched as the dog moved in closer and then, to her shock, licked the boy's arm.

"Stop that this instant!" Margaret hissed. She gave the leash another sharp tug but Alfie stood his ground. He licked the body again, his wet tongue cleaning sand from skin.

Margaret grabbed the leash with both hands and was about to forcibly remove Alfie's paws from the sand, when she felt someone staring at her. She turned, scanning the length of the beach. She was quite alone.

"Come on," she said, this time her words trembling with fear.

She glanced down at the body one last time. The hair across the face had parted slightly.

A dark eye stared up at her. It blinked once.

Then twice.

1
_____

CARRIE KILLIGREW LEANED against the counter, the muscles in her shoulders taut, and scanned the interior of Cove Crafts. She had spent the last hour rearranging the shelves of locally made ceramics and nautical knick-knacks to make them look more appealing. Then she had set about pinning 50% OFF EVERYTHING banners to every available surface, and in the store window.

The chances of making any kind of sale today were slim. Perhaps the last stragglers of the holiday season might drop by for a last-minute souvenir. She hoped so. Because business had been worse than slow this summer.

Little Noah Pengelly had seen to that. Not that it was his fault. Despite the lack of evidence of an abduction, and assurances from the police that Noah had more than likely wandered off, holidaying families had stayed away. And of course, once the media had learned that Porth an Jowl translated from Cornish into English as *Devil's Cove*, well, that was the summer trade shot in the head.

But it wasn't the worry of unpaid bills that was causing Carrie's fingers to tremble as she ran them through her mane of thick, dark hair. It was what was happening on the beach. She had heard the helicopter fly over early this morning. It had woken her up while Dylan had remained face down and snoring gently beside her. It had woken Melissa too, whom she'd sent back to bed with a kiss and a promise they'd watch Frozen together when she returned home from work that afternoon.

A helicopter flying over the cove meant one of two things: either the coastguard was out looking for someone lost at sea, or the air ambulance had been called out to rescue someone unreachable by the usual means.

At first, Carrie had thought it was the former. Then Mabel Stevens from the post office next door had come rushing into the shop to tell her there were police cordoning off part of the beach.

"Margaret Telford found a body," she'd said, her eyes almost bulging far enough to touch the lenses of her glasses. "They're saying it's that poor Pengelly boy."

Exactly who *they* were, Carrie didn't know; it was still early, even for the local gossips. But upon hearing the news, she had been filled with a creeping unease that had since taken hold of her and was refusing to let go.

It was now just after 8 a.m. The shop didn't open for another hour. Pushing herself off the counter, Carrie made her way past shelves of ships in bottles, lighthouse lanterns, porcelain mermaids, and other trinkets, and entered the small storeroom at the back. She filled the kettle and set about making herself her third coffee of the morning.

Mug in hand, she grabbed a canvas bag from the side, then pushed open the rear door and stepped into a small concrete yard surrounded by brick walls.

Pots of strange and exotic succulents lined the ground. Above her head, three wooden beams were covered in thick vines. Bright flowers protruded from hanging baskets.

Carrie made her way to a small picnic table and sat down. Fishing out a pack of cigarettes and a lighter from her bag, she sparked one up and inhaled deeply. As she blew out the smoke in a steady stream, her head filled with cotton. Some of the knots in her shoulders loosened.

It was a bad habit, she knew; and one that Dylan was under the impression she had quit long ago. She *had* quit the day she'd discovered she was pregnant with Melissa, but she had started up again recently. In secret. The same day Noah Pengelly had vanished.

It was just one cigarette a day, here at the shop. One cigarette to help soothe the tension that had been simmering beneath her skin. To distract her from those old, dreadful thoughts that had been resurfacing since Noah's disappearance.

There were police at the beach. Margaret had found a body.

Carrie stubbed out a cigarette and lit up another. So, it would be two cigarettes today. Big deal, she thought.

Taking a paperback from her bag, a crime thriller, she flipped to the bookmarked page and attempted to read. Usually, it took a minute or two for the words to push her dark thoughts aside. But now, they were having trouble getting through.

She put the book down. Sipped some coffee. Sucked on her cigarette.

She and Tess Pengelly had been friends since school. When Noah vanished, she had been there for Tess, visiting her every day she could, bringing home cooked meals, and her leftover prescriptions of sleeping pills and diazepam; anything to help her friend sleep at night. She knew all too well how torturous those sleepless nights could be. She knew all too well how loss tore you apart, inside and out. Which was why, when Noah had still not been found a month later, Carrie had stopped visiting Tess altogether. It felt all too familiar. And much too painful.

Picking up her book again, she forced the words into her mind. Little Noah Pengelly's face pushed them back out.

Was he dead, then? Washed up on the shore along with the flotsam. Poor boy, Carrie thought. *Poor, poor Tess.*

Memories that Carrie had been fighting to ignore lit up her mind like lightning. She was back there, on the beach, running through swathes of people and desperately calling out a name that she had since not uttered in seven years. She could still hear her mother's high-pitched shrieks, her father's usual strong and steady voice now scared and broken. She could still see the looks of confusion, the gradually dawning horror. She could still hear her own screams as hands pulled her back onto the sand, could feel the cough and gag of her lungs as they purged themselves of seawater.

Carrie snapped the book shut and stubbed out what was left of the cigarette. She stood up, swaying on her feet. Perhaps she should walk to the beach, to see what was happening. Perhaps she should call someone—Tess, maybe. No, not Tess; but someone. To find out exactly what Margaret Telford had found.

Or perhaps she should open the shop and worry about her own family's livelihood now they would be relying almost entirely on Dylan's fisherman salary over the winter.

She dumped her coffee cup in the storeroom sink, used the bathroom, then returned to the shop floor. Through the window, she could see Jack Dawkins, the proprietor of Porth an Jowl Wine Shop, who was talking conspiratorially with Mabel Stevens. Poor old Mabel couldn't seem to keep the news of Margaret's discovery to herself. Carrie watched them for a minute as they shook their heads and pointed in the direction of the beach.

Someone strolled past the window. She was too distracted to notice who. Perhaps she would call Dylan, see if he was up yet. To hear his gravelly, just-woken voice tell her everything was going to be all right. That he loved her.

She took a step towards the counter where her mobile phone lay, then froze. Something was happening outside. Mabel and Jack had fallen silent and were both staring across the square, their eyes moving in unison, following something, until they came to rest on the window of Cove Crafts.

An unpleasant, icy sensation slipped beneath Carrie's skin.

At the same time, two uniformed police officers, one male, one female, appeared from the left. They stopped outside the shop door. Carrie watched as the female officer knocked on the glass.

Her first thought was that something terrible had happened to her family. But she had only left them a couple of hours ago; Dylan sleeping, Melissa playing happily in her bedroom.

Now, the female officer was trying the door and finding it locked. The male officer stared at Carrie and mouthed something.

Slowly, Carrie moved to the door.

This had to be about the boy Margaret had found on the beach. It was poor little Noah. He was dead. But why were the police here and not up at the Pengellys' house?

Turning the key, she unlocked the door and opened it.

The male officer spoke first. "Carrie Killigrew?"

Carrie's voice was a whisper. "Yes."

"I'm PC Thomas. This is PC Matthews. May we come in?"

The police officers waited for Carrie to step aside. But she was rooted to the spot. Across the square, Mabel and Jack were watching with hawk-like attention.

"What's this about?" she said, her eyes on the elderly pair.

"Please," PC Matthews said, her voice soft and steady. "It would be better if we could come inside."

Something was wrong. She could feel it in the air, in her blood. This wasn't about the boy. This was about something else.

Carrie stepped aside and let the police officers in.

"Is there somewhere we could sit down?" PC Thomas asked, looking around.

Oh God. Carrie swallowed, suddenly thirsty. She nodded and led the officers through the shop and out to the yard. She indicated the picnic table, noticed the cigarettes sticking out of her bag and quickly pushed them inside.

The police officers stared at the picnic bench, before glancing at each other. They sat down on one side, awkwardly tucking their legs underneath the table. Carrie sat on the other side, staring from one police officer to the other, trying to read their expressions as she fought to control a wave of panic.

There was a moment of silence that seemed to last an hour. Carrie held her breath. She squeezed her fingers beneath her thighs.

"Mrs Killigrew, you may have heard by now about the incident on the beach earlier this morning," PC Thomas said.

Carrie nodded. Her thoughts turned to her friend, Tess, and guilt dragged at her insides.

"Please call me Carrie," she said. "And yes, news travels fast around here. I heard Margaret Telford found a boy. They're saying it's Noah Pengelly."

A look passed between the police officers, but Carrie could not read it.

PC Matthews spoke next. "Mrs Killigrew, we—"

"It's Carrie."

"Carrie . . . Mrs Telford did find a boy on the beach this morning."

"Oh God, poor Noah. Is he . . ." She couldn't say it. To say it would make it true. Noah was just four years old. The same age as her daughter, Melissa. They were in the same class together, just like their mothers had been thirty years ago. They played together. Sometimes Noah would come for a sleepover.

"Mrs—Carrie . . ." PC Matthews was struggling to find the right words. "The boy on the beach, he was . . . The boy who was found isn't Noah Pengelly."

Carrie's mind swayed with confusion. Her gaze swung between the police officers. "Then who was it?"

PC Thomas leaned forward. "Are you able to come with us?"

Carrie stared at him. "Why? What for? What's going on?"

PC Thomas flashed PC Matthews another strange look, who took in a deep breath and exhaled.

"Carrie, I'm not sure how to tell you this," she said. "But we believe the boy who was found on the beach this morning is your son, Callum."

It was as if an invisible fist had punched Carrie in the chest; she couldn't breathe. Her entire body flinched and began to tremble.

"What the hell are you talking about?" she whispered, when she managed to regain control of her airways.

"Your son, Callum," PC Thomas said. "We believe he is the boy who was found on the beach this morning. We'd like you to come with us to make a formal identification."

Any confusion Carrie felt was washed away with anger. Her jaw tensed. Her teeth mashed together, making it difficult to speak.

"You're mistaken," she said in a low voice.

A thick, heavy silence fell and it smothered the small yard. The walls seemed to close in, to grow taller. Inside Carrie's head, thoughts smashed into each other. Her stomach churned; she was going to be sick. PC Matthews leaned further forward until Carrie could feel her breath on her face. When she spoke, her voice was calm.

"Carrie, we have reason to believe this *is* your son, Callum Anderson. I know it must come as a shock, that it must be difficult to believe, but we would really like it if you could come and—"

Carrie leapt up from the table. Her skin was on fire.

"Why are you doing this?" she shrieked. "My son is dead. He's been gone for seven years. You've made a terrible mistake."

The police officers remained seated.

"Carrie," PC Matthews said calmly. "Seven years ago, your son was reported missing. There was an extensive search. No body was ever discovered."

"Jesus Christ, I know what happened!" Carrie spat. "I was there. We never found him because he drowned. He was washed out to sea. He's dead."

PC Matthews shook her head. "Carrie, the boy who was found on the beach this morning is very much alive. We're confident it's your son. Please. Let us take you to him so you can see for yourself."

She could feel tears spilling down her face. She could hear the thud of her heartbeat repeating in her ears. Without warning, a peal of laughter escaped her mouth.

"My boy is dead," Carrie said.

The yard slipped away. Time ceased to exist. Carrie's legs quaked beneath her. A hundred memories of her son flashed before her eyes.

She pressed a hand against the wall to steady herself. Slowly, she shook her head.

"My boy is dead," she whispered.

But a flicker of hope had ignited inside her stomach.

2

THE CORRIDOR WAS QUIET; the only sound the squeak of shoes on polished tiles. Carrie walked on unsteady legs. Officers Thomas and Matthews walked on either side, staying close.

They had driven her to the hospital in Truro, Cornwall's only city, just a few miles east from Porth an Jowl, where she had been made to wait for what seemed like forever in a small visitors' room, with her uniformed chaperones for company. Nobody could tell her any more than she already knew, only that she had to wait a little longer while the doctors performed tests. She'd sat at the table, staring at its surface, trying to quash the hope that was now burning in her chest. Then she'd started pacing from one end of the room to the other in quick bursts, feeling like a caged animal.

Maybe an hour had passed. Perhaps two. Now, as she walked the corridor, Carrie felt as if she had fallen into a dream. Nothing seemed real. Sounds were distant. It was as if she were seeing through someone else's eyes without permission.

They had made a mistake. That was all. A terrible, outrageous mistake. Her son was dead. He'd drowned. He couldn't just reappear after seven years.

I shouldn't be here, she thought, as the corridor stretched out before her. She had a business to run. She had a promise to keep to her daughter.

She needed to call Dylan, to tell him there had been a terrible mistake and that he needed to come get her. Sooner rather than later, please. In fact, drop everything and come right now.

Because she didn't like how she was feeling.

All those old wounds that had never healed but she'd sort of stitched back together and dressed—they were all opening again and bleeding. She was drowning, just like her son had.

Callum. Cal. Her precious boy.

"A mistake," Carrie whispered, making both officers turn and look at her. She stared straight ahead. The corridor was turning a corner. The three turned with it.

The light seemed to grow brighter, hurting Carrie's eyes. They were turning again. Through double doors. Into a ward, past a reception desk, where the duty nurse looked up with curious eyes. Now, they were heading left, along a short corridor with individual rooms on one side.

Outside the last room, three people sat on plastic chairs. Another uniformed police officer, a woman in civilian clothing not much older than Carrie, and a light-haired man in his early forties who was dressed in a charcoal suit. All three stood as Carrie approached.

"Hello Carrie, I'm Detective Constable Turner," the man in the suit said. He nodded to the woman next to him. "This is Leanne Moss, a social worker."

Leanne offered a polite nod. Carrie said nothing; her eyes had found the open door of the room behind and she could see the foot of a bed inside.

Someone was in there. Moving around.

"I'm aware this must come as a shock to you," Detective Turner was saying. He had kind eyes and a genuine smile. "But the woman who called in . . ."

"Margaret Telford," PC Matthews said.

"Right, Margaret Telford. She recognised the boy as your son, Callum. A little older, of course. Since then, we've run a DNA test against samples that were collected at the time of your son's disappearance and stored on our database. The samples match. Now, we'd like you to make a visual identification."

He nodded at the officers Thomas and Matthews, who quickly departed. The other uniformed officer remained.

Carrie returned her focus to the open door.

"My son is dead," she said.

Detective Turner glanced at the social worker, whose name Carrie had already forgotten. Someone was coming out of the room.

A doctor. She had a serious face, with high cheekbones, dark skin, and eyes that were furtive and analytical. She observed Carrie for a second before leaning into the detective and muttering inaudible words. The social worker offered Carrie a sympathetic smile. Detective Turner reached out and placed a hand on Carrie's arm. She flinched.

"They're ready for you now," he said.

The entrance to the room opened like a wide mouth. Carrie stared at it. What was she supposed to do? Her son was dead. She didn't need to go in there to know that. Detective Turner gave her an encouraging nod.

"There has to be a mistake," she said. "This is not my son."

The nausea in her stomach grew worse. Her head began to float away from her body.

Detective Turner stared at the other professionals. He cleared his throat. "If you'd like to go in . . ."

He stood to one side, opening the space between Carrie and the door.

The lights above their heads seemed to burn brighter. The floor became jelly. Carrie opened her mouth and then closed it again. She felt a hand, calming and encouraging on the back of her shoulder. It was the social worker.

"It's all right," she said, her voice maternal and kind. "He's asleep right now. All you need to do is take a peek."

"He was quite distressed earlier," the doctor added, glancing at Carrie. "He's been given a mild sedative."

Carrie stared at the space between her and the open door. Her heart hammered in her chest. Her breaths flew in and out of her lungs.

This wasn't happening. It *couldn't* be happening.

She moved forward, one foot unsteadily in front of the other. She reached the doorway and closed her eyes. Behind her, the social worker squeezed her shoulder.

"It's okay. We're right behind you."

Opening her eyes, Carrie willed herself to step into the room. The others waited in the corridor as she folded into the shadows. A curtain was pulled halfway around the bed. Beside it, a machine attached to an intravenous pole blinked with colourful lights. A bag of clear liquid dangled above. Tubing led from the bag to the bed. The end of the tube was attached to a needle. The needle was inserted into the back of a hand. A hand that was much larger than the one she had held countless times before. She examined the fingers. They looked worn; not the hands of a teenager but those of a weather-beaten fisherman. The nails were surprisingly neat and freshly clipped.

Holding her breath, Carrie moved her gaze from the hand and along the sinewy arm. Panic gripped her body. She looked away again and squeezed her eyes shut.

Behind her, the social worker whispered encouraging words. Carrie's gaze returned to the bed. The boy was asleep. Beneath the cuts and bruises he almost looked peaceful. He was thin. Too thin. Cheekbones jutted from his skin like shards of glass. A mass of straggly dark hair fell across his brow and the pillow. Wide full lips were pressed together. She recognised them instantly. They were his father's lips; a man she had not seen in seven years.

The boy in the bed turned his head slightly. If Carrie had had any uncertainty, it was immediately blown away. Below his left eye, just adjacent to his temple, was a perfectly round mole.

"Your beauty spot," she whispered, the voice coming from a memory she thought she'd forgotten.

It was him.

He was painfully underweight. Bruised. Battered. Older. It was impossible. But it was him.

The ocean had swallowed him for seven years. Now, it had spat him back out. He was changed. Damaged. But he was her son. Callum Mark Anderson. No longer nine years old but still her Cal.

She nodded. Tears found their way to her eyes. And then it was as if her body had been taken by the ocean, too. Everything was swept away. And she was drowning in joy and confusion and grief.

"My boy," she managed to say. She fell to her knees.

3

THE VISITORS ROOM was small and simple, furnished with a table and chairs, and a sofa. Carrie sat at the table, nursing a polystyrene cup of cooling coffee she had no intention of drinking. Detective Turner sat at the opposite end while Doctor Singh filled Carrie in on her son's condition.

"As you may know, Callum was brought in early this morning," she said in a voice that was serious but not uncaring. "He's dehydrated and somewhat malnourished. We currently have him on fluids via intravenous. We've taken blood and urine samples, and we've run X-rays." The doctor paused, shooting a glance at the detective, which did not go unnoticed by Carrie. "While there are no signs of recent bone injuries, there are signs of old ones. Possible fractures in both arms and a break in his left ankle. Did Callum sustain any of these injuries prior to his disappearance?"

Carrie tried to think back. Her mind was full of fog, impenetrable. She shook her head. Her son was alive. He had not drowned.

"I'm not sure."

Doctor Singh raised an eyebrow.

"I mean, no. He's never had an accident in his life. Nothing to bring him to hospital." Carrie glanced at the doctor, then at the detective.

Doctor Singh went on. "Callum's chest was clear, his lungs empty of water, which suggests he had not been in the sea for long and more than likely lost consciousness on the beach."

"Where did he come from?" Carrie's voice sounded far away, like an echo from a dream. None of this seemed real. How could she be talking about her son as if he were alive? She'd spent the last seven years burying him, over and over again. Convincing herself every morning that she would not walk into his room and find him asleep in his bed.

"I can't tell you that," Doctor Singh said. "Callum hasn't spoken a word since he arrived this morning."

"Surely he must have said something."

"We've booked him in for a CT scan in the morning to check for possible brain injury. If that's clear, then it's possible his silence is an indication of post-traumatic stress. So, we'll need to do a psychiatric assessment."

"Psychiatric assessment?" Carrie's gaze shifted between the doctor and the detective once more. She wanted nothing more than to be with her son. To close the seven-year gap that lay between them like an endless chasm. "What happened to him?"

"I'm afraid I don't have the answer to that. But try not to worry. These tests are standard procedure." The doctor stood. "Callum is stable for now. Once he's awake, we'll be able to find out more. I'll come by later."

She nodded briefly and excused herself from the room, leaving Carrie alone with the detective.

Carrie shook her head. She was asleep. That was it. Having one of those dreams in which Cal was alive. Any moment now she would be woken by a gut punch of grief.

But she felt awake. Wide awake. Her son was alive.

Detective Turner leaned forward. "Crime scene investigators are down at the beach right now. They may not find much, but—"

"Crime scene?" The words caught in her throat, like she'd swallowed a dry pill without water. Of course, a crime scene, she thought. *Did you really think he's been floating around the sea for the last seven years?*

The detective was saying something. She watched his lips move up and down. It took her a second to tune into his voice.

" . . . his health is a priority, of course. We don't want to put him under any undue pressure . . ."

"Someone took him," she whispered.

" . . . and the fact the X-rays revealed old fractures and you say he never sustained any injuries before he vanished. And of course, the fact he's been gone for seven years . . ."

"Someone took my boy." An icy finger of dread woke her from her dream state.

"We don't know what happened yet. And until Callum can tell us, we have to keep an open mind."

Carrie caught her breath. She felt the muscles tighten in her shoulders. When she spoke next, her voice was a trembling whisper. "Was he . . . Did they . . ."

Detective Turner shook his head and offered her a reassuring smile. "Callum has undergone a thorough examination at the SARC. There was no evidence of sexual assault. The hospital's taken blood and urine samples. We'll test for any substances in his body. Toxicology can take a while but we'll have the results soon. Because Callum was in the water, any DNA evidence would have been washed off, but we've taken nail clippings and of course, when Callum is up to it, we'll be able to take a statement."

Carrie sat back in her chair. Someone had taken her son. They had managed to keep him hidden all this time. It seemed impossible. A sliver of doubt inserted itself into her mind.

"What if we're wrong?" she whispered. "What if it isn't Cal lying in there?"

She knew it was him. It had to be. But how could he have reappeared after all this time?

"There's something we can do to ease your mind," Detective Turner said. From a briefcase, he produced a pair of latex gloves and a small plastic kit. "We have the DNA match from the database but I can take a sample from you, one that will prove the boy asleep in that hospital bed is your son."

Turner gave a polite smile. Slipping on the latex gloves, the detective produced something that looked like a cotton bud and asked Carrie to open her mouth. She watched the detective as she felt the swab roll against the inside of her cheek. Then it was gone, placed inside an evidence bag, which the detective now sealed.

Once he had packed and labelled the swab, Detective Turner sat down again. "I'd like you to tell me about the day Callum disappeared."

Carrie frowned. She didn't want to talk about that. She wanted to return to the ward, to be there when her son woke up.

"It might help to talk about it, to jog your memory."

"My memory doesn't need jogging," Carrie said, her jaw tightening. "I've relived that afternoon, over and over. Every day. Ever since he disappeared." She looked away, stared at her coffee. "Can't you just take a look at the old file?"

Detective Turner rubbed his stubbled jaw. He eyed Carrie's coffee enviously. She slid it towards him and watched as his face flushed with embarrassment.

"I'll be going over it," he said, taking the cup. "But I'd like to hear from you."

Carrie watched him through narrowed eyes. She had told the story many times. Relived it every night when she went to sleep and every morning when she woke.

"Sometimes you can stare at the same photo, over and over," Detective Turner said. "Then suddenly you see something you've never noticed before."

Carrie glanced at the door, wondering if Cal would wake soon, if he would remember her when he did.

"It was a Saturday," she said, avoiding the detective's gaze. "The fifth of August. Two weeks into the school holidays. It was a scorching hot day; blue sky, calm seas. The town was overrun with tourists. Cal always loved it when they came. He was excited to see the town so alive. You're not from around here, are you?"

Detective Turner shook his head. "I grew up in London. Got transferred down this way a few years ago."

Carrie was surprised. She had already guessed he was no native, but she struggled to hear a London accent.

"Well, I guess Porth an Jowl is no different from any other tourist town. For the locals, summer is hell, but it makes you a living and keeps you in food and clothes when winter comes. And winter is the real hell. Cold winds. Constant rain. Most of the town shuts down for six months. No wonder Cal loved the summertime."

For a second, she was lost in thought, memories of Callum as a child overwhelming her. It was hard to imagine him lying just a hundred metres away in a hospital bed, seven years lost. One minute, nine years old, the next, sixteen. What had he looked like in between? How had his face changed? His body grown? In a few years, he would not be a child at all but a young man. Those seven years were lost. She would never see him grow from a child into a teenager.

But she could live with that. She had thought she would never see him alive again.

"Cal's father, Kye, we had already separated. We were both seventeen when I found out I was pregnant, eighteen when I had Cal. Neither of us were ready to be parents. We were children having children. We finished things when Cal was two, but we remained friendly. Then Kye went off to work on the oil rigs. He'd send money for Cal every month without fail. And whenever he came back, he'd take him to his grandparents for the weekend. But it wasn't the same; Cal missed his dad."

She hesitated for a second, smothered by memories.

"Kye had sent some extra money so Cal could buy a body board. He'd been wanting to learn to surf. That afternoon, we went down to the beach. It was busy. Hundreds of people with their kids and dogs filling the sand. We found a spot further out near Devil's Gate, that rocky outcrop on the left before the beach turns the corner. Cal wanted to get right out on the water. But the tide was on its way in and the currents can get a little tricky around there. I told him to wait. He wouldn't have it. So, I said he could have five minutes. I'd watch him." She paused again, aware that her voice was trembling. "I should have gone in with him."

Across the table, Detective Turner stared at her with soft, brown eyes. He did not judge, merely listened.

"I looked away, just for a minute." She hung her head. Tears streamed down her face. "One minute, that's all. He was there. Then he wasn't. I panicked. I got up. Ran to the shore. I searched the water, the beach. There were so many people but he wasn't among them. And then I saw his body board floating out on the water . . . After that, it's just images. And screams. My screams."

Carrie gazed across the room, her face that of a condemned woman. "There was a search. The police, the coastguard, local people. They all blamed me. The bad mum not looking out for her child. That's what everyone thought. So did Kye. My parents . . . But blame didn't bring my boy back. Eventually, people stopped looking. Kye stopped calling. Mum and Dad left town. But I stayed. I couldn't leave. How could I?"

"Mrs Killigrew—"

"Carrie."

"Is there anything else you remember from that day? Before you went to the beach or during your time there. Anything that seemed strange. Anyone acting out of the ordinary?"

Carrie thought about it for a long time. She shook her head.

"Are you still in contact with Callum's father?"

"Not for years. I couldn't even tell you where he is."

"What about your parents? Where are they now?"

"Last time I heard from them, they were halfway across the world. They like to travel. I call it running away."

"Do you have a way of contacting them?"

"A mobile number. I haven't used it in a while."

"Perhaps now might be a good time."

"They can wait." Carrie leaned forward, her eyes glowering. "Detective, someone took my son away from me. They let me think he was dead all this time. They let me blame myself. You need to find him. You need to find who did this to my boy."

Detective Turner nodded. "We'll do everything in our power to find out what happened."

A thought struck Carrie, making her feel suddenly uneasy.

"What about Noah Pengelly?" she said.

The detective opened his mouth and closed it again. "I believe his mother has already visited the hospital. An officer will speak to the family and let them know it isn't Noah who's been found."

"They'll tell her it's Cal?"

"Not yet. We won't be telling anyone that for now."

"You think there could be a connection?"

"Your son's appearance will be treated as a separate case," Detective Turner said. "But a team will be set up to compare cases and look for any connections."

Carrie nodded as she felt a sudden selfishness embrace her. She was sorry for Noah. For Tess. But her boy was alive. She didn't yet know what he'd been through or how much he'd suffered, but she knew she wasn't going to let anyone hurt him again.

If they tried, she would kill them.

"So, what's next?" Carrie asked.

Detective Turner stared at her. "We wait for Cal to wake up."

4

DARKNESS HAD FALLEN over Porth an Jowl. The sky was clear, revealing a glittering blanket of stars and a waning moon. An unsettling hush crept through the streets and into people's homes. The beach, however, was a hive of activity. The crime scene investigators in their white suits crawled over the beach like astronauts exploring a Martian landscape. Police tape cordoned off a large area and a handful of uniformed officers stood with their arms folded across their chests as they kept guard.

Over on the far right, The Shack was dark and silent, closed for business while the CSI team worked.

"They won't find anything. The tide's already been in and out." Seventeen-year-old Jago Pengelly sat on the promenade railings, dressed in baggy jeans and a black hooded top, with his feet tucked under the lower bar, and a mop of black hair falling across his eyes.

Beside him, three months his junior and with a skateboard balanced on her knees, Nat Tremaine rubbed the back of her freshly shaved head. "They always find something on those stupid TV shows."

She sucked on a hand rolled cigarette and blew the smoke

through her nostrils in a steady stream. She passed the cigarette to Jago, who flicked off the ash and brought it to his lips.

There were other people watching from the safety of the promenade; late night dog walkers, inquisitive neighbours who lived on the seafront and had come out of their houses for a better view. A news van was parked on the roadside and a gaggle of journalists milled up and down, interviewing residents and eyeing the beach.

Jago watched them with contempt.

"Vultures," he growled, his face lost in a fog of smoke.

Nat followed his gaze towards the journalists. "I'm surprised they haven't made it to your house yet."

"Yeah, well good luck getting my mum to talk. She's been out of it ever since the police came by."

"Valium?"

"And the rest." He spat the words out as if they were poison. His mother was barely present these days, instead sleeping her life away in a drug-induced haze. He knew why. She was starting to give up. She was starting to believe that Noah was dead.

Jago passed the cigarette back to Nat. She took one last drag, pinched it between thumb and forefinger, and flicked it off into the distance.

On the beach, the CSI team was finishing up and gathering equipment. Jago and Nat watched as they crossed the police line and headed back towards the promenade.

"Maybe you should go talk to them," Nat said. She took out her pouch of tobacco and a cigarette paper and began rolling another cigarette. "They might be able to tell you something."

Jago watched as a couple of journalists and a cameraman broke free from the gaggle and raced towards the CSI team, who were now climbing into their van.

He shook his head in disgust.

"No one's going to tell me shit."

"But you're Noah's brother. His family. So, it's not him up at the hospital, but whoever it is, maybe they've been with him. Maybe they'll know where to find him."

Jago returned his gaze to the police officers still guarding the crime scene perimeter. "Probably just a coincidence."

"Come on, you don't believe that. Noah disappears and two months later some other kid washes up on the beach and no one knows who he is . . ." The cigarette rolled and sealed, Nat passed it to Jago. She stared off into the distance for a second before her eyes lit up with an idea. "Hey, remember that kid who went missing down in Zennor last year? Maybe this is him."

Jago fumbled in his pocket for a lighter. "That kid probably fell off a cliff. Stupid parents too busy taking holiday snaps to notice him gone."

They were both quiet, watching as the CSI van growled to life, pulled onto the road, and drove away.

"Show's over," Jago said.

The inhabitants of Porth an Jowl began returning to their homes, the frustration on their faces illuminated by the streetlights.

Most of the journalists were also turning around and returning to their vehicles.

"Who do *you* think it is?" Nat said.

"How would I know?" Jago took another drag on the cigarette then passed it to Nat. "I bet Margaret Telford knows. She was the one who found him. I should go around there. Talk to her."

"She won't be allowed to tell you anything."

They were quiet again. Jago closed his eyes. His head filled with images of his little brother. One minute, Noah had been playing in the garden. The next, he was gone. As if a tear had opened in the fabric of the universe and he had stepped through it, never to be seen again. The police had found no evidence of abduction. They believed he'd wandered off into the wood behind the house while his mother had run his evening bath upstairs. There were several abandoned mine shafts in the area. If he had wandered westward through the trees he would have come to the lighthouse at Desperation Point, and a sharp drop into the ocean.

There were many hazards for a little boy wandering alone in the wilderness. Jago refused to believe his little brother had succumbed to any of them.

Nat was staring at him. He caught her gaze and held it.

"What?"

"You should come back to college," she said. "It's not the same without you. Everyone's so dull, it's dragging me down."

Jumping from the railings, Jago stretched out his spine, then began crossing Cove Road. He wasn't in the mood for college talk. What was the point? The only thing he was in the mood for right now was getting drunk.

Behind him, Nat dropped her skateboard to the ground, hopped on with her right foot, and pushed off the ground with her left. Scooting ahead of Jago, she turned ninety degrees and brought the skateboard to a halt.

"Come on, dickhead. Are you really going to leave me riding the bus to Truro and back every day with those troglodytes? What about university? What about getting out of this shit hole of a town?"

"What about leaving me alone?" Jago said, the words firing from his mouth. Guilt pinched his lungs as he saw Nat flinch.

"I'm only saying because I care," she mumbled.

Jago looked away. It wasn't as if he hadn't thought about returning to college. He thought about it all the time. Everyone had started back last week without him. He'd missed his end of year exams back in July thanks to Noah's disappearance. The college dean had attempted to call twice this week already.

How could he even begin to think about leaving Devil's Cove when he was failing? How could he think about leaving even if he was top of the class?

He froze. Up ahead, the face of his little brother smiled at him. Jago stepped forward to examine the missing persons notice taped to the street light. Sea salt had eroded the paper. Noah's image, a picture of him beaming with joy as he clutched his new blue teddy bear, was fading away.

Jago looked back at Nat, who was now staring at the ground, an angry scowl pulled down over her features.

"You know, you're more fun when you're being morose," he said, shrugging off his backpack. He pulled on the zip and delved inside to remove a fresh poster and some tape. "All this emotional *feelings* crap is creeping me out."

Carefully removing the old poster, he set about attaching the new one. Nat came up beside him.

"Yeah, well you're more fun when you're not being a total ass." A hint of a smile rippled across her lips. But only for a second. She pointed her head in the direction of the promenade.

Someone was crossing the road and heading straight for them. The man was in his late thirties, good-looking in an unconventional kind of way, but he had a hunger in his eyes that made him look predatory. Like a shark.

Even in the dim street light, Jago recognised him immediately. Anger rose from his stomach.

"It's Jago, isn't it?" the man said, as he approached. "I don't know if you remember me? Scott Triggs. I write for The Cornish Chronicle."

Jago regarded him through narrowed eyes. "I remember you."

Scott smiled and unfolded his arms, adopting a casual stance. "So, what do you kids make of all this? The police haven't released a statement yet but I'm guessing if you're here, that isn't your brother up at the hospital."

Jago's hands slowly curled into fists.

"Do you think I could get a quick interview? Just your thoughts and feelings about this new turn of events," Triggs said. He pulled a mobile phone from his pocket and activated the voice recorder app as he nodded at the newly pinned poster. "It won't take long. I can get the story in tomorrow's paper. It might spark interest in Noah's

story again. Jog memories. Maybe someone will remember something and come forward."

Nat stepped down on the edge of her skateboard and flipped it
up into her hands. She tugged Jago's arm.

"Come on," she said. Before you say something you regret."

The journalist activated the voice recorder and held it up. "It
must have been devastating to learn the boy they found this
morning wasn't Noah. Were you visited by the police?"

Jago stared at the voice recorder then at the journalist, his eyes
slowly narrowing.

"Were they able to shed any light on the identity of the boy on
the beach?" Scott Triggs waited for an answer. When it didn't come,
he frowned. "Who do you think the boy could be? Do you think
there's a link between your missing brother and the appearance of
this mystery boy?"

Nat tugged harder on Jago's arm. He resisted, shrugging her off.

"Jago… This isn't a good idea."

But Jago wasn't listening to her. He took a step towards the
journalist. "The last time we spoke to you, you promised your story
would help. That it might spur someone to come forward," he said.
"Instead, you made my family look like a bunch of inbreds. You
insinuated it was our fault that Noah disappeared. Why would I
speak to you again? Why am I even wasting my breath on you right
now?"

He leaned in closer, his teeth mashing together.

Scott Triggs took a step back. "Hey, I only write the stories. I
can't stop my editor from barging in and changing my words."

Nat pulled on Jago's arm again. "Come on, dickhead. I don't
fancy having my face in the papers."

Jago took another step forward. "You had no intention of
helping my family when my brother disappeared. You have no
intention of helping us now," he said. "So why don't you fuck off?"

He locked eyes with the journalist for a second more, before
turning away. Jago stalked out of the car park.

Nat turned to follow. She paused, staring at Scott Triggs. "Here's a quote for you," she said, then lifted her middle finger. Dropping her skateboard to the ground, she hopped aboard and took off.

Jago had made it through the town square and was now marching up the hill. Fire burned in his veins. He had wanted to plant a fist right in the centre of that journalist's face. He had wanted to keep hitting until his face was nothing more than bloody pulp.

Behind him, Nat was catching up fast. He quickened his pace. He was going to go home. He was going to get drunk until Noah's beautiful eyes faded into an alcoholic haze. And Nat wasn't invited.

He sped up, ignoring her pleas to slow down. He would drink until there was only darkness. He would drink until even he had ceased to exist.

5

EARLY SUNDAY MORNING sunlight seeped through cracks in the blinds, waking Carrie. She didn't know when she'd fallen asleep or for how long, but now her muscles complained at the discomfort of sleeping in a chair. It took her a moment to remember where she was and why she was there. A burst of adrenaline raced through her body, waking her immediately. She sat up and glanced at the hospital bed.

It wasn't a dream. Her son was alive. And he was awake.

His eyes were half open, blinking as they gazed at the ceiling. Then, very slowly, he turned his head.

Carrie's body trembled.

She tried to speak but her words got stuck. Tears filled her eyes, threatening to spill down her face, to flood the room and drown them both. She fought them back. There would be time for tears, but right now she needed her son to recognise her. To understand that she was his mother.

Dropping her feet to the floor, she leaned forward.

Cal watched her, his face blank. His eyes devoid of emotion. A sliver of ice slipped under Carrie's clothes. It was like staring into a black hole. Into nothingness. There was no recognition there. No familiarity. For a second, despite the DNA test results, despite the mole beneath his left eye, she wondered if this really was her son.

He looked like him. An older version of him. But he was staring at her as if she were a stranger. Carrie turned away to glance through the open door. Unaware that Cal was now awake, the police officer remained sitting outside, staring off into space.

Turning back to Cal, Carrie attempted to relax the muscles in her face, to push the fear away.

"Cal?" she whispered. "It's okay. You're safe. You're in hospital."

The boy in the bed continued to stare at her with blank eyes.

Doubt filled Carrie's veins. She swallowed, her throat suddenly dry. "It's me. It's your mum. Don't you recognise me?"

The boy blinked. Something passed across his face. Not recognition but something else. A darkness.

Carrie's heart threatened to burst out of her chest. "Cal? Is it really you?"

Nothing. Not even the blankness this time. Perhaps they were wrong. The test results had been somehow mixed up.

The boy returned his gaze to the ceiling. Beside the bed, the machine beeped and a light flickered. Some of the sugary liquid from the IV bag was released and began making its way to his body.

Carefully, Carrie got to her feet. She took a step forward.

"It's me. Your mother. Don't you remember?"

Cal's head turned sharply. This time there was something in his eyes. He watched her as she stepped closer. He was so small for a sixteen-year-old. Not just underweight but physically small. As if his growth had somehow been stunted.

Carrie took another step closer. Who had snatched her son away from her? What had they done to him? Waves of horror and sadness and anger rose from the pit of her stomach.

"Cal . . ." Tears came. "Cal . . ."

She rushed towards him, arms outstretched, wanting nothing more than to sweep her son into her arms and take away his pain.

Cal's eyes grew wide and black. His arms flew up to his face then down to his sides. He scrambled back, taking the IV pole with him, ripping the cannula needle from his skin and splattering blood on the sheets. Before Carrie could stop him, he flew from the bed and hurled himself into the corner of the room. He crouched down, splaying his hands against the wall, baring his teeth like a wild animal. The machine beside the bed began to emit a series of loud beeps. Carrie was paralysed, watching in horror.

"It's okay," she breathed. This was not her son. This was a wild animal, backed into a corner, ready to defend itself if necessary.

"Cal, it's me."

The sound of hurried footsteps reached her ears. A second later, the uniformed officer entered the room with two nurses.

"I didn't mean to—" Carrie began as the nurses brushed past her. They stopped at the foot of the bed and stared uncertainly at each other. In the corner, Cal's eyes shot from one person to the other. His chest heaved up and down. His hands pressed tightly against the wall. He was still bleeding. The police officer took Carrie by the arm. She shrugged him off.

"It's all right." One of the nurses, a middle-aged woman with a kind face and a steely calm borne from years of experience, smiled at Cal. "No one is going to hurt you. We just want to make sure you're safe."

She shot a glance at Carrie. "I think it's best you wait outside."

Wiping tears from her face, Carrie glanced at her son; the wild animal pinned in the corner. Numbly, she nodded and allowed the police officer to escort her from the room. Once outside, she peered through the window and watched as the nurses slowly coaxed Cal back onto the bed.

Within minutes they had him tucked up again. He was even allowing one of them to attend the bloodied wound where the cannula had been torn out.

Behind Carrie, the police officer talked into his radio, passing on the message that the boy was awake. More footsteps echoed along the corridor. Doctor Singh veered around the corner. She stopped outside the room and peered through the glass.

"I see our young adventurer is awake."

Carrie wrapped her arms around her chest.

In the room, Cal was calmer now. One of the nurses bandaged his hand while the other shifted the machine around to the other side of the bed.

Carrie could see the fear on Cal's face as the needle came closer. She wanted to go to him. To stroke his forehead like she used to when he was upset. Back when he knew her as his mother.

A sob escaped her.

"He doesn't know who I am," she said.

Doctor Singh regarded her through analytical eyes. "Did he speak to you?"

Carrie shook her head.

"Let's see what the CT scan shows before we go making any presumptions." Doctor Singh offered her a sympathetic smile. "It's early days, Carrie. Very early days."

Wiping a tear away, Carrie nodded. But now she couldn't shake the feeling that a terrible mistake had been made. How could her own son not recognise her?

They watched through the glass as the nurses finished up. Cal was lying back once more. He was alert, watching their every move, but he was calmer. For now.

The doctor turned to Carrie. "By the way, your husband and daughter are waiting for you. They're in one of the visitors' rooms. Your husband seems quite curious about what's going on."

Carrie felt a sudden flutter of panic in her chest. She had spoken to Dylan briefly yesterday afternoon. It had been difficult to explain to him what had happened. It had been even harder to force him to stay at home with Melissa and wait for her to call again. Clearly, his patience had worn thin.

Carrie nodded, feeling as if she were drifting away from reality, still wondering if she would wake up any second now.

"I'll have one of the nurses take you to them," Doctor Singh said. "Perhaps your husband can convince you to go home for a couple of hours and get some rest."

"I need to be here. For him. I need to make sure he's safe."

"Callum is perfectly safe here, Carrie. A police officer is stationed right outside his room. No one is going to hurt him."

Carrie stood up. Her legs trembled beneath her. Through the glass, she could see the nurses finishing up.

Cal shifted his gaze and found hers. There was a flicker of something. Then it was gone.

"Go home," Doctor Singh said. "Come back this afternoon. We'll have some more results for you then. Besides, Callum is going to need you more than anyone else. And that means your health should be your priority."

"But I . . ." Carrie was quiet for a second. Giving Cal one more look through the window, she turned back to the doctor.

"What if he doesn't remember me?"

The doctor frowned for a second, then she reached out and gently squeezed Carrie's arm. "We'll do everything we can to make sure that doesn't happen."

6

The Killigrews' house, a detached cottage with a slate roof and well-tended garden, was situated on Clarence Row, halfway up on the west side of the cove.

The drive back from the hospital in Truro had been fraught with strained silence. Even Melissa, who normally refused the notion of peace and quiet, had sat mutely in the back of the car. Like her father, she was blonde-haired and blue-eyed. But where his skin was tanned and weathered from a life at sea, she had the pale complexion of her mother.

Before leaving the hospital, the police officer—Carrie still could not remember his name—had warned her that the press would be moving around the cove, attempting to find out what they could about the boy on the beach.

An official statement would be released to them later today to confirm that it was not Noah Pengelly. Cal's name would not be mentioned yet. It was in the investigation's best interests that Carrie and her family did not approach the press or answer any questions if the press came to them.

Pulling up outside of their home just after eleven, Carrie was relieved to see the street was empty. Much of Porth an Jowl's population would be attending Sunday service down at the church. No doubt, rumours would be flying from pew to pew. Secrets were hard to keep in a town as small as Porth an Jowl. Especially when air ambulances and crime scenes were involved.

Helping Melissa out of the car, Carrie wondered how long they had until the identity of the boy on the beach was revealed. She'd barely had time to let the news sink in herself. She and Dylan had yet to talk about it.

She glanced at him as they walked up the garden path. His narrow, intense eyes were giving nothing away. But she could tell by the tension in his firm jaw and the small vein that had popped up on his left temple that all was not well. And why would it be?

Once inside, Carrie switched on the television in the small but comfortable living room, turned to a channel dedicated to eye-popping cartoons, and sat Melissa in front of it.

In the kitchen, Dylan made coffee, then the two sat at opposite ends of the dining table. Both were silent, staring into the space between them. Occasionally, Carrie would glance up, hoping to catch Dylan's thoughts in his expression. But if she had learned one thing over their five-year relationship, it was that Dylan wasn't much for volunteering his feelings.

Her mind wandered back to Cal. She hoped he was all right at the hospital. The doctors and nurses would be taking good care of him, but what he really needed was the comfort of his mother. She thought back to early this morning, to his waking and not recognising her. Worse than that, he'd seemed afraid of her.

She longed to get back there. To make him remember.

She watched Dylan sip his coffee. Finally, he looked up.

"How can they be sure it's him?" he said. It was not the response Carrie had hoped for.

"They had his DNA on a database from before. They matched a sample. It's him."

Dylan's deep, furtive eyes shifted from side to side. He ran his fingers through his days old beard. "Where the hell has he been all this time?"

Carrie could only shake her head. They were quiet again for a while. The sound of the TV filtered into the kitchen.

Dylan reached a hand across the table. Carrie slipped her fingers between his.

"How are you holding up?" he asked.

"My son was dead. I'd dreamed over and over about this moment. About him coming back. I wished for it so much I thought I'd go crazy. And now he's here, in a hospital bed, very much alive. I can't get my head around it."

A look passed over Dylan's face, so brief that Carrie barely caught a glimpse of it. He stared at the table, then back up at her.

"How's Melissa doing? Did you tell her?" she asked.

"I didn't know what to say."

Carrie glanced over her shoulder, out into the hall. She'd barely had time to absorb the news herself, never mind think about how it would affect her daughter, who had been an only child. Until now.

"Perhaps we should wait to speak to Melissa," Dylan said.

"Why?"

"Because we need some time to get our heads around this. Everything's going to change. And we don't even know if . . ."

"If what?"

Dylan's fingers, which had been stroking the top of her hand, stiffened. He shook his head. "It's just a shock, that's all."

He was quiet and sullen, staring at the floor.

Carrie's thoughts returned to Cal. He would be scared. She needed to be there for him, at the hospital.

She stood, leaving her coffee untouched and Dylan's hand reaching for her across the table.

"I need to take a shower, change into some clean clothes."

Nodding, Dylan got to his feet. He hovered for a moment, unable to meet her gaze.

"I'll make something for dinner," he said. "Melissa can help."

"I may not be back."

"Then we'll save you some."

Carrie nodded again. She turned to leave.

"Hey." Before she could argue, Dylan had moved around the table and wrapped his arms around her waist. He pulled her to him. She resisted for a second, then lured by the warmth and smell of his body, she folded into him, pressing her cheek against his chest.

Carrie looked up, meeting his gaze. He brought his lips to hers and they kissed.

"Your son is alive," he said. "What a head trip."

Her mind racing, Carrie slipped from his embrace and hurried upstairs. She went to the bathroom, turned on the shower, and while she waited for the water to heat up, she ducked into the bedroom to grab a change of clothes. She paused. She would have to buy Cal an entire new wardrobe. She had kept just a few of his clothes from when he was a child. Embracing them and smelling the trace of his scent had got her through her darkest days.

At the hospital, Cal had not allowed her to get close enough to discover if he still smelled the same.

Heading back to the bathroom, she stopped dead centre in the landing. She found herself gazing at Melissa's bedroom. It had once been Cal's. For a while, she had kept the room just as he had left it. The bed unmade. Dirty clothes on the floor. An assortment of dinosaurs and toy soldiers littered across the room like bodies on a battlefield.

Then two years later, along came Dylan. It had been a fiery, intense introduction to a relationship. After three months, she'd discovered she was pregnant. At first, she was horrified. It was the guilt mostly. The idea that she was replacing her son with another child. Then the beauty of having *another* child began to take hold. The idea that the house might once again be filled with laughter and life became all consuming.

Melissa was born. Then came the day when Cal's room became hers. It had been a difficult, painful day, putting Cal's things into boxes and into piles to donate to charity. Carrie had kept just a few of his belongings. His favourite toys. The clothes that reminded her the most of him. By then she had already begun to accept she would never see him again. That her son was dead.

Opening the door to Melissa's room, she peeked inside. It was hard to picture how it had once looked. Where would Cal sleep now? There was the cramped spare room that served as her office. There was perhaps just enough room to fit in a bed and a small chest of drawers.

Returning to the bathroom, she stepped out of her clothes and into the shower. The water was hot against her skin.

Perhaps they would move. The four of them. Into a new home. The trouble was, empty houses were hard to find in Porth an Jowl. Perhaps they would move elsewhere, then. There were plenty of other places they could live. Away from all the bad memories that had kept her here like a prisoner.

She would broach the subject with Dylan in the morning. For now, the only thing she could think about was getting back to her son.

7

A LIGHT DRIZZLE fell over the cove, darkening the pavements. It was Tuesday afternoon, a little after two.

Scott Triggs had spent the morning staking out the hospital entrance. Yesterday's police statement had revealed nothing he hadn't already discovered himself. The boy on the beach was not Noah Pengelly. Every effort was being made to identify him. It was too soon to speculate about a connection between the boy and Noah. Patience and discretion were vital at this early stage of the investigation. More details would be released soon. Blah. Blah. Blah.

While most of the press would report what information they'd been given before respectfully waiting until the next statement, Scott had other ideas.

It was a feeling in his gut. An intuition that the police weren't being truthful about the boy's identity. A quick visit to Margaret Telford had confirmed his suspicions. Although she had refused to answer his questions, her expression had spoken volumes. She knew exactly who that boy was.

Now, his car was parked a few houses down from the Pengelly

house, which was located at the centre of the top tier of homes on the west side of Porth an Jowl. Behind the houses lay Briar Wood. Beyond that, miles of farmland. He stared through the rain-speckled windscreen and tapped his fingers against the steering wheel. This story was big. If he moved fast enough and from the right angle, this story could be his. An exclusive. Exactly what he needed to climb out of the cesspit that was local news and onto the national press.

Towns like Porth an Jowl were all the same. All you needed to do was target the local gossips, butter them up, and *bam*—they would be lining up to spill every juicy detail.

Tess Pengelly had almost tripped over herself when he'd asked for her story. She'd said she'd do anything to help find her son. With just a little coaxing, she had spilled the details of her dead husband's alcoholic ways and her own troubled upbringing. She'd labelled the police investigation into her son's disappearance as 'hopeless' and she'd criticised her fellow locals for not caring whether her son had lived or died. The fact that Tess had taken a cocktail of booze and tranquillisers before he'd asked for an interview had not served her well.

Scott had lied to Jago. Every word of that story had been his own. Now, he wondered if Tess Pengelly would agree to share her thoughts about this new development. Maybe, if she was wasted enough. But if Jago was home, Scott could forget it.

His thoughts turned to the eldest Pengelly boy for a second. That dropout had given up on his education and was likely to follow in his dead father's drunken ways. That's what happened if you stayed living in a hell hole like Devil's Cove—you got drunk, turned into your parents, then you died.

Scott smiled, still proud that he'd been the one to announce the town's true name to the world. Picking up his phone, he checked the time. Another ten minutes had already passed. He couldn't sit here, wasting time. He was an early bird with a worm to catch. The question was, how did he catch it?

Margaret Telford wasn't talking. Turning up at the Pengelly house would likely end in a brawl on the doorstep with Jago. Who else in Devil's Cove could he turn to?

Just as the question formed in his mind, the answer came into view. Two houses along from the Pengellys', a door opened and a crooked old man stepped out. He leaned on a walking stick with one hand and held onto a dog leash with the other. At the end of the leash was a brown and charcoal Yorkshire Terrier. It was clear the man had once been tall and formidable in his youth, but time had warped him like a tree branch.

A memory stirred in Scott's mind. He had spoken to this man before, when Noah Pengelly had disappeared. Scott had been attempting to interview the Pengellys' neighbours with little success, until he had bumped into the old man in the street. He'd seemed guarded at first, but a few compliments about his dog and a couple of leading questions had quickly revealed him to be the quintessential local busybody. The kind who knew everybody's business. A misanthrope who couldn't wait to spill his neighbours' secrets but would be enraged if someone were to spill his own.

Scott watched the old man guide the dog through his unkempt garden and onto the street. He closed the gate and began to head in Scott's direction.

Grady Spencer.

Scott never forgot a gossip's name.

He moved fast for an old man with a stick, already clearing the space between his house and Scott's car. In a second, he would pass by, taking the town's secrets with him. Grabbing his mobile phone from the dashboard, Scott hopped out of the car. The drizzle hit his skin in a depressing mist.

"Mr Spencer?"

The old man stopped in his tracks, looking over his shoulder with a suspicious eye. He turned, tapping his stick against the pavement, and looked Scott up and down.

"Who wants to know?"

His voice was sharp and rasping, unpleasant on the ears. At his feet, the little dog drew its upper lip into a snarl.

Scott moved towards him with an extended hand. The dog broke into a high-pitched yap. "Scott Triggs. Cornish Chronicle. We talked before about Noah Pengelly."

A look passed over Grady Spencer's face. His eyes narrowed. "Don't remember."

Scott smiled. Lying sack of shit, he thought. He could tell the old man was going to need some buttering up. The dog worked last time. Giving the terrier his full attention, Scott crouched down and flashed another smile. "I remember this cute little fella. He had an unusual name. What was it?"

Grady Spencer leaned over him. The dog continued to growl.

"Caliban." The old man pointed a knotted finger at Scott. "You want something from me."

"I do?"

"You're after something. A story."

Grady Spencer stared at him with something like triumph.

Straightening back up, Scott raised his eyebrows in mock surprise. The old man was a regular Sherlock Holmes. "You may be right. In fact, I'll let you in on a little secret. I'm onto a big story."

For a second, the old man stared up at the sky, squinting as rain splashed on his skin. He had no umbrella, no rain coat, just an old jacket that had seen better days and hung over his bent frame like a sheet on a dryer.

"The boy they found on the beach," he said, returning his gaze to Scott. His eyes were ice blue, the whites shot through with thin red veins. "That story was yesterday's news."

"Not entirely true," Scott said. "They still haven't identified him, have they? Or at least, that's what they're saying."

Grady Spencer narrowed his eyes.

That got his attention.

"I think the police know exactly who that boy is. I think they're keeping his identity a secret."

"And why would you think that? Got a hunch, have you?"

"Something like that. Think about it. They still haven't found Noah Pengelly. It's been two months now. Then there's the kid that disappeared last year down in Zennor. He's never been found either. Now an unidentified boy appears on the beach. I did my homework —a couple of children were reported missing in the surrounding area in the last couple of months, but both were found unharmed. They'd just wandered off, got lost or something. So, who is this mystery boy? Where has he come from? Maybe the police think the unsolved disappearances are connected. Maybe this boy has confirmed that."

Scott paused for a moment, thoughts turning in his mind. Grady Spencer watched him, his thin lips pressed together. By his feet, Caliban stopped growling.

"What are people in town saying, Mr Spencer? Has Margaret Telford spoken to anyone?"

The old man's lips curled into a sneer. "I don't give two shits about what that old witch has to say. She tried to report me. Said I let Caliban foul up the streets. Meddling cow. A dog has got to do its business. It's natural."

"I see. I paid her a visit earlier. She was very rude to me as well."

"Always been a stuck-up cow, that one."

"You'd think she didn't want the people of this town to know who'd been found. And I'm sure the people of this town would feel better about letting their children out to play if they knew it was safe, don't you think?"

"I don't give two shits about the people in this town, either," Grady said. "You ask me, they should keep their kids shut up in their houses. Keep 'em out from under my nose."

Scott turned away for a second. This old man was a real charmer. A loner with no friends. No family. Or if he did, they probably visited once a year, and for them that was probably once a year too much.

For the first time since he'd stepped out of the car, Scott felt the rain seeping through his clothes. Time to wrap this up.

"Who do you think they found on the beach, Mr Spencer?" he asked. "Obviously, it's no one local. But I had a feeling this morning that Margaret Telford knew the boy's identity. In fact, I'd bet my life on it."

The old man was quiet for a second, staring down at his dog. When he looked up again, his face had taken on a mischievous expression.

"People around here, they stick together," he said. "They don't like outsiders. Especially ones that come sticking their beaks into things that aren't their business."

Scott felt his body deflate. Had he misjudged the old man? Was he really going to join the rest of the cove's inhabitants in respecting the police force's request for discretion?

Grady Spencer cracked a smile, exposing crooked brown teeth.

"But I don't give two shits about them, do I?" he said. "And I know exactly who the police came calling on after they found that boy. Heard it from Mabel Stevens, I did."

Bingo. "And who did Mabel Stevens say it was?"

Grady Spencer sniggered then pressed his lips together. He tugged on Caliban's leash, pulling the dog to his feet.

"Not my business, is it?" he said, walking away. "But Cove Crafts has been closed since Sunday."

The old man picked up his pace, heading away from Scott and into the rain.

Scott watched him go. His heart raced with excitement. He had to move fast. Before more journalists came snooping around. This was his story. His exclusive.

No one was going to take it from him.

Returning to the dryness of his car, he pulled his phone from his pocket. There was just one bar of signal. Just enough to get him online so he could find out exactly who owned Cove Crafts.

8

THE RAIN CONTINUED into the afternoon, growing heavier as it spread across the county. Carrie pulled up in the hospital car park and sat for a moment, looking up at the large complex of square buildings. Her gaze shifted to the canvas bag sitting in the passenger seat.

She had returned to the hospital on Sunday afternoon to find Cal asleep again. She had sat in a chair in the corner, anxiously watching him, studying every line and contour of his face. It was her son. She was sure of it. But when he had woken two hours later, he had reacted as if she were a stranger. Feeling doubt creeping in again, she had kept her distance from the bed. Cal had returned the favour by not throwing himself into a corner like an animal.

The CT scan had revealed no injuries to his brain, further cementing Doctor Singh's theory that Cal's behaviour was borne from trauma. Carrie had felt a confusing mix of relief and horror. Someone had done terrible things to her son. They'd hurt him. Broken his bones. Scarred him. How long had he endured such tortures?

If only Cal would speak. If only he would allow her to come

close so she might hold him in her arms and take away the horror. A psychiatric evaluation had been carried out yesterday morning. Carrie had sat in the cafeteria, clutching a plastic cup of coffee. Although she had been told much of the initial evaluation would be observational, it hadn't stopped her from feeling shut out.

When she'd been allowed back in the room, Cal had continued to ignore her. Each time she had tried to speak, he had turned away to stare at the silent images of the television on the wall.

She could not get close to him, yet he would allow nurses to give him his medication and prop up his pillows.

Late last night, Carrie had returned home feeling defeated and bereft. She had missed Melissa's bedtime for the second night in a row. Dylan had wanted to talk. Carrie had shut herself in the bathroom, turned on the shower, and wept.

Now, she stared at the bag on the passenger seat, forcing a smile to her lips. She reminded herself that it was early days. Her son had been dead for seven years. Now he was alive. Even if Cal never spoke to her again, she had to be grateful.

Leaving the car, she skirted around the main entrance, where a gaggle of journalists was still gathered, desperate to know the identity of the boy found at Devil's Cove, and headed for a side entrance she'd been instructed to use.

She walked the corridors until she came to Trembath Ward. The duty nurse smiled as she passed by the reception desk. Carrie nodded stiffly then looked down at the trail of wet shoeprints she'd left in her wake.

A uniformed police officer sat outside Cal's room. He smiled politely as Carrie approached.

"Anything?" she asked him.

"He seems more interested in TV than talking," the young officer said.

Carrie paused in the doorway. Cal was sitting up in bed, his eyes trained on a cartoon show and his brow pulled down with concentration. He had a little more colour, she thought, and the shadows around his eyes seemed lighter.

Drawing in a breath, she let it out and knocked softly on the door. Every muscle in Cal's shoulders grew taut.

Carrie hovered in the threshold, as if an invisible force was keeping her out. It took her another ten seconds to push through it. She stepped into the room, the bag swinging slightly in her hand.

"How are you doing?" she said at last.

On the bed, Cal's hands curled into fists and wrapped themselves around his body. He shot her a glance before returning his attention to the TV screen.

Carrie inched forward.

"Cal?"

Nothing. Not even the flicker of an eyelid.

She came to a halt at the foot of the bed.

"I brought you something."

Cal's eyes turned to meet hers. They were dark and round, just like his father's. But they were not the eyes of a child. They were the eyes of someone who had seen terrible things. He looked at her for a second more then dropped his gaze to the bag.

Carrie cleared her throat. "I found a few of your things from when you were a child."

Slowly, she set the bag down at the bottom of the bed. She opened it up and peered inside. A plastic dinosaur lay on top. It was a Tyrannosaurus Rex, about fifteen centimetres tall, painted green and yellow, with its mouth stretched open in a terrifying roar. She held it out as if offering her hand to a wild animal.

"Do you remember, Cal? You used to carry him around everywhere. He used to sleep under your pillow at night. What did you call him?" She stared at her son, her eyes fixed on his mouth, waiting for him to speak. Cal stared at the dinosaur. His right hand unclenched and moved down to his side. "It was Rex, wasn't it? We used to joke that it was a dinosaur not a dog."

Carrie extended her arm, bringing the toy closer. Cal was still staring. *Good.* This was progress. She took a step forward, offering the toy to him.

"Here."

Immediately, Cal shrank back against the bed frame, bringing his knees up to his chest and balling his hands into fists. Carrie took a step back. "I'm sorry. I didn't mean to scare you." She could feel tears forming at the corners of her eyes. Failure pressing down on her chest.

She set the dinosaur down on the mattress. Returning to the foot of the bed, she waited a minute until Cal had peeled himself from the bed frame. His gaze moved from Carrie to the dinosaur and back again. Another minute passed by. Carrie held her breath, not daring to move.

Cal leaned forward. In one quick movement, he shot out a hand and snatched up the dinosaur. He stared at it for some time, turning it over in his hand. Then he closed his fist over it and returned his gaze to the bag.

Carrie's heart hammered in her chest.

"How about this?" she said, her voice faltering as she removed an unframed photograph from the bag. "Do you remember? It's you and me. It was taken just after your sixth birthday. You see the bike you're sitting on? It was your birthday present. We were trying to teach you to ride without the stabilisers. You were scared but you kept trying. And then suddenly, you did it. All by yourself."

She held out the photograph as far as she could. In it, a six-year-old Cal sat on his blue bike beaming with pride. She knelt next to him, an arm wrapped around his waist. She was younger, happier.

What a different picture it was now.

Cal regarded the photograph, the crease in his brow deepening. He returned his gaze to the television.

She placed the photograph on the bed and waited for Cal to snatch it up. He remained unmoving, eyes trained on the television screen.

Out of ideas, Carrie turned and watched the television for a while. Every minute or so, she could sense Cal's gaze seeking her out. She avoided it.

She was a failure.

How could her son not know who she was? She should have kept a close eye on him that day at the beach. She wondered what life would be like now. Grief would not have thrown her into Dylan's arms. Melissa would never have been born.

It was an uneasy thought. One that filled her with confusion and guilt. Cal was staring at the photograph again.

Holding her breath, Carrie took a step back. She watched as he plucked the photograph between finger and thumb and held it up in front of his face.

He stared at it for a long time. Then at her. Then back at the photograph. When he looked at her again, there was something in his eyes that hadn't been there before. Carrie's heart thumped. Was it recognition? She returned his gaze in exhilarated silence. Yes, she was sure of it. He was *remembering*.

And then his eyes grew frightened and darted to the open door.

Carrie turned. A second later, she heard footsteps echoing in the corridor. Detective Turner appeared, waving a hand as he passed the window. He came to a halt in the doorway.

Cal glanced at Carrie, and for a second, he looked just like the frightened little boy who used to call for her in the middle of the night after having a bad dream.

"I'll be right back," she told him.

In the corridor, Detective Turner muttered to the uniformed officer, who stood and walked away.

An uneasy feeling sank its teeth into Carrie's mind. Through the window, she could see Cal on the bed. His head swivelled on his shoulders as he turned to watch her.

"How is he?" Detective Turner asked.

A smile spread over Carrie's face. "I think he recognised me."

"That's great. Has he said anything?"

The smile faded. "He won't talk. Or can't. The CT scan was

clear so it's nothing physical. I'm still waiting to hear from Doctor Singh."

"The psychiatric evaluation?"

The words sounded so clinical. Images of padded cells taunted her mind.

Detective Turner's eyes softened. "How are you holding up?"

Carrie shook her head. She honestly didn't know how to answer the question.

Both adults stared through the glass at the boy in the bed.

"It's a lot to take in," Turner said. "After all, it's not every day you find out your son isn't dead."

Carrie flinched at the words.

"Sorry. Probably not the best way to frame it." Detective Turner cleared his throat. "Callum's reappearance has set tongues wagging at the station. Detective Sergeant Mills will be leading the initial investigation. She's very keen to speak with him when he's ready."

"She's not the only one," Carrie breathed. She turned to face the detective. "Have you found out anything? About who took him?"

A moment of silence passed between them.

The detective adjusted his tie. "It's early days yet. Until we've fully established that this is a criminal investigation, we—"

"What other kind of investigation could it be?" Carrie stared at him, not quite believing his words. "Or do you think my son has just been gallivanting around the county these last seven years, eluding search parties and investigations, and TV reports? This is hardly America, Detective Turner. You can drive from one end of Cornwall to the other in two hours."

She fell silent, realising she had raised her voice. She glanced back at Cal through the window. He was watching her, his knees still tucked up to his chest, the toy dinosaur gripped in his right hand.

"That's not what I'm saying," Turner said. "The toxicology report came back today. It was clear. So, unless Cal can tell us what happened, or our enquiries lead somewhere, we have nothing else to go on."

He paused, for a moment, staring at Carrie with serious eyes.

"If Cal was snatched, we don't want his abductor knowing that it's him we've found. Which is why the longer we can keep your son's name out of the press, the larger window of time we'll have. But unless something comes up very soon, we'll have little choice but to release his name. Rumours are flying. Media interest is growing. It won't be long until someone finds out the truth and then any control we have over what information gets released will be gone."

Carrie turned away. Her head spun and her limbs ached. Exhaustion was taking hold.

"Our best chance of finding out what happened to Cal is for Cal to tell us," Detective Turner said. "But until he's able to, we'll keep searching for answers." He touched Carrie lightly on the shoulder and turned to leave. A few metres up the corridor, he stopped. "Your DNA test results came back, by the way. They were a match."

When she was alone, Carrie folded her arms across her chest and stared through the glass. Cal was no longer watching her but was transfixed by the toy dinosaur.

He really was her son. Her flesh and blood. Her Cal.

She was about to go back inside when she heard more footsteps approaching. She looked up, expecting to see the uniformed officer returning, but it was Doctor Singh.

As she came closer, Carrie felt a chill slip beneath her clothes.

"Good afternoon, Carrie," the doctor said. "Could we go somewhere and talk?"

The exhaustion sinking into Carrie's bones vanished and was replaced by fear.

9

EVENING FELL OVER THE COVE. The rain had ceased an hour ago. Clouds had melted away to reveal a blazing sunset that seared the ocean. The beach had finally reopened and music was filtering out from The Shack, floating through the air to reach Carrie's ears as she stepped out of her car and stared at her home. She listened for a moment. There was something strangely soothing about the muted beat. A slice of normality, she supposed. Life continuing as usual. For some.

Her discussion with Doctor Singh played in her mind as she stepped onto the pavement. It had been an unpleasant conversation, one that left her with difficult decisions to make.

But decisions could wait for a few hours, until she had slipped into a hot bath and put some food in her stomach. She knew she should check in on Melissa, who had barely seen her mother in three days. She knew she needed to have a conversation with Dylan about how their lives had been turned upside down and inside out.

But if she didn't get some sleep soon, she would be no good to anyone. Not to Melissa. Not to Dylan. Not to Cal.

"Carrie Killigrew?"

She stopped at the gate. Climbing out of a blue Renault was a man in his late thirties. He was dressed in jeans and a shirt, and carried a bag over his shoulder. A journalist. She'd had enough experience to recognise one immediately.

She glanced back at the house. This wasn't supposed to be happening. Not yet.

The man approached. Carrie moved quickly, stepping through the garden gate and shutting it behind her.

"Scott Triggs. I write for The Cornish Chronicle." The journalist reached a hand across the gate. "I wonder if I could ask you a few questions."

Carrie stared at his open hand. "About what?"

"About what's been happening here in Devil's Cove. It must be a terrible reminder for you. It must bring back awful memories."

Carrie felt a flash of anger heat her insides. When Callum disappeared, the press couldn't wait to paint her as a terrible mother; one who had neglected to watch her son on a busy beach with known dangerous currents. She had a sudden urge to inform this journalist that her son was not dead. That he was alive and recovering at the hospital. That she was not a terrible mother.

Instead, she shook her head. "I don't know what you're talking about. If you'll excuse me."

"I couldn't help but notice your shop has been closed these last few days," Scott Triggs said. "Were you just at the hospital?"

Carrie's heart thudded. Fumbling for her house keys, she marched along the garden path.

"It's him they've found, isn't it?" Scott Triggs called out. "It's your son, Callum Anderson."

The keys slipped from Carrie's fingers and hit the ground. She stooped to pick them up, then fought to get the right key into the lock. How had he found out?

Scott Triggs stood at the gate, a triumphant smile on his lips.

"Let me tell your story," he said. "Give me an exclusive and I'll make sure you're paid substantially for your time. More than that, I can clear your reputation."

At the door, Carrie froze. She turned and glared at the man.

"Don't you want that, Carrie? For the world to know you're not the terrible mother they think you are?"

Carrie turned the key between trembling fingers. She pushed open the door and staggered inside.

"Leave my family alone," she hissed.

She slammed the door hard, sending ripples through the house.

Upstairs, Melissa began to cry.

At the end of the hall, Dylan stepped out of the kitchen. His face was lined and shadowy with stubble.

"What is it?" he said.

Leaning against the door, Carrie let the tears come.

Dylan moved up to her.

A moment later, she was in his arms, sobbing uncontrollably into his chest.

"How are we doing?"

After settling Melissa back into sleep, Dylan had sat Carrie at the kitchen table and watched over her as she picked at leftovers. Now, they nursed glasses of red wine under the dimmed lights of the living room. Exhaustion weighted Carrie's limbs. She didn't want to talk. She wanted to sleep.

She shook her head. "Physically, he's doing better. There's no brain damage. His heart is fine. He's hydrated. They're getting nutrients into him. He'll need some dental work but his body is okay. The psychiatric evaluation suggests post-traumatic stress, just like Doctor Singh said. Perhaps some learning delays." She paused, suddenly overwhelmed by horror. Who had done this to her son?

Beside her, Dylan nodded. He looked tired, Carrie thought. Perhaps she wasn't the only one not getting any sleep around here.

"How about you? How are you doing?" she asked him.

He was quiet for a long while, staring into his wineglass. Finally, he looked up.

"I'll be honest," he said. "I'm having a hard time taking it all in. What happened to him? Where has he been all this time?"

The muscles at the base of Carrie's neck contracted. She took a sip of wine. "Detective Turner says it's early days. We might not know until Cal's able to tell us."

"When will that be?"

"I don't know, I'm not a doctor." She glared at him, then dropped her gaze to her lap. "Sorry. I'm tired."

Dylan swallowed the contents of his glass. He reached for the wine bottle and offered it to Carrie, who shook her head. Shrugging, he filled his glass to the top.

"What will happen now? I mean, for us. As a family?"

Carrie stared at him. It was a strange thing to say; as if Cal was some separate entity who was about to come and tear this family apart. She may not have seen her son in seven years. She may have believed him to be dead all this time, but he was her blood. He was as much her family as Dylan or Melissa.

"The hospital's main concern is Cal's physical health," she said. "Because Cal is doing better, Doctor Singh says he'll likely be discharged in a few days."

Dylan's glass hovered below his lips. "But he's not well. Mentally, I mean. Shouldn't they be worried about that?"

"They *are* worried. But it's a general hospital not a psychiatric ward." She hesitated, taking a moment to steady her breath and drink some wine. "We have two choices. Cal is sent elsewhere for inpatient care where he can receive more therapeutic treatment to deal with the trauma he's experiencing. Or we can bring him home."

Dylan stared at her. "What does Doctor Singh think?"

"Doctor Singh says whatever decision we make should be in Cal's best interests."

"That doesn't answer my question."

"It's not Doctor Singh's decision to make. If we bring him home he won't just be dumped in our laps. He'll be assigned a community mental health team. We'll have lots of support. Therapists. A social worker."

"But we don't know what he's been through. How do we know that bringing him here so soon will help? And what about Melissa?"

"I'm sure she'll be happy to have an older brother looking out for her."

"But we don't know if . . ."

Carrie turned to face him. "We don't know if what?"

"He's been gone a long time," Dylan said quietly. "God knows what's been done to him. What if it's not safe? What if he's dangerous?"

Anger ignited Carrie's blood. "*Dangerous?* Did you forget Cal is the victim in all this? Besides, the way he looked at me today . . . He's my son, Dylan. His place is here with me."

"And Melissa is *our* daughter," Dylan said, leaning forward. "She's four years old. It's our job to keep her safe. Bringing Cal home when we don't know where he's been or what's happened to him doesn't sound safe to me. There's a journalist outside our home, for Christ's sake!"

The living room closed in on Carrie. She could feel her anger boiling and churning. Any second now, it would erupt from her mouth and she would regret every word it spat out. She turned away and focused on her breathing.

"What about inpatient care?" Dylan said, looking away. "Would it really be so bad for a few weeks? Cal would get the care he needs. We'd have time to get to know him. I mean, we're talking about him moving in and I haven't even met him."

"They don't have those kinds of facilities in Cornwall. They'll send him away. Out of the county." A tear slipped down Carrie's cheek. "He's only just come back to me, Dylan. I can't have him taken away again."

Silence, heavy and stifling, fell between them.

"We were talking about having another child," Dylan said, at last. He looked up with sad eyes.

Carrie nodded. "You always said you wanted a son."

She searched his face. There was no happiness there. No joy. Only worry and doubt. And she understood why. Everything was going to change. It already had.

"We'll still be a family," she whispered. "Just a bigger family."

Slowly, Dylan stood. "I'll run you a bath."

Without making eye contact, he padded to the door. He stopped still. Carrie looked up. She longed to go to him. To fold into his arms.

"I need to meet him," Dylan said. "I need to see for myself that he's safe for Melissa to be around. I want to talk to the doctors."

Carrie nodded. It was a start. "We'll go tomorrow. As a family."

She watched as Dylan left the kitchen and listened to his footsteps ascending the stairs.

She looked down at her hands. Her fingers were trembling.

Cal's face flashed in her mind.

"Don't let me down," she whispered.

10

BRIAR WOOD WAS a small but dense space, populated by swathes of indigenous trees; mostly oak and birch with the occasional pine. In summer, it was green and lush. Now, with autumn looming, the leaves were turning to rust. Yesterday's rain had not returned. The afternoon sun slipped through the canopy and shimmered in small clearings. Birds sang out from branches. As winter approached, most would migrate and Briar Wood would fall empty and silent. Just like the town below.

Nat and Jago had spent the last fifteen minutes walking in a wide berth, eyes on the ground or up in the branches. Jago had devised several different routes in which to search, each one heading in a different direction then looping back to the same spot behind the fence of his backyard.

When Noah had vanished, the police had discovered one of the slats in the fence was loose. After forensics found nothing out of the ordinary, it was concluded that Noah had discovered the loose slat and gone exploring in the wood. Desperation Point was just a couple of hundred metres to the west.

But little Noah had not taken his own life. He had not slipped off the edge, either.

Someone had taken him, of this Jago was convinced.

Nat was not so sure.

An extensive search of Briar Wood had already been conducted by the police two months ago. A local search party had been put together shortly after but had also found nothing. The police were adamant—if there was evidence hidden in Briar Wood it would have been found by now.

They hadn't said it outright, but Nat believed they had reached the same conclusion as everyone else. Sometimes accidents happened to little boys who wandered off by themselves.

Now, as she and Jago turned direction and headed north through the trees, she wondered if they were achieving anything other than wasting time.

It was not the first time the thought had crossed her mind.

She glanced across at Jago, whose face was pulled into a frown as he searched the ground up ahead. The news that the boy on the beach was not his little brother had hit him hard. He hadn't said anything but Nat could hear it in his heavy breaths. She could see it in his slow gait. And he was quieter than usual, bordering on mute.

To have his hopes raised then dashed like that, the pain must have cut deep into his heart. Nat knew a little of how that felt herself.

Perhaps that was why they were out here in the woods again, retracing steps they'd taken several times before.

"You know you missed another great day," she said, when Jago's silence became annoying. "Yeah, we learned all about Michelangelo. Did you know he was a millionaire? All that bullshit about him being a starving artist when all along he was raking it in. That could be us one day."

Jago walked on as if he hadn't heard a word she'd said. "Yeah, of course, you'd have to get out of this shit hole first. Even if we don't go to uni next year, we could still go somewhere. Find a mentor or something. Learn everything we can from the greats." Nat quickened her pace. There was another reason she'd been considering this route lately. University fees. She didn't have the money to pay them. And seeing as how she hadn't seen her parents in five years, she doubted they would happily hand over the cash.

She walked on. "What do you think? I'm thinking London or Manchester. Somewhere big and busy. Somewhere cool."

They rounded a large holly bush. The ground beneath their feet descended a little. Jago walked ahead.

"Jesus, I wish you'd come back to college." Nat pulled out her tobacco pouch and a cigarette paper. "That prick, Sierra Davis, was giving me a hard time about my hair. Like a girl never shaved her head before. Big fucking deal. Better than her ridiculous highlights. I mean, hello! It's not the nineties. God, I hate her so much. All summer I had the pleasure of not seeing her damn face and now there she is, every class, in *my* face. If I wrote a shit list, she'd be right at the top. Number one."

Jago paused, turned his head slightly. "You know for someone you hate so much, you can't seem to stop talking about her. Someone might start thinking you had a crush."

Nat felt her face heat up. "Whatever. There's just so much to hate, that's all."

Jago turned direction, weaving his way through a copse of birch trees. Following behind, Nat rubbed her hand over her head. It had felt liberating to shave off her locks. She liked how smooth her scalp felt against her fingers. How she didn't have to bother with brushing and styling and spraying or gelling. Besides, shaving her head had felt like a statement. A big 'fuck you' to conformity.

Of course, shaving her head had given the people of Devil's Cove further reason to whisper behind her back.

When she'd been first shipped out to live with Rose Trewartha, the cove's resident foster carer, she'd quickly learned that most people referred to her as 'the looked after child'. As if she were the only kid to have been removed from her family. After a year of living in the cove, she'd learned to ignore the whispers and the looks. It seemed that, unless you were born and raised here, you would always be an outsider.

Which was just fine with Nat. She had learned a long time ago that most people couldn't be relied upon.

In six months, she'd be turning eighteen. Rose would stop receiving money for her care and would have no legal obligation to continue giving her a home.

She suspected Rose would never see her put on the streets. She had grown attached to Rose, and she knew Rose was very fond of her also. But how long would it be before some other wayward stray showed up needing a home?

Besides, Nat was getting out of here. She was moving to the city to live an artist's life.

She looked up. While she had slowed down with her thoughts, Jago had pressed on. She quickly caught up to him.

"Anyway," she said. "Sierra Davis can kiss my ass. Along with the rest of them. In less than a year, we'll both be out of here. Half of those losers will never leave. They'll get knocked up or become alcoholics. Meanwhile, we'll be cool as fuck, and they won't be able to stand it."

Jago did not respond. He stomped on. Nat caught up with him again. "You want to talk about it?"

"Not really."

Jago shot her a glare and she was momentarily taken aback.

"Hey." She grabbed his arm, bringing him to a standstill. "What's going on?"

"What do you think is going on?" he said, his voice low.

Nat already knew. She'd experienced Noah's disappearance right by Jago's side.

"That boy on the beach has really got you rattled," she said.

"I don't want to talk about it. I had Mum going on all last night. So, it wasn't Noah. It doesn't mean that he's dead. It doesn't mean we won't find him."

Nat said nothing. She watched Jago wipe beads of sweat from his forehead then stare off into the distance. Anger flashed in his eyes. He'd always had anger in him, Nat thought. Long before Noah disappeared. Long before Nat had arrived in town and moved in next door. Long before they had formed a reluctant friendship; two outcasts forming one unstoppable force against convention and conformity.

They were silent for the next few minutes until they had gone full circle and could see the backs of houses through the trees. They reached the wooden fence that ran alongside and stopped outside Jago's backyard.

Nat stared at the loose slat that remained unfixed. Just in case he comes back this way, Jago had said. Her gaze shifted to the house on the left, where Rose would no doubt be inside cooking up some culinary delight to feed to Nat later. Then onto the next house, where the curtains were old and stained, the windows filthy, and old junk in the yard peeked over the fence. Moss grew on the stonework. Slates were missing from the roof.

"Come on," Jago said, tapping her shin with his boot. "Let's walk out to the lighthouse."

He got moving again. Nat stood for a moment longer, staring up at Grady Spencer's house, before running to catch him up.

11

CARRIE STOOD at the foot of the bed, feeling victorious. The Pokémon cards she'd found in the box of Cal's keepsakes had acted like a key to a locked door. She had arrived at the hospital later than planned but it had been worth every delayed minute.

She'd slept badly, lying awake on her back and staring up at the ceiling, desperately thinking of ways to deepen the connection she'd made with Cal.

At 4 a.m., the memory had come to her; Cal and Jago flat out on their stomachs on the living room floor, feet waving in the air, as they laughed and joked while doing battle with the monsters on their Pokémon cards. Cal had been obsessed with them for a long while, building his collection and swapping duplicates with friends at school until his collection was almost complete.

The house still dark, Carrie had climbed out of bed and crept downstairs to the living room, where she'd left Cal's keepsake box on the side cabinet.

Now, she watched as Cal sat up cross-legged on the hospital bed, shuffling through the cards, his expression somewhere between confusion and delight.

He was remembering. He looked up at Carrie for a second and she saw the child he had once been; bright-eyed and filled with excitement. A ripple moved across his lips.

Carrie caught her breath.

Had he smiled?

She wanted nothing more than to rush forward, to hold him against her, to kiss his cheek. But she knew better.

Instead, still holding her breath, she moved slowly to the visitor's chair next to the bed and sat down.

Cal's head snapped up.

She held his gaze.

Held it for what felt like an hour.

Finally, Cal relaxed his shoulders.

Carrie could barely contain her joy as she watched him continue to sift through the cards. Occasionally, he would stop to examine one at length.

"Do you remember?" she said.

Cal glanced up at her. He nodded.

Tidying the cards in a neat pile, he placed them on top of the bedside cabinet next to Rex the dinosaur and a handful of other plastic figures that Carrie had brought in yesterday. Little memories from a long time ago all neatly lined up in rows.

Cal stared at them all.

Something had changed in the last twenty-four hours. It was as if he had reached deep into his unconscious and pulled out missing pieces of a puzzle. The way he kept looking at her today—he knew her. She was his mother.

The realisation could not be described with words. It was an intense heat billowing from her heart, travelling along her veins to her extremities. And now she was about to do something that could jeopardise it all.

"Cal, would you look at me?" she said, softly. He turned to face her, his face still etched with curiosity. Carrie swallowed. "There's someone who I'd like you to meet. Someone who I care about very much."

She looked at the door again and nodded to the figure hovering in the hall.

A second later, Dylan entered. He came to a halt halfway between the door and the bed, eyes darting across the room.

"This is Dylan," Carrie said.

Cal looked up. His face grew very still.

Dylan cleared his throat. "Hello, pal. Pleased to meet you."

His gaze flicked back to Carrie. He reached out a hand towards Cal. Cal backed away, pressing up against the bedframe.

"You don't have to be afraid," Carrie soothed. "Dylan is a kind man. He won't hurt you."

She nodded at Dylan, who shrugged a shoulder and shoved his hands in his pockets. This wasn't going to be easy on both sides.

"Do you remember what I told you yesterday, Cal? About Dylan and me. We're married. We love each other. Do you remember that?"

An expression passed over Cal's face, like rainclouds suffocating a blue sky. With his right hand, he plucked a photograph from the bedside cabinet and thrust it at Carrie. His eyes grew dark and angry. It was the picture she'd given him two days ago. The one of his old family. Across the room, Dylan stared at the floor.

"I know it's hard to understand," Carrie said, her jaw aching with tension. "A lot has changed since you've been . . . gone."

Cal curled his free hand into a fist and pressed it into the bed. He leaned forward, bringing the photograph closer.

"Cal, baby. I know everything is confusing right now. Everything is different. But I'm here. We all are. We're going to help you through this. When you come home with us, things will be better. You'll see."

As quickly as the anger had ignited in Cal's eyes, it was extinguished. Dropping the photo to the bed, he hung his head and turned away from the adults.

Carrie's shoulders sagged. She caught Dylan's eye, who shook his head.

"This was a bad idea," he muttered.

Carrie shot him a look. "He's not deaf, you know."

They were quiet for almost a full minute. Doubt wrapped itself around Carrie's body. She'd made some progress with Cal, but was it enough? In two days, maybe three, he was going to be discharged. What would happen if they took him home?

When. She corrected herself. *When we take him home.* She looked from her son to her husband, who were both avoiding her gaze. Hopelessness engulfed her, threatening to spill from her eyes. She shook it off. No. This had to work. *She* had to make it work.

"Go get Melissa," she said.

Dylan shot her a doubtful look. "I don't know if that's—"

"Please, Dylan. Go get her."

Muttering to himself, he turned and left the room.

Now they were alone, Cal turned to face her.

"Give him a chance," Carrie said, smiling. "You'll see when you get to know him that he's kind and caring. And he makes really good pizza."

Cal didn't look convinced. With one eye fixed on his mother, he pulled his knees to his chest and wrapped his arms around his shins.

"There's someone else I want you to meet," Carrie said, choosing her words carefully. "You have a little sister now. Her name is Melissa."

A moment later, the quiet was filled with footsteps and excited chatter. Cal's head turned to the door. His brow grew tight and wrinkled.

Beside him, Carrie reached out a hand. "It's okay."

Dylan entered the room, carrying Melissa in his arms, who was busy telling her father all about the adventures of Dora the Explorer. Her eyes roamed the room and found Cal. She stopped talking.

"Hi, sweet pea," Carrie smiled. "Did the nurses take care of you?"

"I tried on a step-a-scope and listened to my heart."

"You did?"

Melissa nodded. Cal watched her silently from the bed.

"Melissa, this is Cal," Carrie said, trying to keep her voice calm and steady. "Do you remember me talking about him?"

Melissa nodded, her stare fixed on the boy in the bed.

Carrie turned to Cal. "And this is Melissa. Your sister."

The siblings regarded one another like Man seeing the moon for the first time.

"Can you say hello?" Dylan said, kissing the top of Melissa's head. The little girl watched the boy through large, round eyes.

"Hello," she said.

Dylan set her down on the floor. She leaned into his legs, hooking one arm around the back of his knees.

"I don't have a brother," she said. "I'm an only child."

"That was before," Carrie smiled. "Now you have a big brother to take care of you. Isn't that great?"

Melissa looked uncertain.

"Come here, sweet pea. Come say hello."

Taking a slow step forward, Melissa fixed her gaze on Cal, as if she expected him to leap from the bed and attack her at any second.

Carrie took her by the hand and swept her up into her lap. She kissed her on the top of the head, then on her cheek. Melissa squirmed. Cal stared.

"This is all a little strange, isn't it?" Carrie looked at both her children. "But soon, it will feel like things were always this way."

She glanced at Dylan, whose face was lined and drawn. On her lap, Melissa shifted around. She had already lost interest in Cal and was staring at the collection of toys on the cabinet.

"Dinosaurs," she said.

Cal reached out a hand. His fingers hovered for a second,

twitching up and down. He picked up the T-Rex and, curling a fist around it, turned back to Melissa.

She stared back at him with hopeful blue eyes.

"Perhaps Melissa could play with one of your toys," Carrie said.

Cal tightened his fist around the dinosaur. After a moment, he reached across with his free hand and picked up a small red car. The paint was cracked and peeling off in places. He regarded it for a moment, before placing it on the bed.

"Thank you, Cal." Carrie smiled. Inside her chest, her heart heaved and swelled. She scooped up the toy car and handed it to Melissa. "What do you say?"

Melissa turned the car over. Her eyes wandered to the T-Rex in Cal's fist.

"Thank you," she said.

This was good. This was progress. Cal could listen and understand. More than that, he recognised the needs of others. Whatever had happened to him, he'd still retained his empathy.

Carrie found herself smiling. Dylan removed his hands from his pockets. Their eyes met.

"All right, then," Carrie said.

12

Meetings took place between doctors and the mental health team. Therapists were consulted. Carrie and Dylan were interviewed and assessed. There would be follow-up checks, of course, and home visits, but all agreed it was in Cal's best interests to continue his recovery with his family.

And so, days later, on a cloudy Sunday afternoon, Cal came home. His transfer from hospital to house had been meticulously planned. Sneaked out of a side entrance to avoid the press, he and Carrie were transported to an ambulance and driven out of Truro to a roadside service station, where Dylan was waiting with the car. The staging had seemed elaborate to Carrie, but necessary.

The police would be issuing a statement to the media tomorrow, announcing Cal's identity. And then the circus would really begin.

Carrie had protested, begging Detective Turner to delay the statement. But the decision had been made by his superiors. Cal had still not uttered a single word. The initial inquiry into his reappearance had come up empty. Unless he could tell them what had happened, there wasn't much of a case to investigate.

Carrie glanced over her shoulder. Cal had spent the entire journey from the hospital glued to the rear passenger window, his shoulders heaving up and down, his breaths steaming up the glass. Doctor Singh had provided him with a pair of dark glasses for the journey. It seemed that Cal's eyes were light sensitive, suggesting that wherever he'd been, he'd had limited exposure to daylight. A low vitamin D count had confirmed this.

Now, as the car pulled up outside the house, he turned and stared past Carrie.

"This is your home," she told him. "Do you remember?"

He remained silent and unmoving, his expression unreadable through the glasses.

Dylan killed the engine and unhooked his seatbelt. "I'll take Melissa in first and make sure the coast is clear," he said.

Carrie watched as he climbed out and a second later, helped Melissa out of her booster seat. The two hovered by the garden gate as Dylan checked the street. Giving Carrie a quick nod, he swept Melissa into his arms and carried her towards the house.

Carrie twisted around and faced Cal, attempting to peer through the dark lenses of his glasses. All she saw was her own face, worried and lined, peering back.

"Are you ready?"

Cal remained still.

Getting out of the car, Carrie took a second to scan the street herself. Sunday afternoon had been a good choice to return home. People didn't venture out much past lunch time. Satisfied no one was watching, she opened the rear passenger door.

"You have to undo your seatbelt," she said.

Cal glanced down and touched the seatbelt.

"It's the red button, you have to push it."

Had he really forgotten?

She watched as he slowly depressed the button, releasing the seatbelt. He jumped at the click. Carrie waited as he climbed awkwardly out of the car. She reached a hand to steady him before closing the door, then cast another quick glance at her neighbours' houses. The thought of the press descending tomorrow made her stomach tumble and flip. She just hoped it would be over and done with in a day or two, with another story coming along to steal the attention.

She gently grasped Cal's elbow, who was also nervously scanning the street. He flinched but did not pull away.

"Come on." Together, they walked to the house. When they reached the doorstep, Cal froze.

"It's okay," Carrie said. "You're home now. You're safe."

Behind his dark glasses, she couldn't tell if Cal remembered the house at all. She gave a gentle push on his elbow and they stepped inside. Cal stopped still again. She felt the muscles beneath his skin tighten. Dylan and Melissa were in the kitchen. Melissa was talking incessantly, as if it were a perfectly ordinary day. Dylan was quiet, just as he'd been in the car. And for days now.

Pushing worry from her mind, Carrie took Cal's jacket and hung it up. "I'll show you around," she said. "Maybe it'll jog your memory." Cal was unmoving. "You can take those glasses off now. You don't need to wear them indoors."

His movements slow and unsure, Cal reached up and carefully removed the glasses. Blinking, he stared at the hall, his eyes coming to rest on a wall of family photographs. He leaned into a picture of Carrie, Dylan and Melissa, that had been taken last Christmas.

Carrie took the glasses from him and gently tugged him away from the picture.

The first stop on the tour was the living room.

"It looks a little different than before," she said. "The walls used to be blue, I think."

Now they were a burnt orange. The carpet was long gone, the exposed floorboards varnished. Even the furniture was different.

Cal hovered in the doorway, reluctant to go in.

Next, Carrie led him to the kitchen, where Melissa sat at the table, preoccupied with paper and colouring pencils. Dylan was busy pulling food out of cupboards. A fresh chicken sat in a dish, ready for roasting. Both he and Melissa looked up as they entered.

It had been given a fresh coat of paint but the kitchen mostly remained unchanged. Cal looked around, his eyes coming to rest on Melissa, who was busy drawing a picture of what looked like a horse.

"You used to do the same thing," Carrie said. She felt a sudden stab of sadness. Seven years. Lost forever. But she had thought her son was dead. Seven years was more than a fair exchange for his return.

Dylan cleared his throat. "Do you like chicken, Cal?" he asked.

Cal flinched and stared at the floor.

"I'm sure he does," Carrie said. "Everyone likes chicken."

"Except vegetarians," Melissa said, looking up.

Both Dylan and Carrie stared at each other.

"And where did we learn such a big word like that?" Carrie said.

Melissa swapped her blue pencil for a red. "School."

"Well, aren't you my little super brain?"

Leaving the kitchen, Carrie led Cal upstairs. She took the steps slowly, watching him as he moved. She was being overcautious, she knew, but he seemed so fragile. As if one misstep would break him into a thousand pieces.

He glanced up, catching her eye. His face was expressionless.

She wished she could tell what was going through his mind. This had to be strange for him, just as it was for Dylan and Melissa.

They reached the top of the stairs and paused on the landing.

"This is the bathroom," Carrie said, pushing open the first door on her left. It was a tiny room, white tiles on the walls, turquoise linoleum on the floor. There was enough space for a bathtub and shower, toilet and sink. "You used to love taking a bath. You had this little toy boat with a motor. It went around and around. You'd pretend you were . . ."

She clamped her jaw shut. *You'd pretend you were a pirate sailing the ocean. The ocean that took you from me.*

Cal stared at the empty bath.

They moved on. Cal slowed to a halt outside the next door. A colourful sign was fixed in the centre: MELISSA'S ROOM.

Carrie thought she saw a flicker of recognition in his eyes. She pushed the door open.

Melissa's room was large and colourful. Her bed sat up against the far wall. Large cushions were scattered across the floor. Boxes of toys overflowed on the opposite side. In the window, a row of dolls and soldiers stood guard.

"Do you remember this room?"

Cal stepped inside. He turned a half circle.

"I know this is weird," Carrie said. "This used to be your room. But Melissa has so many things, she needed the space."

She watched, her heart in her throat, as Cal continued to turn. His gaze rested on the toys standing on the window sill. His hand slipped into his right pocket and pulled out his toy T-Rex.

"Let me show you your new room," Carrie said.

Cal didn't move. His eyes flicked from left to right. Was he remembering something?

"Cal?"

His eyes found hers. If he was upset, his blank expression hid it well. He followed her out to the hall, where she led him to the next room. There was no sign on this door. It was as blank as Cal's face.

"This is your new bedroom," Carrie said, opening the door. She stepped aside. The room was half the size of Melissa's, with just enough space to fit in a bed, a wardrobe and a chest of drawers.

"I know it's not much right now. I thought maybe we could work on it together."

Cal stared at the room. His fist tightened around the T-Rex.

Brushing past him, Carrie went to the wardrobe, where a few garments hung inside.

"I bought you some clothes." She removed a red hooded top

and held it up. "I'm not sure if you like them. I don't really know what sixteen-year-old boys wear these days."

Cal stared at the hooded top, then at Carrie. His blank face was beginning to unnerve her. And then it changed. It was subtle. A narrowing of the eyes. A tightening of the lips.

He turned and left the room.

Carrie stood for a moment, feeling like the world's shittiest mother as she heard him open the door to Melissa's room.

"Cal…" She followed him, arriving in time to see him cross the room and push Melissa's toys on the window ledge to one side. He set the plastic dinosaur down and turned it to face the room. He took a step back and glared at Carrie.

"I'm sorry," she whispered. *Sorry for giving up hope. For believing you were dead. For replacing you.* "I know it's different. I know things have changed. But it's going to be okay. We can make it work."

A crease in Cal's brow caught Carrie's attention. Good, she thought. It may have been anger he was feeling, but at least he was feeling something.

"As soon as you're well enough, how about we take a trip into Truro and go shopping for your room? You can choose the curtains. The quilt. We'll get some posters, whatever you like."

She suddenly realised she had no idea what Cal liked. Or if he had any idea either.

"What do you think? You can paint the walls any colour you want. We'll make it yours. Any way you want it."

Cal looked up. He stood still for a while longer, swaying from side to side. Slowly, he turned back to the window, picked up the Tyrannosaurus Rex, and returned it to his pocket.

Carrie's shoulders loosened a fraction.

Mother and son stared at each other.

"Let me show you the garden," Carrie said. "I think one of your footballs is still around somewhere."

Cal followed her out of the room like an obedient puppy.

As they descended the stairs, the question Carrie had been desperate to ask him, forced its way into her mouth. It was too early. The doctors had warned her: only ask when he's ready. She sealed her lips. The words pushed against them.

What happened to you?

13

DINNER WAS roast chicken with potatoes and greens. Dylan and Carrie sat at opposite ends of the kitchen table with the children in between. Melissa held one of her dolls and was busy braiding its long hair while staring at Cal every few seconds.

"Sweet pea, what have I told you about bringing toys to the table?" Carrie said.

Melissa let out a long sigh. "Not supposed to."

"Exactly. So, can you please give me Cara?"

Glancing at her father, then back at her mother, Melissa heaved her shoulders and begrudgingly handed over the doll.

"Thank you."

Carrie dumped the doll in her lap. Beside her, Cal was watching Dylan carve the chicken. His eyes focused on the carving knife as it glided through the cooked white flesh.

"Are you hungry?" Carrie asked him.

He remained silent, his attention on the meat.

Carrie looked up at Dylan, who raised an eyebrow.

"Well, I hope you're hungry, Cal," he said. "I've cooked enough food to feed a fishing fleet."

Cal placed his hands on the edge of the table. Rex the dinosaur was still clutched in his left hand.

"That's not fair!" Melissa cried, pointing a finger in his direction. "No toys at the table."

"She's right," Dylan said.

"No toys at the table!" Melissa repeated, this time directly at Cal.

He stared at her.

"It's true, Cal," Carrie said, leaning in. "It's the same rule we had when you were younger. Toys are for playtime. Could you please put it away?"

Cal removed his hands from the table, slipping the dinosaur inside his pocket.

"You're supposed to give it to Mummy," Melissa said. She waited for him to do so. When he didn't, she screwed her little face into an angry scowl. "Why doesn't he speak? He's being rude."

"And now *you're* being rude," Carrie said. "You know why. We've already talked about it."

"But he's still got—"

She fell silent at the sight of her mother's glare then pushed her lip out to its fullest extent.

"Okay, who wants chicken?" Dylan said. He began dishing out slices of the white meat.

"Chicken is a bird," Melissa said, pulling her face into a scowl.

Carrie suppressed a smile.

"Here you go, Cal." Dylan set a plate in front of him. "Help yourself to potatoes."

Cal stared at the chicken on his plate. He lowered his head and inhaled through his nostrils. His eyelids grew heavy then fluttered.

Dylan smiled. "Smells good, huh?"

As quick as lightning, Cal grabbed the chicken from his plate. He opened his mouth wide and crammed the meat inside. He lunged again, grabbing a potato from the dish. It was hot and he winced, dropping it on his plate. He grabbed another one and dropped it into his lap.

Dylan's jaw dropped. Carrie drew in a breath. Across the table, Melissa's eyes grew as round as the dinner plates.

"Cal, no," Carrie said, trying to keep her voice calm and low. "That's not how we eat here. Use your knife and fork."

His cheeks full, grease smeared across his lips, Cal stared down at the cutlery. Slowly, he picked up his fork and turned it over.

"And we wait until everyone has food on the plate."

Clamping his jaw shut, Dylan spooned potatoes and vegetables onto the other plates and passed them around.

Cal finished chewing the food in his mouth. He swallowed, hard. His eyes fixed hungrily on the rest of his dinner but he made no move to eat it.

"Okay, good," Carrie said. "And now everyone has their food we can eat."

She watched as Cal stared at his fork. His animalistic behaviour had shocked her. Again, she found herself asking the same question. What had happened to him these last seven years? She felt a sudden wave of nausea rack her body.

"Sweetheart, are you okay?" Dylan stared at her from across the table, concern lining his features.

She nodded. "Fine. Let's just eat."

She speared some chicken. She waited until Cal had done the same. He watched her, as if waiting for permission. She nodded. They both began to eat. Across the table, Melissa's gaze moved from mother to son.

"Eat up, sweet pea," Dylan said.

Her lower lip still poking out, Melissa picked up a fork and began to eat.

Carrie's shoulders relaxed a little. *Okay. This is good. Close enough to a normal family as we're going to get for one day.*

"Angus wants me back on the boat this Thursday," Dylan said, with a mouthful of potato.

Carrie frowned. "I thought you were taking this week off. You said you were going to be around."

"I know. But they're already a man down. If there's not enough men, things get tricky. You know what it's like. Besides, I've already taken a week off. Plus the shop's been closed and next week is the last of the season. Things are tight. We need the money."

"I know that. It's just . . ." Carrie lowered her voice, which she knew was stupid because her children weren't deaf. "It's our first week together as a family. A newer, bigger, family."

Dylan nodded as he harpooned a potato. "I'm sorry, but it can't be helped. I'm here till Thursday. That's another few days. The press will be gone by then."

"You don't know that."

Carrie glanced at Cal, whose face was lined with concentration as he fumbled with his knife and fork.

"We'll talk about it later," she said. She returned her attention to her son. "How's the food?"

Cal's mouth was full. He had almost cleared his entire plate, while the others had only just started.

"You might want to slow down there, buddy," Dylan said, smiling. "It's not going out of fashion anytime soon."

Melissa's eyes grew wide as she watched Cal force an entire potato into his mouth. Then, picking one up from her plate, she copied him, pushing it all the way into her mouth with two fingers.

"Melissa Killigrew, what do you think you're doing?"

Melissa glared at her mother. Across the table, Dylan covered his mouth with his hand.

"It's not funny," Carrie said, before covering her own mouth and turning away. Encouraged, Melissa picked up some chicken with her hand and crammed it into her mouth.

Before Carrie could chastise her, her attention was drawn to movement behind Dylan's head. A man stood outside the kitchen window, a camera held up to his face, snapping pictures of the Killigrews at dinner. Carrie recognised him in an instant. It was the journalist from the other day.

Dylan spun around. "Fucking asshole!"

"Don't swear in front of the kids." Carrie's eyes were frozen on the journalist, who slowly lowered his camera.

Dylan sprang to his feet. "I'll kill him. I'll put him in the ground."

The man began to back away.

"Don't go out there," Carrie said. "Don't make this worse."

But Dylan was already moving to the back door in large strides. He threw open the door. The journalist turned and ran. Dylan chased after him, bellowing at the top of his lungs.

At the table, a terrible, high-pitched wail escaped from Cal's lips. Slipping from the chair, he ducked beneath the table and started to scream.

Melissa dropped her fork with a clatter.

Carrie jumped up, just one thought racing through her mind: *Dylan was going to do something stupid.* She needed to go after him.

She froze, her eyes moving from the open door to her son's feet sticking out from beneath the table. Cal's screams were like metal tearing.

"Everything's okay," Carrie soothed. "There's nothing to be scared of, I promise."

Melissa's open mouth formed a perfect circle. Cal stopped screaming and began whimpering like an injured animal. Shouts and yells came in through the open door. Carrie found Cal's feet again. She crouched down. He was on his knees, his trembling body folded over, his head touching the ground.

"Cal…" Carrie felt her heart break a little. She reached out a hand but didn't touch him. "It's okay. You're safe. No one's going to hurt you."

The shouts were growing louder, more intense. She felt a flash of anger. Why couldn't Dylan ever deal with things calmly?

"Mummy?" Melissa's round face peeked underneath the table. "What's Cal doing?"

"It's okay, sweetie. He's a little frightened, that's all."

Carrie reached out and placed a hand on Cal's back. He flinched. She held it there and whispered soothing words in his ear. "It's okay. I've got you. You're safe."

She could hear footsteps, returning to the kitchen. Poking her head out from beneath the table, she saw Dylan close the door and move to the kitchen window. He pulled the blinds, plunging the room in darkness, then flipped the light switch on the wall.

Dylan's face was red, his pupils black and wide.

"What are you doing under there?" he said, his voice still angry.

"Cal got scared from all the shouting."

Guilt flashed across Dylan's features. He drew in a deep breath.

"I'm sorry." He stood, watching Carrie rub Cal's back.

"What happened?" she asked.

Cal's whimpering had quietened to a baby-like moan.

"Bloody journalists, why can't they just leave us alone?"

"What *happened*?" Carrie repeated, this time her voice sharp and waspish.

"It doesn't matter. He's gone now."

"Did you hit him?"

"No, I did not." Dylan unfolded his arms and held his hands out in front of him. "His camera may have had an accident, though. The idiot must have butter fingers."

At the table, Melissa's eyes moved from her father to her mother. A broken camera was better than an assault charge, Carrie supposed. But the last thing she wanted was for the press to paint them as an aggressive family.

"How did he know about Cal?" Dylan said, hovering by the kitchen sink. "The police aren't releasing their statement until tomorrow."

Carrie shook her head. It was a good question. She wondered for a moment if Margaret Telford had spoken to the journalist. Or if Mabel Stevens had told him about the police showing up at Cove Crafts. In a town as small as this, a secret was not a secret for very long. At least they'd got Cal home safely.

Carrie stared at his cowering frame beneath the table. "Can you take Melissa out of here? Let me get him calm."

"But I'm still eating," Melissa complained.

Dylan crossed the kitchen and swept his daughter and her dinner plate up in his arms. "Well, I guess you get to break the house rules and eat your dinner in the living room!"

He glanced uncertainly at Carrie as he passed by.

Carrie returned her attention to Cal. His face was still buried into the floor and his hands still covered his ears.

"I've got you," she soothed, her hand gently running up and down his spine. "Everything is going to be all right."

She bit down on her lip, hoping she spoke the truth.

14

Scott Triggs was furious. He sat in the driver's seat of his car, the door open, one foot resting on the curb as he dabbed his scraped elbow with a tissue. His camera sat in his lap in two pieces. Dylan Killigrew was nothing more than an inbred thug. He had a good mind to report him to the police.

Dumping the bloody tissue on the passenger seat, he picked up the main bulk of the camera, popped a button, and pulled out the memory card. Dylan was also an idiot, and come tomorrow, Scott would make sure the world knew about it.

He had the photograph he needed to go with his exclusive—the Killigrew family sitting around the dinner table with a ghost. He already had a draft of the story prepared and he'd even crafted a headline: The Boy Who Came Back From The Dead. Now, he needed to phone the press room and talk to his editor-in-chief before tomorrow's paper was finalised and sent off to print.

Wincing as the graze on his elbow rubbed against the car seat, he pulled his phone from his pocket. He looked up. A thought occurred to him. This story was potentially much bigger than the reappearance of Callum Anderson. What if his disappearance was somehow connected to the disappearance of Noah Pengelly? If he was right, if he could discover the link, this story could be the one to send his career skyrocketing into the big leagues.

Judging by the lack of other journalists, Scott was confident he was the only one to have discovered Callum's identity. But with the police having announced tomorrow's press conference, it meant he had a small window of time.

Scott stared across at the Killigrew house, an idea forming in his head. Slamming the driver door shut, he dumped the camera pieces on the passenger seat and started the engine. He spun the wheel, pulling away from the kerb. Turning onto Cove Road, he took a left and headed uphill. As he drove, he dialled the press office of The Cornish Chronicle.

"Charlie, it's Scott," he said into the phone, indicating left and turning onto another small row of houses. "Put Mike on the line. Have I got a story for you!"

There was just one parking space remaining on the roadside. He wedged the vehicle into it, bumping the car in front, and killed the engine as the editor-in-chief's voice spoke in his ear. It took exactly thirty seconds to convince him to hold the front page.

"You've got two hours, Triggs," the older man said, his voice wheezy with excitement. "Don't you dare let me down."

Scott grinned from ear to ear. "You offend me, Mike. When have I ever disappointed you?"

Hanging up before the man could reply, he climbed out of the car and looked up at the Pengelly house. As usual, the curtains in all the windows were closed, making it impossible to tell if anyone was home.

Crossing the road, Scott checked the rest of the street. No one else was around. Sunday in Devil's Cove was like a ghost town. Just as well, he thought, as he pushed open the garden gate and made his way along the path. The last thing he needed was nosy neighbours getting in the way.

As he drew closer, he saw the front curtain twitch. Before he could press the buzzer, the door opened. He had hoped to see Tess Pengelly in all her sedated glory. To his dismay, Jago Pengelly stood in front of him, thunder rolling across his face.

Damn it, Scott thought. He wasn't going to get the quote he had hoped for. But time was running out. Which meant right now he would take any quote or reaction he could get. And he was willing to take one on the chin in exchange.

"Don't you give up?" Jago said, spitting out the words.

"God loves a trier." Scott smiled as he pulled out his phone and switched to voice recorder mode. His thumb hovered over the record button. "Do you mind?"

Narrowing his eyes, Jago moved to close the door.

Scott held up a hand. "I have something to tell you. Something you'll want to hear."

Jago paused, staring at him. "Not interested."

"Really? Then why are you still standing here?"

"Good point." He moved to close the door again.

Scott thought about using his foot as a wedge then quickly decided against it. There was no time for a trip to A&E.

"I know who the boy on the beach is," he said, catching his breath. In the doorway, Jago's body tensed.

Got him. Scott held up the phone.

"Do you mind?" he asked again.

Jago stared at him, anger flashing in his eyes. He was going to say no. He was going to tell Scott to leave before he regretted it. The boy's gaze travelled from the phone and back up to Scott's face.

"Who is it?" he asked.

"Do I have your permission to record this?"

"How do I know you're not lying to me? How do I know this isn't bullshit just to get me to say something stupid?"

"Because tomorrow morning my story is going to be a front-page exclusive. And it'll be out before the police hold their conference."

Jago pushed the door open a little. He turned and looked over his shoulder into the house.

"Bullshit."

"It's true."

"You're lying."

This wasn't working. Scott chewed his lip. Time for a different tactic. Shrugging his shoulders, he slipped his phone back inside his pocket. "All right. Suit yourself. I just thought you'd want to find out first-hand before the rest of the world does."

He turned to leave.

"Wait." Jago looked back into the house once more before stepping onto the path and closing the door behind him. "I'm listening."

Scott pulled the phone from his pocket again.

"Do I have your permission to record this conversation?"

Jago shrugged. "Whatever."

Scott's pulse raced as he tapped the record button. He took in a deep breath and blew it out. There was no point in having a heart attack when he was about to hit the big time.

"So, who is it?" Jago asked, looking impatient now.

"Actually, I believe it's someone you know." Scott watched with glee as confusion clouded Jago's face. "Someone who you used to be friends with, so I hear."

"What the hell are you talking about?"

His pulse still pounding, Scott took another breath. "This is going to come as a surprise, but the boy they found on the beach is Callum Anderson."

Jago's face grew a shade paler. His jaw swivelled open. His eyes grew wide. Then they narrowed. Scott glanced down to see the boy's hands curling into fists. "It's true. I've seen him with my own eyes. Just now, sitting at the dinner table with the rest of his family."

"Cal is dead, you sick asshole. He drowned. What are you trying to do?"

He stepped forward, his fists clenching and unclenching.

"It's true," Scott insisted. "I have pictures."

"Show them to me."

"I can't. That idiot Dylan Killigrew broke my camera."

Jago was inches from Scott's face now. The journalist took a large step back.

"I don't believe you," Jago said, although the uncertainty in his eyes told a different story. "You're just trying to get me to say something I'll regret so you can put it in the papers."

"Can you share your thoughts?" Scott said, holding his phone between them as if it might protect him. "Do you think Callum Anderson knows where to find your brother?"

Jago shook his head. "Get out of my garden."

"If Callum does know something about your brother's whereabouts, why hasn't his family come forward to the police?" Scott took another step back. He felt Jago's anger gathering energy like a storm. The boy's knuckles grew deathly white.

"Come on, Jago. You need to give me something," he said.

Before Scott could utter another word, Jago swung at him. A fist connected with Scott's chin. His vision turned white, then yellow. He stumbled back, tripping over his feet.

At the same time, his phone slipped from his fingers and fell to the ground. Jago shot forward, raising his foot and bringing it crashing down, over and over.

Scott watched in horror as his phone came apart in pieces.

"Stop that!" he roared.

He stooped to pick up the remnants.

Jago was faster. Snatching up the pieces, he flung them into the road and they rained down on the tarmac.

"Fuck your exclusive," Jago said. His eyes blazed with fury. "Cal is dead. You'll be joining him if you don't leave now."

His chin throbbing, Scott leaned forward. His body trembled with anger.

"Listen to me, you little prick. Come tomorrow, I'll make sure you and your mother look like the backwater inbreds you are. You want to know who's responsible for your brother's disappearance? You are! Maybe if you'd kept a better eye on him, he'd still be—"

Jago's fist connected with his nose. Scott flew back, blood spraying in the air. Pain shot up his spine as he hit the ground.

Leaning over him, Jago raised his fist again.

Scott drew up his hands.

"Jago, stop!"

Tess Pengelly stood in the doorway, a faded blue bathrobe wrapped around her skeletal body. Her hair hung in lank tresses around her shoulders. Black shadows circled blank eyes. She held onto herself as if the action was the only thing keeping her together. Scott watched as Jago slowly lowered his fist.

"Come back inside," Tess said, her eyes trained on her son.

Scott pulled himself up on his elbows. Blood flowed from his nose and splashed on his shirt. He looked up at Jago, who slowly turned to face him. Without saying another word, the boy moved towards his mother. Only when Jago had disappeared inside, did Tess acknowledge Scott's presence.

She looked like a ghost, he thought; the life draining out of her a little more with each day that Noah was missing.

Tess opened her mouth to say something. She closed it again. She turned and looked down the street, then disappeared inside the house, closing the door behind her.

Pinching his nose to stop the blood flow, Scott pushed himself up with his free hand and staggered to his feet. Well, this is just great, he thought, as a wave of pain turned into nausea. He stumbled back to the road, where his phone lay in pieces.

So he'd failed in getting the quote he'd wanted from the Pengellys, but he still had the picture of Callum Anderson. And he had the story ready to go on his—"Shit!"—phone.

Blood was still flowing. He could taste it at the back of his throat. A fresh wave of pain pulsed from the centre of his nose.

"Think, Triggs," he hissed. He was running out of time. If he could get to a phone, he could call the press room again and dictate the story to Charlie. But he still needed to send the photo from his memory card. He could do that from his laptop, but not without an Internet connection.

The alternative option was to get in the car and drive like a maniac back to the office, hopefully without getting himself killed. But he couldn't drive until his nose had stopped bleeding.

He pinched the bridge of his nose harder. A bolt of white hot pain brought tears to his eyes.

Screw the Pengellys! And screw the Killigrews, too! They'd not only destroyed several hundred pounds' worth of his property, but they'd thrown his big break into jeopardy.

There was no way he was letting them win. Tomorrow, that front page would be his and their names would be dragged through the mud.

His eyes wandered up and down the street as he tried to think of a plan. They came to rest on the dirty walls of the cottage two doors up.

Grady Spencer.

It was probably too much to expect the old codger to have the Internet, but he might have a phone. Scott could call the press room and tell them he was on the way. If they refused to wait a little longer, he'd threaten to give the story to someone else.

Pushing open the garden gate, he cast one last glance at the remnants of his shattered mobile phone, cursed Jago Pengelly's name, then hobbled towards Grady Spencer's house.

"Okay, you old bastard," he said. "You're my only hope."

15

Grady Spencer's garden was a mess. The lawn was choked with weeds. Thick brambles sprouted from the hedgerow. The path to the front door was old and cracked.

Scott cleared his throat, dabbed at his bloody nose with a tissue, then knocked on the door.

Immediately, the air filled with high-pitched yaps. Scott grimaced. If that rat started getting nasty again, he'd kick it where the sun didn't shine.

He waited a few seconds more, then impatiently rapped his knuckles on the front door. Caliban's barking rose to a higher pitch.

A moment later, he heard locks being drawn back, followed by chains being removed. The door opened a crack. Grady Spencer's unpleasant face stared out. At the foot of the door, Caliban pushed his snout through the gap and drew back his lips into a snarl.

"Ah, it's you," the old man sneered. "What happened to your face? Ask the wrong questions, did you?"

"Something like that," Scott said, his voice nasally. "Listen, I need your help."

"Always wanting something, aren't you? What is it now?"

As Scott quickly explained his situation, Grady Spencer regarded him with a disdainful look. At his heels, Caliban continued to growl.

"Was I right, then?" Grady said. "About the boy? It was that Anderson child."

Scott hesitated. Screw it, he thought. Tomorrow the story would be everywhere. He doubted even Grady Spencer could move fast enough to leak the news to another journalist.

"You were right," he said, nodding. "The boy on the beach is none other than Callum Anderson. You're a real detective."

Grady Spencer arched an eyebrow. "You being clever?"

"Just honest." Scott tried to peer past the old man, into the house. An odour wafted out; a smothering concoction of dust and mould. "So, can you help a friend out and let me use your phone? I'll mention your name in the story as a thank you."

He had no intention of doing so. The glory of revealing Callum Anderson to the world was his alone.

Grady regarded him for a moment, his breaths laboured and filled with liquid. Down at his feet, Caliban let out a shrill yap.

"You best be quick," the old man said, opening the door to its full extent. Caliban growled, earning himself a swift tap of Grady's foot. Scott paused, staring into the hallway. A dingy light hung from the ceiling, illuminating stacks of magazines and papers piled up against dirty walls. A staircase led up to the top floor on the left, its carpet threadbare and turning to dust.

"Not fancy enough for you, is it?" Grady said, his upper lip curling at the corners.

Scott smiled. "A man's home is his kingdom."

He stepped over the threshold and into the hall. The smell of decay filled his nostrils, intensifying the pain caused by Jago's fist.

Grady Spencer closed the door and slid the bolt across.

"Is that necessary?" Scott said, eyeing the locks.

"Door doesn't shut by itself. Been trying to get someone to fix it for months." The old man brushed past him. Caliban trotted alongside.

As he followed Grady through the house, Scott's journalistic eyes grew wide and round. If the stacks of newspapers and magazines in the hallway were a subtle clue, the rest of the house screamed at him at a deafening volume. He had entered a hoarder's domain. Open doors revealed rooms filled with boxes and crates stacked in precarious towers. Cupboard doors hung open revealing bags upon bags of unknown items that threatened to burst forth like a broken dam. Scott didn't know what he felt the most—pity for the old man or disgust.

The end of the hall lay in shadows. He followed Grady through a door on the right. The kitchen was large and high-ceilinged. The perfect size for Grady Spencer to fill it to the brim with crap. Scott watched as he shuffled over to a large table, which was covered in more books and magazines. Where the hell did this guy eat? Making a space on the table, Grady pulled out a chair and brushed it down with the back of his hand.

"Sit there."

"I really just need to use the phone, if that's all right."

Grady's eyes narrowed.

Still pinching the bridge of his nose, Scott reluctantly sat down. He was going to have to shower as soon as he got home.

"That was some clout the Pengelly boy gave you," Grady said, with a chuckle, as he picked up the kettle from the stove and brought it over to the sink, which was surprisingly free of dirty dishes. "Deserve it, did you?"

"The boy's unhinged. Just like his mother." Scott pulled a fresh tissue from his pocket and dabbed his nose. The bleeding was slowing, but the pain was growing more intense. He had painkillers in the car but there was no way he was leaving until he had spoken to someone at the Chronicle.

A growl from beneath the table made him look down. Caliban glared back and bared his fangs.

Scott wondered if he should use the old man's bathroom to clean up his face before driving to the office. Plus, he'd gone hours without pissing and now his bladder was throbbing in complaint. His eyes swept the room, taking in the disarray. If the kitchen was this unsanitary what hope did he have of not coming away from Grady's bathroom with some incurable disease?

Across the room, Grady dumped the kettle on the stove, turned a dial to release the gas, then struck a match. There was a sharp *whoosh* and blue flames shot out in a wide arc.

"Is that thing safe?" Scott asked. The stove had to be at least thirty years old.

"My house is still standing, is it not? You a tea drinker, boy?"

Scott smiled. It had been several years since he had been referred to as a boy. There was no time for tea and gossip. He had a career-changing story to write. Where was the damn phone?

Grady was staring at him expectantly. No tea, no phone. It was suddenly obvious that was the deal.

Damn it.

"Sure," Scott said, his whole head throbbing now. He had no intention of imbibing anything made in this house. Perhaps he should just leave. Take his chances in the car and hope for empty roads. He glanced at the kitchen door.

"So, you saw the Anderson boy with your own eyes?" Grady removed two cracked mugs from a cupboard. Even from where he sat, Scott could see they were covered in a fine layer of dust.

"That's right. You'll read all about it tomorrow. So, if I could just use your phone . . ."

Ignoring him, Grady opened the refrigerator door. Terrible smells came out but he didn't seem to notice. He pulled off the top of a carton of milk and brought it to his nose. "You ask me, that boy should have been taken away from her when she had him. What did she know about looking after a child? She *was* a child."

Scott looked up. Perhaps there was some more meat for his story here. "What about Callum's father?"

"Kye Anderson. Scum, like the rest of his family. Only thing they're good for is collecting money from the state." He shuffled over to the table, a rancid odour of stale urine trailing him. "You ask me, it was Carrie's own fault she lost her boy. Maybe if she kept a closer eye on him, she wouldn't have had all those years of grief. Women like Carrie Killigrew only care about one thing; what men think of 'em. That boy deserved better than he ever got from her."

He glanced over his shoulder. "Maybe wherever he was, he was loved. Bet she hasn't even thought about that. Bet she hasn't even thought to be grateful."

On the stove, the kettle began to whistle.

Scott stared at the old man, noting the anger on his face. And something else he couldn't quite read. Was it pain? Grief? Grady Spencer turned his head sharply and locked eyes with him. Scott forced a smile to his lips. The throb in his bladder intensified.

The old man shuffled over to the stove and, removing the kettle from the burner, began pouring hot water into the mugs. There was something here. Scott was suddenly sure of it. His intuition was singing like a choirboy.

"What do you mean by that?" he asked. "That wherever Cal was, he was loved?"

Grady poured milk into the mugs. "Didn't mean a thing. Sugar?"

"No thanks. So where do you think Carrie's son has been all this time? Do you think someone local could have taken him?"

The drinks made, Grady shuffled over to the table. As he moved, tea slopped over the sides of the mugs and splashed on the faded linoleum. Setting them down on the table, he pushed a pile of magazines off a chair and onto the floor.

He sat, staring squarely at Scott, then smiled, revealing cracked, yellow teeth.

"Trouble is these days, everyone thinks they know everything. Everyone thinks they're too clever for their own good." He glanced down at Caliban, who had moved to sit by his side. He reached down and allowed the dog to lick his hand. Scott grimaced. "Just like with the Pengelly boy. Everyone has an opinion about what happened to him, too. But they're all wrong."

There was a strange look in the old man's eye. A spark of something. Was it danger? Excitement?

"Oh? And how would you know that?"

Grady leaned back, an unnerving, triumphant look on his face.

Scott leaned forward, pressing down on his bladder. The urge to piss grew unbearable.

"Mr Spencer, is there something you'd like to tell me?"

Spreading his lips into a full-toothed grin, the old man began to laugh. And then the smile vanished. "There are things I could tell you that would make your hair turn white. Stories that would make you curl up in a corner and cry like a baby." He paused, his pupils growing large and black, like pools of oil. "But you've heard enough tales from me for now. We'll save those for another time."

He smiled again.

Blood rushed in Scott's ears as he stared at the old man. Suddenly, he wanted nothing more than to be a hundred miles away from Grady Spencer and his claustrophobic kitchen.

But he needed to make that phone call before it was too late. And now he was about to piss himself. *God damn it!*

"Could I use your bathroom?" he asked, as a searing pain shot through his bladder.

Grady watched him, that strange smile still on his lips. He nodded to the kitchen door. "First on your left at the top of the stairs. The chain's rusty. Be gentle when you give it a pull."

Scott jumped to his feet. "Thanks. Perhaps you could point me to your phone as well?"

The old man stared.

Unable to wait any longer, Scott raced out of the kitchen, glad to be away from Grady Spencer for now. All the mess and bad odours were making him queasy. Heading through the hall, he reached the stairs and took them two steps at a time, careful not to touch the railings with his hands.

The upstairs landing was gloomy and dank. Curtains were drawn over the single small window. The stench of mildew choked the air. Pushing open the first door on the left, Scott was relieved to find that, except for the mouldy walls, the bathroom was relatively clean. He made quick work of emptying his bladder then gave the chain a gentle pull as Grady had instructed. He washed his hands while trying not to imagine the origins of the strange stains at the bottom of the sink, and splashed water over his face to wash away the dried blood.

Catching sight of his reflection in the mirror, he winced. His nose was swollen to almost twice the size. A dark bruise was blooming on his chin. Nothing was broken, though. *Good job,* he thought, looking around for a towel before deciding to dry his face on the sleeve of his shirt.

He turned to leave. Something caught his eye.

A bright blue rubber boat sat on the edge of the cracked bathtub. Its little funnels were painted bright red. On the front of the boat were two large cartoon eyes. In other circumstances, Scott would have laughed at a grown man being in possession of something so childish. But the sight of the toy sent a sliver of ice slipping down his spine. He leaned forward and picked up the boat, turning it over in his hands.

Perhaps Grady had grandchildren that sometimes came to visit. But what parent in their right mind would bring a child into a house like this?

Replacing the boat on the edge of the tub, he stepped back onto the landing. Something was wrong. He'd felt it in the kitchen, a kind of energy teasing the hairs on his skin. He'd felt it when he'd looked directly at Grady Spencer, when the old man had spoken so cryptically about Noah Pengelly.

Scott's eyes roamed the landing. The door next to the bathroom was ajar. He glanced back at the stairs and cocked his head.

He would take a quick look. Just poke his head around the door. Then he would go. He'd find a pay phone along the way. He should have done so in the first place. Scott stepped through the open door and peered inside.

It was a large bedroom. The curtains were open, but the filthy window panes let in little light. To Scott's surprise, the room was almost clutter free. The furniture was old and rickety, the carpet bald. The double bed in the centre had seen better days.

Wrinkling his nose at the overpowering stench of urine and stale air, Scott moved silently into the room. There was nothing out of the ordinary here. Just an old man's bedroom in need of a good bleaching.

He shook his head. Perhaps the knock to his head and unbalanced his instincts. His mind returned to the toy boat.

And that was when he saw it.

In the corner of the room.

A cage. It was too big for that stupid terrier. In fact, it was better suited to a much larger dog. A German Shepherd perhaps. A Doberman.

Or a child.

Scott moved up to the cage and bent his knees. The inside was cast in shadows but he could see something lying on the floor inside. Slipping his hand in between the bars, he fumbled around until his fingers found what they were looking for.

He drew them out. His heart smashed against his ribcage. In his hand were old comic books, their pages curled as if read many times. Fear blossoming in his stomach, Scott stumbled back. He stared at the comics still clutched in his hand.

What did he do?

He could run downstairs and out the front door, and head straight to the police. And tell them what exactly? That Grady Spencer was somehow behind the disappearance of Noah Pengelly? A handful of comic books was not evidence. Finding Noah, dead or alive, was.

Or he could get to the press room and make sure his story was on tomorrow's front page.

A voice from downstairs shattered his thoughts.

"You get lost up there, did you?"

Goosebumps prickled Scott's arms. *Fuck.*

He gave the comics one more glance then stuffed them down the back of his jeans. He found Grady Spencer back in the kitchen and sitting at the table. He looked up when Scott entered, that strange, disconcerting smile on his lips.

"Your tea is going cold," he said. "I didn't make it for nothing, did I?"

Scott remained standing. He should have chosen the door. He should have been on his way to the police station.

"I need to go," he said, his throat running dry.

The old man leaned forward, watching him closely. "You wanted to use the telephone. You said it was urgent."

"I remembered something I have to do back at the office."

"I let you in my home and I made you tea. You haven't taken a single sip." Grady's eyes grew even darker. The shadows in the room seemed to reach out to him. Then the old man threw a hand in the air. "Suit yourself." Reaching over, he picked up Scott's still full mug. He shuffled across the kitchen and dumped it in the sink.

Now there was some distance between them, Scott sucked in a breath. If Noah was here, he had to find him. He may have behaved like an asshole most of the time, but Scott was not a monster. Besides, he thought, as he turned and glanced at the kitchen door, he could already see the headline: JOURNALIST SAVES MISSING BOY FROM HOUSE OF HORRORS.

Perhaps he would be the hero in this story after all.

He'd need to distract the old man. Use physical force if necessary to subdue him. Then he would search the house from top to bottom. Noah had to be well hidden. His mind whirring, Scott wondered if the house had a basement.

"The trouble with you journalists," Grady said, standing by the stove, "is that you think you can waltz in and out of people's lives, asking your questions and making up the answers without a care in the world."

Scott was half-listening, half-watching the door. He tried to mentally picture the hall. Stairs were on the left. Two doors on the right: a living room and a dining room.

"Oh, you think you're changing the world, changing people's lives," Grady continued. "But all you're really doing is poking your nose in where it doesn't belong. Sniffing around like some filthy animal, spreading disease with your words."

There had been another door, hadn't there? On the left, just past the stairs. Scott had the sudden urge to run out and see.

"You don't understand a town like this. You think you can pull wool over our eyes any time you please. Well, we're not all so naive, Mister Journalist. Some of us saw you coming a mile away. Some of us saw what a scourge you were, coming in here, trying to drag up trouble when things needed to be left alone."

Scott looked up, startled to see Grady Spencer beside him, his face twisted into a frightening grimace.

"He's my boy," the old man snarled. "Mine."

The kettle struck the side of Scott's head, sending him crashing against the wall. He slid down it. The room went white. Then red. Pain ripped through his skull.

Grady brought the kettle down again, smashing it into his face. Bones snapped. Blood spurted.

Scott slumped forward. The world went dark.

16

THE HOUSE WAS QUIET. Carrie stood in the landing, listening to the creaks of the old cottage. A blanket of tiredness wrapped around her. It had been a strange day. A joyous day. One filled with fear and doubt. But one filled with wonder and a feeling she could not put into words.

Tiptoeing to Melissa's room, she pushed open the door a few inches and peered in. Melissa lay on her side, long hair covering her face. She purred softly like a kitten.

Carrie smiled. Melissa had coped well with the new addition to the family. It wouldn't be an easy transition, Carrie knew that, but Melissa was young. She would soon grow to love having an older brother to watch out for her.

Closing the door, Carrie moved noiselessly until she stood outside Cal's bedroom. The door was open a crack. He had been afraid to be left alone in the dark and confused by the bedtime routine. Carrie wondered just how much he could remember of his old life. She pushed the door open a few inches more and poked her head inside.

Her heart stopped. The bed was empty.

She looked down the hall and peered into the bathroom. The door was open, the lights switched off.

She saw him moments later.

He was curled up beneath the bed with his back to the room, naked except for his underwear. The pyjamas she'd given him still lay on top of the mattress. Carrie winced as she looked at the myriad scars and marks on his skin.

"Cal?"

He remained still, his shoulders gently moving with each breath. She wondered if she should wake him, to get him into the bed where he would be more comfortable. But waking him might cause another panicked outburst. It had taken Carrie over an hour to calm him down following the incident at dinner.

She hung in the doorway for a minute more, listening to his breaths, then moved along the landing.

Dylan was barely awake, a John Grisham novel slowly slipping from his hands. Carrie climbed into bed beside him. He lifted one arm and she slipped into the crook.

"Everyone okay?" Dylan's voice was heavy with sleep.

Carrie rested her head on his bare chest. The steady beat of his heart filled her ears. It was calming, quietening the anxieties that plagued her mind.

"Cal is under the bed," she said.

Dylan opened an eye. "What's he doing under there?"

"Sleeping."

They were both quiet for a moment.

"I'm sorry about earlier. I shouldn't have lost my temper like that, not in front of you or the kids." Dylan brushed strands of hair from Carrie's face. She remained silent. "What about tomorrow when Cal's name is released to the papers? What's going to happen then?"

Carrie sighed. She didn't want to think about it. Not now. She just wanted to sleep.

"I guess we'll find out in the morning."

Dylan had both eyes open now. He put the book down and kissed the top of Carrie's head. "I'm worried about leaving you on Thursday."

"So, don't leave."

"Carrie…"

She sat up. "I know. We need the money. But can't you wait just a few more days?"

"You know I can't. The fish aren't going to wait for us and nor are the other fleets. If we lose a few days, it could mean the difference between food on the table or going hungry."

Carrie turned away.

"I need you here," she said.

Dylan sat up. "I *am* here. And I'll only be gone for a few days."

"A lot can happen in a few days."

Carrie drew in a deep breath and held onto it. She hated how helpless she sounded. Like she couldn't cope on her own. The truth was, she wasn't sure if she could. She had no idea what was going through Cal's mind. She had no idea if she had the strength or the knowledge to deal with his trauma. But he was her son. It was her responsibility.

Dylan turned to face her, his tired eyes softening.

"Look, if you don't think you can cope, I'll see if I can get someone else to replace me. It means we'll be eating beans three times a day for a while, but you're right. I should be here."

He kissed her shoulder, then her neck. Carrie felt her skin tingle. She shut her eyes. Dylan was right. Holiday season was over. The shop would soon be closed until next spring. Business hadn't been great this summer as it was. There was maybe enough money in the bank to cover things, just. But if Dylan stayed home any longer they'd be in trouble. The last thing she wanted was for her family to go hungry.

I can do this, she told herself.

She'd survived Cal's disappearance. She'd survived thinking he was dead for seven years. Hell, she'd survived two childbirths. She could manage a few days on her own.

She turned to face him, bringing her lips to his.

"You're right. You should go. I don't like beans."

Dylan smiled. "You're sure?"

His fingers glided along her bare shoulder and down her arm. She kissed him again.

"I'm not made of glass, you know."

Dylan's fingers moved further down. He kissed her, harder this time. She pressed into it. Then pulled away.

"I want to," she whispered. "But Cal... What if he needs me?"

"No fair," Dylan breathed in her ear. He nibbled her lobe. "Fine. I'll add it to your tab."

"My tab?" Carrie punched his arm.

Dylan flashed her a wicked grin. "I never told you about that?"

"No, you didn't."

They were both quiet for a second, the fire they had started still burning. Then Dylan extinguished it.

"What are you going to do about Cal's dad?"

Any anxiety Carrie had put to one side came flooding back.

The last time she had spoken to Kye was ten months after Cal had disappeared. He'd made a brief return from the oil rigs. She and Dylan had yet to start their relationship. A chance meeting with Kye on the seafront had led to too many drinks and too much grief brought to the surface. They'd gone back to Carrie's house and slept with each other, their bodies connected by sadness. Kye had left the next morning. Carrie hadn't heard from him since, and as far as she knew, he hadn't returned to Porth an Jowl. But he had a right to know that Cal was back. That his son was not dead.

"I'll get in touch with his parents," she said. "I think they're in Falmouth now. They'll know where to find him."

"And what then?" Dylan asked.

"Well, I guess Kye will want to see Cal."

Silence grew between them. Carrie no longer felt tired. Her

mind was awake, racing, remembering, worrying. She glanced across at Dylan, who shared a similar expression. His gaze met hers. He traced a finger over the back of her hand.

"And what about your parents?" he said, quietly.

Carrie pulled away. What was he trying to achieve tonight?

"What about them?" she said. "They haven't bothered with me in years."

"But still—"

"I'm not having this conversation. Jesus, Dylan."

She lunged for the bedside lamp and switched it off. Lying down, she turned on her side and stared at the bedroom door. If her parents wanted to find out about Cal, they'd have to do it through the press. If they wanted to see him, they'd have to make the first move. She was done with them.

An angry tear slipped from her eye and ran across the bridge of her nose to soak into the pillow. Behind her, Dylan reached over and switched off his bedside light.

"I'm sorry," he whispered.

He lay next to her but made no move to wrap his arm around her like he usually did.

Carrie lay on her side, overwhelmed by anger, wanting nothing more than to feel her husband's skin against her own.

17

MONDAY MORNING BROUGHT grey skies and light rain. Carrie had been awake for a short while, lying next to Dylan as she stared up at the ceiling. She hadn't slept well; a mixture of excitement and anxiety overwhelming her brain.

She knew she should contact Kye's parents. Not just to locate him but to tell *them* that their grandson was alive. They would be overjoyed to see him. But she was unsure about having Kye back in her life again. Or if Cal was ready for more upheaval. He barely seemed able to cope with returning home to his mother and a larger, newer family.

Perhaps it was best to delay reaching out to them by another week. But by then Cal's name would be plastered all over the newspapers. And did she have the right to make that decision, anyway? After all, Kye was Cal's father, not Dylan.

Turning on her side, she watched Dylan sleep for a little while. He always looked so peaceful in his slumber, the weathered lines at the corners of his eyes softer. He was a handsome man. Looking at him now, she felt the same tingle she'd experienced when they'd first spoken at The Shack. She had known of him since they'd been children but they hadn't been friends in school. Being a few years older, Dylan had frequented different circles. It was only after Kye had left that they'd exchange more than just a few words.

Dylan had been good to her in those early days. The pain of her loss was still raw but he never shied away from it. He was there when she needed to talk. Sensible enough to keep his distance when she needed to be alone. And so far, he hadn't grown tired of her sometimes-difficult ways. But now, lying next to him, Carrie couldn't help but worry that Cal's appearance was already causing a rift between them. Not because Dylan was uncaring. But because everything had changed.

Climbing out of bed, Carrie threw on a pair of shorts and one of Dylan's old T-shirts, and made her way out to the landing.

Melissa was awake, sitting in the centre of her bedroom floor, surrounded by toys.

"Morning, sweet pea." Smiling, Carrie crept into the room and sat beside her daughter. "How's my little pumpkin?"

Melissa shrugged her shoulders. Usually, she greeted Carrie with a babble of conversation and too much energy for an early morning. Today, she turned away and turned her attention to her game; a scenario involving one of her dolls and a police car.

"Everything okay?" Carrie ran her fingers through her daughter's long hair.

Melissa pulled away. "I'm hungry. I want pancakes."

Carrie sucked in a breath. Okay, here we go, she thought. She had expected some rejection from Melissa—it seemed a natural part of the process of moving from only child to youngest sibling. But she hadn't expected it to sting so sharply.

Planting a kiss on Melissa's head before she could escape, Carrie stood. "Well, I'll see if the pancake fairies are visiting today. I have a feeling you may be in luck."

Leaving Melissa with her toys, Carrie returned to the landing and moved along to Cal's room. The door was still open a crack. She knocked softly.

Cal was not in his bed. Had he slept beneath it all night? She moved into the room and cocked her head.

He wasn't under the bed. He wasn't in his room.

Ignoring the quickening of her heartbeat, Carrie returned to the landing and checked the bathroom. Finding it empty, she hurried back to Melissa.

"Have you seen your brother?"

Melissa looked up, a scowl creasing her features.

"I don't have a brother," she said.

Panicking now, Carrie hurried downstairs and made a quick search of the house.

Cal was not there.

The ground shifted beneath Carrie's feet. She felt as if she were falling. It was the same feeling she'd experienced that day on the beach. Falling through blackness with no end in sight.

"Cal?" She spun a full circle. He was gone. She had lost him again. "Cal, are you here?"

What did she do? She wondered if she should call the police or if she should go looking for him. But what if he came back and she wasn't here? Moving quickly, she grabbed the phone from the kitchen wall. She had to find him before he disappeared forever.

She dialled 999 for the emergency services. As she waited, her gaze shifted to the kitchen window.

A surge of relief flooded her senses.

Hanging up the phone, she wrenched open the kitchen door and stumbled into the backyard.

Cal stood, shivering in his underwear in the centre of the lawn and staring up at a charcoal sky.

Carrie ground to a halt. She watched him for a second, taking in the old scars and marks that littered his wet skin. Pain stabbed at her heart.

"Cal?"

His head shifted in her direction. His body grew taut.

"What are you doing?" She stepped closer.

Cal's gaze lingered on her before returning to the sky.

"Come on, come inside," Carrie said. "You'll hurt your eyes."

Cal didn't move. He continued to blink away the raindrops, oblivious of his shivering body.

"Come inside now before you catch a cold."

This time, Carrie didn't wait for an answer. She took him by the arm and gently guided him back to the house. In the kitchen, she grabbed a clean towel and began drying him down.

"You scared me," she said, as he watched her work. "I thought you were gone."

When Cal was dry, Carrie dumped the towel on the side.

"You should put some clothes on. I'll make some breakfast. Do you like pancakes?" She felt suddenly ashamed that she couldn't remember. Cal stared at her. "Go on. Go and get warm."

He stood for a second longer before heading back upstairs.

When she was alone, Carrie stared at her hands. They were trembling. Her heart thumped with dizzying palpitations, as if she had just completed a marathon.

He was still here. Cal had not disappeared. She had not lost him again. She allowed a moment for her body to relax, then began pulling out pancake ingredients from the cupboards.

She looked up. She could hear voices. A few at first, then suddenly more, rushing in like a swarm of bees.

Leaving the kitchen, she hurried into the hall. The voices were coming from outside. She knew who they belonged to before she rushed into the living room and threw back the curtains.

The press had arrived in all their glory. There had to be at least twenty of them gathered outside. A news van pulled up. A camera crew spilled out of it. At the sight of Carrie in the window, photographers turned in her direction and began snapping away. The chorus of voices, all hungry for a story, rose in volume.

Carrie snapped the curtains shut.

"Dylan!"

"I see them!" he called from upstairs.

"Keep the kids away from the windows!"

She took the steps two at a time.

Dylan was out of bed and on his feet. Melissa wandered out of her room, toys swinging from her hands.

"Who are those people?" she asked.

"Pains in the butt," Dylan said, sweeping her up in his arms.

Carrie brushed past them and entered Melissa's bedroom. She stared down at the gaggle of people, who were now all staring up and taking more pictures. She closed the curtains.

Returning to the landing, she saw Cal standing in his bedroom doorway, now dressed, his eyes round and his shoulders hunched. His bedroom overlooked the backyard. Unlike the idiot from yesterday, it seemed these journalists were at least playing by the rules and staying off her property.

"It's okay, Cal. They'll go away soon." Carrie turned to look at Dylan, who was busy pretending he'd stolen Melissa's nose.

"Well," he said, glancing up, "looks like we're staying indoors. Who's up for a pizza and movie day?"

Melissa squealed with delight.

Cal stared at the floor and squeezed Rex in his fist.

"Why can't they just leave us alone?" Carrie said.

"They will. Soon. Something more exciting will come along."

Glancing worriedly at Cal, who was now swaying from side to side, Carrie bit down on her lip.

"I hope you're right."

18

Jago opened his eyes then squeezed them shut again as pain pierced his skull. He groaned, turning over on the bed. An empty bottle of vodka lay next to him. Clothes were strewn across the room, along with a jumble of magazines, art books, and old sketch pads. He sat up, vaguely aware of a TV blaring from somewhere in the house. Rubbing his eyes, he fumbled for his mobile phone on the bedside table. It was just before midday and he'd missed three calls from Nat.

He couldn't remember going to sleep, which meant he'd passed out again. It wasn't a good thing, he knew that. But vodka washed away his pain. At least until the morning. Until right now. Grief punched him in the gut and knocked the breath from his lungs.

Doubling over, he pulled his knees up to his chest and waited for the sensation to pass. Noah was gone. Jago was forced to relive the realisation every single morning.

The hammering in his head grew louder. So did the volume of the TV. It was deafening, as if his mother had cranked it as loud as it would go.

Dragging himself from the bed, he threw on yesterday's clothes and stood for a minute, attempting to push through the wave of nausea that rolled up to greet him.

When the risk of throwing up had passed, he moved to the window and pulled open the blinds.

The late grey morning seeped in. He winced as his eyes adjusted to daylight. Rain was coming down in a depressing drizzle, dampening the overgrown garden.

His mind flashed back to yesterday evening and his encounter with Scott Triggs. The man was a liar. He had to be. Because Callum Anderson was dead.

After returning indoors with his mother, Jago had fed her lies, telling her the journalist was only after more quotes. Once she was dosed up for the night, he had gone to his room and started drinking. Memories of Cal had swum in his mind, mingling with his memories of Noah. After drinking enough vodka to numb the edges of his pain, Jago had begun to wonder if the journalist had been telling the truth.

Was the boy on the beach really Cal? He'd drowned seven years ago, pulled under by the currents.

The more he'd thought about it, the more ridiculous it seemed. And yet, for a few minutes, he'd almost convinced himself to stumble down to the Killigrew house and find out for himself. The need to kill his pain had stopped him.

Now, some of the doubt he felt last night returned.

It had to have been a lie because it was too ridiculous to be true.

Leaving his bedroom, he stumbled onto the landing. The TV was booming out from his mother's room. He wondered how she could sleep through it, even with the cocktail of pills and booze she swallowed each day.

"Mum, turn it down!" he growled. His hangover was well and truly kicking in, clawing at the base of his skull. He smacked his lips together. He was dehydrated. Somewhere deep in his stomach, a rumble of hunger echoed and he tried to remember the last time he'd eaten. Yesterday at breakfast, maybe. Or had it been the day before?

"Mum!"

Anger buzzed inside him as he stalked towards his mother's door. He knocked once. Waited. Knocked again. When she still didn't answer, he threw open the door and stomped inside.

The air in the room was rank with alcohol. Much like his own. The curtains were closed, the bedsheets pulled back. In the corner, an old portable TV flashed in the shadows, showing a news bulletin. The reporter's voice stabbed at Jago's ears.

Grimacing, he crossed the room, looking for the remote. Unable to find it, he moved up to the TV and twisted the volume dial. He froze, instantly recognising the images on the screen.

The news reporter was standing outside a familiar looking house. The image cut to a shot of the beach, then to one of the town square. Jago reached for the volume and turned it back up.

For a second, he wondered if the story was about Noah. Then, as the reporter continued to speak, a picture flashed on the screen.

His jaw dropped open. He was staring at a photograph taken at least seven years ago. It was a picture of Callum Anderson. His childhood friend, who had tragically drowned one summer afternoon. But Cal was not dead, the reporter was announcing. Cal was very much alive.

Jago stood. The room spun around him.

Scott Triggs had been telling the truth. Cal was alive.

It was impossible. Where had he been hiding these last seven years? A surge of hope rushed through Jago's body. If Cal was alive, did that mean Noah was alive, too? And if Cal was alive, did it mean that he and Noah had been together? That he knew where he could be found?

"Mum, have you seen this?" he called. She had to be downstairs somewhere. A sliver of ice pierced his brain, jolting him fully awake. He turned and surveyed the mess in her bedroom. Normally, she would be asleep now. If you could call it sleep. She rarely woke before mid-afternoon. Jago's heart skipped up and down as he glanced at the television. Where was she?

Leaving the room, he raced downstairs, sweeping from room to room.

"Shit," he breathed.

His mother wasn't here. But he knew exactly where she'd gone.

19

BY THE TIME morning passed over into afternoon, the press was showing no signs of leaving. Much to Carrie's annoyance, she had spotted neighbours talking to various journalists as she'd peeked through her bedroom curtains. She would be having strong words with Dottie Penpol and Elvira Trevithick once she was free to leave her home, no doubt about it.

The children seemed to be handling the situation better than the adults; Melissa played happily with her toys while Cal watched television. All his favourite shows were gone. Now, he flicked between a cartoon aimed at a much younger audience and a violent heist movie. Carrie tried to persuade him to watch something more appropriate but he refused. She left him alone; it was difficult enough dealing with the shit show outside without Cal having another meltdown.

Dylan had spent most of the morning pacing the living room floor and occasionally peering through the curtains. Eventually, he'd moved upstairs.

He and Carrie had barely spoken a word in the last hour. So

much had changed in the last week. Their entire world, she supposed. Dylan's life had been turned upside down without any choice in the matter. And now he was father to a stepson he wasn't meant to have. A stepson who'd been through an unknown horrific experience. Who was traumatised. Who couldn't even speak.

Carrie wondered what Dylan really felt about that.

He was trying to be supportive, she could see that, but his outward veneer was beginning to crack. Being trapped inside the house like an animal in a cage wasn't helping, either. Especially when you were surrounded by journalists wanting to put your picture in the paper.

She'd been through it already and knew exactly how it felt. Back then, she'd been young and naive. The devastation of losing Cal had far exceeded the shame of being accused of being a bad parent. Now, with Cal back home, the media attention seemed somehow more intrusive. More dangerous.

But Dylan was right. Sooner or later, a different story would attract their attention and Cal's reappearance would be old news.

"You kids okay?" she asked from the living room doorway.

Cal's eyes were still fixed on the television. On the screen, a car chase was in progress. Melissa sat on the carpet a metre away from him, drawing pictures in her sketchbook. Neither of them looked up. Taking their silence as a sign they were both fine, Carrie padded into the hall. She could hear the journalists babbling outside. No doubt having a good chat about her family. Comparing notes, perhaps, as they waited for the Killigrews to emerge.

Another sound reached her ears. The thud of Dylan's feet as he paced up and down their bedroom. She thought about going up to him then changed her mind. When Dylan paced, it almost always meant he needed to be left alone, until he'd either worked out the problem or his legs had grown tired. Carrie was restless herself. There was only so much sitting down she could do. Besides, the darkness of the house was insidious, creeping beneath her skin and filling her with gloom.

Perhaps she should move everyone into the kitchen, she thought, where there was still light and privacy. Or perhaps she should throw open the living room curtains and give those damn journalists the finger. *Yeah, sure. Great idea.*

As she turned to gather her children and ferry them into the kitchen, the journalists' din swelled with excitement. She heard cameras clicking and flashing. The din grew into a frenzy.

Heading into the living room, Carrie moved to the window and pulled back a curtain.

"Oh, shit," she breathed.

Melissa drew in a shocked gasp. "You said a bad word!"

Carrie snapped the curtains shut and raced back out to the hall. "Dylan! Get down here, now!"

The words had barely left her mouth when there was a hurried rapping on the door.

"Shit. Fuck."

Dylan was descending the stairs, looking tired and angry. "What's wrong?"

The rapping came again, this time harder, more urgent.

Carrie shook her head. "I have to open it."

"Why? Who's there?"

"It's Tess."

"Are you kidding me?" Dylan was beside her now, staring at the door. "You can't open it. The journalists will have a field day."

"I can't ignore her."

"Yes, you can. If you open that door, you might as well invite the whole damn lot of them inside."

Carrie folded her arms and met her husband's glare. "She's lost her son, Dylan. You know why she's here."

"But we don't know where her son is. We don't know that Cal does either. We don't even know where he's been."

"I know that. I'm not letting her near Cal. But I can't just let her stand there. Imagine what the papers will say."

The knocking came again. Then the doorbell, harsh and shrill in their ears. Dylan let out a heavy sigh. He shook his head and took a step back. "I hope you know what you're doing."

"Not really. Go in with the kids, make sure they're okay. And Dylan?"

"Yeah?"

"Please, stay in there. No more smashing journalists' cameras, not while they're all watching."

"I'm not promising anything."

Carrie watched him disappear into the living room. She turned to the front door and drew in a deep breath. She held it for as long as she could then let it out.

Then she unlocked the door and pulled it open.

A wave of noise crashed over her.

Tess Pengelly stood on the doorstep, a pale representation of the person she used to be. Her hair was a mess. Dark shadows were tattooed beneath her eyes. She wore clothes that hadn't seen a washing machine in days. Behind her, the journalists hung over the garden gate, pushing and shoving each other, all barking questions.

"Tess . . ." Carrie's voice was lost beneath the din. "What are you doing here?"

Tess stared at her with hollow eyes that moved behind Carrie into the hall.

"Where is he? Does he know anything?" she said, her voice exhausted and trembling. "I need to see him."

Carrie remained unmoving in the doorway. Two months ago, Tess had been healthy and happy. Then Noah had disappeared, snatching away his mother's zest. This was the first time Carrie had been face to face with Tess since making the decision to step away.

Apart, they were better able to deal with their individual loss. But together, their grief pulled like magnets. It was unbearable. And Carrie hadn't wanted to make Tess feel worse.

Or herself, for that matter.

Now, with Tess standing before her, desperation seeping from every pore, Carrie felt guilt crushing her chest. But Cal had come home. It was her duty to protect him.

"I'm sorry, Tess," she said, shaking her head. "Cal isn't ready for that yet. We've only just got him home."

"Please," Tess begged. She winced as, desperate to listen in, the journalists fell silent. Only the clicks of pictures being snapped could be heard. "I need to know if he's been with Noah. If he's been with my boy. Please, let me see him."

Carrie shook her head again. Guilt squeezed her lungs in its fingers, making it hard to breathe. "I can't. I'm sorry. We don't know where Cal has been. He's not ready to talk yet." She hung her head. "Not even to me."

Tears spilled down Tess's face. The sadness in her eyes, the desolation, grew dark and angry.

Carrie lowered her voice to a whisper. "I'm sorry, Tess. I promise you, as soon as Cal is better, I'll ask him about Noah."

"My son is out there somewhere," Tess said through clenched teeth. "Scared. Alone. God knows what's being done to him. If Cal knows where he is, he needs to tell me. I need my boy. I need Noah to come back home."

Carrie sensed movement.

Dylan came up behind her. He nodded at Tess.

"Close the door," he said, quietly. "You can't help her, not now."

Carrie turned back to Tess. "As soon as Cal's talking again, I'll ask him. I promise you. But that's all I can do."

The anger in Tess's eyes spread to her whole body. Her face twisted and contorted. Her hands curled into fists.

"All you can do?" she said, her voice rising. "Someone took my boy! Your son can tell me where he is, I know he can. I can't wait until he's better, Carrie. My boy could be dead by then!"

"Carrie . . ." Dylan placed a hand on her shoulder.

She shook it off. Her eyes moved from Tess to the journalists. They were loving this, she thought. She could just imagine the stories in tomorrow's papers.

"I'm sorry," she said, avoiding her friend's wretched gaze, and moved to close the door.

Tess wedged her foot between the door and the jamb. "You close that door and you're letting my son die!" she cried. "Do I have to get on my knees and beg you in front of all these people?"

Carrie shook her head. "Move your foot, Tess. Don't give these journalists a story. They are not here to help you. This will only make things worse."

Tess began to cry uncontrollably. Her foot remained wedged in the doorway.

"Tess, you need to leave," Dylan said, his tone gentle yet firm. "I'm sorry, but Carrie's already told you. When Cal is well enough, we'll make sure he tells us what he knows. Until then, you need to go home."

The two glared at one another.

"I'm not going anywhere until I see Cal."

Behind Tess, the journalists became one unified roar. Jago Pengelly appeared among them, pushing his way into the garden.

Relief surged through Carrie's body.

Jago hurried along the path. Tess turned and, upon seeing him, sagged like a deflated balloon.

"Mum, what are you doing?" Jago said, his voice soft. He slung his arm around her shoulder. She leaned into him.

"I need to know where he is," she said. Her voice was bereft of any emotion.

Jago kissed her head. "This isn't going to help, Mum. Come on, let's get you into bed."

"I'm sorry," Carrie said again. This time, Tess didn't look up.

Jago nodded. "It's okay. I'll take her home."

He whispered something in his mother's ear and kissed her temple. Turning her away from the Killigrew house, he guided her along the garden path. A second later, they were absorbed by the journalists, who all turned to fire questions and snap pictures.

Carrie's heart ached as she watched them disappear. She felt Dylan's hand on her waist, his thumb caressing the small of her back.

"You did the right thing," he said.

For a moment, she stood with her head resting against Dylan's chest. What if Tess was right? What if Cal did know the answer to Noah's whereabouts? What if waiting for him to speak, to tell them what he knew, would make it too late to find Noah alive?

There had to be a way to get Cal to open up. To communicate where he had been all this time. To tell them if Noah was being held in the same place.

With the front door closed and locked, Carrie and Dylan returned to the living room. Cal no longer sat in front of the television but stood in front of the windows, peering through the curtains.

"Come away from there," Carrie said, surprised by the irritation in her voice.

He released the curtains but remained where he was. Carrie searched his expression. There was nothing there. No clues. No answers. The last seven years were locked deep inside his mind. They were going to need more than asking questions to find out the truth.

Part of Carrie didn't want to know the truth. Because she knew it would be horrific. And that horror would devolve into nightmares that would last a lifetime. And she would have to relive the guilt of losing him, over and over. Because wasn't she responsible? Responsible for the terrible things that had happened to him since?

She thought of the scars and marks on his body. Of the X-rays of broken bones and fractures that hadn't been there before he'd disappeared. Did Noah look the same? Did he bear the same scars? The same broken bones? Or was his skin now rotting away, parting like dead petals to reveal those pearly white bones beneath?

Suddenly, Carrie wanted to scream at Cal. To demand the

truth. Instead, she shifted her eyes to the television, then to Melissa, who was oblivious to the world as she drew pictures of animals.

"I'll make something to eat," she said, even though she suspected no one was hungry.

20

It was the pain that woke him. White hot and piercing. Like a pickaxe through the head.

Scott Triggs opened his eyes. He was on his back. In the dark. There was a light source seeping in from somewhere as the darkness was not entirely impenetrable.

He turned his head left, then right, waiting as his eyes adjusted to the gloom. He tried to move. To sit up. The pain in his head forced him back down. It was followed by a nauseating wave of dizziness. Smells reached his nostrils. Something sharp. Something damp. Something deeply unpleasant.

Now he was more awake, his nerve endings sprang to life. The ache in his head began to spread across his face. The bridge of his nose throbbed. He was pretty sure it was broken. He ran a tongue along his teeth. At least two were missing.

Like a light snapping on, he remembered what had happened.

Panic grabbed hold of him. He tried to pull himself up on his elbows. His hands would not move. He realised with sickening clarity his wrists were strapped down.

Terror gripped him by the throat. Scott pulled against the restraints but they held fast.

He kicked his legs but his ankles were held down, too.

That old bastard had knocked him out cold and had him tied up somewhere in the dark.

Tears sprung to Scott's eyes. He fought against the bindings like a wild animal but only succeeded in making them tighter. He was going to be sick. He turned his head and vomited, spraying the contents of his stomach over the surface of the table, or whatever the hell it was he was strapped to.

He fought to free himself again then lay very still, blood pounding in his ears. Why was this happening to him?

Get a grip, he told himself. If he was going to get out of here he would need a clear head.

He spent the next few minutes trying to draw in deep breaths and let them out in steady streams. He willed his heartbeat to slow down, for the adrenaline in his veins to dissipate.

He stared upward. Now that his eyes had adjusted to the gloom, he could make out the ceiling a couple of metres above his head. He turned his head to the left. He couldn't see much apart from shadowy blocks. Were they shelves? Wherever he was, the room was big. A basement, perhaps? Was he beneath Grady Spencer's house?

There had to be something nearby that he could grab. He lifted his head to get a better view. As far as he could tell, the table was in the centre of the room and surrounded by space.

Almost like an altar. The thought sent his pulse racing again.

There was nothing he could reach. Nothing that would help him to escape.

Resting his head back against the table, he tilted his chin up to the ceiling and looked behind him. On the peripheries of his vision, light crept out from beneath a door.

It was his way out. If he could free himself.

How was he going to do that?

Terror returned to Scott as a fresh wave of pain wracked his body. He fought against the bindings once more, spasming and thrashing on the table like an epileptic in the throes of a seizure.

He was trapped. A prisoner. Scott drew in lungsful of air and screamed. His voice was deafening, bouncing off the walls. He sucked in another breath and screamed again.

Surely someone had to hear him. He was on a residential street for Christ's sake!

Silence suffocated him like a shroud.

Tears filled his eyes. His nose for a story had finally put him in dire trouble. That old bastard was going to kill him. He wouldn't be able to fight back. No one was coming to save him because no one knew where he was.

Scott wept. His body trembled uncontrollably. He didn't want to die! Not yet. He still hadn't had a story make it to the front page. This was supposed to be it. This story, right here in Devil's Cove. Except now he was part of the story. As the tears streamed down the sides of his face, he wondered if this was how he would finally make it to the front page. *As* the news.

Above his sobs, he heard a noise. Footsteps, slow and shuffling, descending wooden steps.

Keys jangled. A lock was turned. The door creaked open. A switch was flipped and dull, yellow light illuminated the room. Scott squinted as a naked lightbulb flickered above his head. Instinctively, he tried to raise his hand to cover his eyes. The bindings dug into his skin. He waited for his eyes to adjust then looked wildly around the room.

He had been right. He was in a large basement. Shelves, filled with boxes, lined the walls. The floor was stone. The ceiling, rock.

His hands and wrists were tied with straps to a workbench, which was old and worn. He winced at the vomit next to his head as he strained to face Grady Spencer.

The old man stood in the doorway, silent and unmoving.

Watching him.

"Why are you doing this?" Scott hissed. He could just make out his silhouette, black against the yellow light. "People know I'm here. If I don't get back to the office soon, I'll be missed. They'll come looking for me."

Grady Spencer made no move to enter the room. He stood, quietly observing from the doorway.

"Why don't you say something?" Scott cried. "Let me off this table!"

He began thrashing again, knocking his head against the bench. Searing pain tore the breath from his lungs.

"Please," he begged, his voice cracked and desperate.

Grady Spencer lurched into the room, moving to the left, disappearing from Scott's view.

Then, Scott heard wheels, squeaking and stiff, rolling against the ground, followed by a metallic clatter.

His entire body went cold. He pulled against the straps, bunching his fingers into tight fists. Tendons in his neck threatened to tear. Veins in his forehead popped.

He screamed as tears shot from his eyes. "Let me off this damn table or I'll rip your fucking head off!"

The sounds moved closer. Grady leaned over him. Scott glanced to his side to see a metal trolley. On top of the trolley was a tray. In the tray, neatly lined up, were razor-sharp instruments.

Scott's heart stopped. His bladder released itself.

"I'll kill you," he wailed.

Grady Spencer leaned over him, a gleeful smile on his lips.

"Kill me?" he laughed. "And how do you intend to do that? Cry me to death?"

Tears slipped from Scott's eyes as he examined the instruments on the trolley. A scalpel. A hacksaw. Gardening shears. Something that looked like forceps with blades.

"Please, let me go," he sobbed.

Grady Spencer smiled. "You journalists are all the same. Polite with your pleases and thank-yous, ever so friendly when you need to be. Just to get your story. Just to get your name on the front page." His gaze moved from Scott to the trolley of torture instruments. "There are all kinds of ways to get on the front page without interfering in other people's lives."

"Please," Scott said, begging now. "I won't say anything. I'll leave right away. You'll never hear from me again."

The old man's voice was cracked and cruel. "After tonight, I suppose I won't. Now, where shall we begin? Left hand, or right?"

Scott's blood ran cold.

"Please." He couldn't breathe. It was as if someone had sucked all the air out of the room. "Please, let me go."

Grady ran a finger along the tools in the trolley. He fingered the gardening shears, changed his mind, and selected the hacksaw.

Scott's eyes fixed on the rows of sharp, steel teeth. They were stained and rusted, as if they had been used many times.

"Left, or right?" Grady repeated, this time with a raised eyebrow and a casual tone, as if he were asking Scott to choose between coffee or tea.

Something in Scott's mind snapped. He began screaming and thrashing on the table. Hot tears shot from his eyes. Grady Spencer stood and watched. His shoulders heaved with a sigh.

His energy spent, Scott slumped to a standstill. He stared at Grady Spencer, realising he was staring into the eyes of a killer. He should never have knocked on the old man's door. He should have climbed into his car, started the engine, and driven back to Truro with half a story.

"It was you, wasn't it?" he said. "You took the Killigrew boy. You've been keeping him here all this time."

Grady Spencer flipped the hacksaw over in his hand. His expression grew sour.

Scott twisted his head to peer around the basement. "Did you take Noah, too? Is he here?"

Beside him, the old man shook his head. "Once a journalist, always a journalist. You can't stop asking questions, can you?"

Scott turned away from him.

"Noah!" he screamed. "Noah Pengelly, are you here?"

His voice echoed around the basement. He turned back to Grady Spencer.

"Listen to me, you sick bastard, someone will find out. Someone will notice me gone. And when they come searching, they will find you and they'll lock you up." He pulled against the restraints. "Let me go. If Noah is here, I can take him with me. I'll say I found him wandering somewhere."

The old man paused, staring down at the hacksaw. Slowly, he placed it back in the tray. "I've changed my mind, You're giving me a headache."

Picking up the forceps with one hand, he thrust them into Scott's mouth. Metal scraped against his teeth. He felt a terrible pressure as his jaw was forced open. Scott tried to scream then began to choke. He tried to pull away, but the old man had a surprising amount of strength.

In that instant, he knew he was going to die. There was nothing he could do to stop it. He couldn't even beg for his life.

"That boy is mine," Grady Spencer said, picking up the shears and snapping them open. "I found him. Finders keepers. He belongs to me."

He moved the shears towards Scott's tongue.

"You shouldn't have put your nose where it doesn't belong," Grady said, a wicked grin spreading across his face. "Maybe I'll take that, too."

Scott squeezed his eyes shut and prayed for a quick death. But after the first few cuts, it was clear Grady Spencer had other ideas.

21

The room was rectangular and bland-looking, replete with beige carpet, white walls, and a sad looking cheese plant in the corner. Carrie was glad to be away from the house. The press had returned early that morning. A few had even camped out in the street, sleeping in their cars. They were fewer in number than yesterday, but there were still enough to cause a scene when she and Detective Turner had bundled Cal into the back of her car and driven to the police station in Truro.

Now they sat around a table in this characterless room; Carrie and Cal on one side, Detective Turner and a woman named Carla Vincenti on the other. A video camera on a tripod stood in the centre of the room, recording them.

Detective Turner had already introduced Carla, explaining that she was a registered intermediary. Today she would be evaluating Cal's abilities and needs so she could then advise investigating officers on how best to proceed with their questioning.

Carrie had initially been reluctant to subject Cal to any sort of assessment so early on, but yesterday's visit from Tess Pengelly had weighed heavily on her conscience.

"We'll keep this simple, today," Carla had assured her before sitting down. "Strictly no questions from the detective, just a few simple get-to-know-you exercises that will help me ascertain Cal's level of understanding."

Even with the intermediary's assurance, Carrie was still reluctant. But she sat and she watched as Carla introduced herself to Cal and then began her evaluation, asking him a series of simple yes or no questions.

So, your mum tells me you like dinosaurs," she said, smiling. "Do you like dinosaurs, Cal?"

Cal stared at her with blank eyes. Beneath the table, he fiddled with his plastic T-Rex. Carla moved on, asking more questions and jotting down notes. Cal continued to stare without responding.

Next, Carla produced a set of picture cards and asked Cal to make choices by pointing to the appropriate card.

His hands remained under the table.

"It's too early," Carrie interrupted. "He's not ready for this."

Detective Turner frowned. Carla held up two more cards. One was an image of a house, the other a cave.

"Which one do you live in, Cal?" she asked. She gave no more verbal prompts but held out the cards and nodded encouragement.

Beneath the table, Cal's hands grew very still. His head turned as he stared at the picture of the cave. His nostrils flared. His eyes grew dark and narrow.

"What is it, Cal?" Carrie said, glancing at the cards then back at her son.

"Mrs Killigrew, if you could just—" the intermediary began.

Carrie held up a hand, silencing her, then placed it on her son's shoulder. "What do you see?"

Cal pulled away, staggering to his feet and knocking back his chair. Carla glanced nervously at the detective, who remained seated and calm. All three watched as Cal backed away, until he had trapped himself in a corner. He slid down to a crouched position and wrapped his arms around his shins.

Carrie was on her feet and moving towards him. She stopped a metre just in front.

"It's okay," she soothed. "I'm here. You're safe."

Cal stared at her, his eyes burning into her skin. For a moment, he looked as if he might launch himself at her. Then he lowered his head and began to rock.

"We're done here," Carrie said, glaring at Detective Turner. "I'm taking him home."

It took five minutes to coax Cal out of the room and through the building. As they reached the car, Turner caught up with them. When Cal was safely in the passenger seat, Carrie turned to the detective.

"I'm sorry," he said. "But we have to try."

"You saw what happened in there," Carrie said, trying to keep her voice level. "He needs more time."

Turner nodded as he glanced back at the station. "I agree. But his reaction was interesting, don't you think? Those pictures triggered something. I think we need to go back in there and try again."

"No."

"The longer we wait, the harder it could become to find out what happened to your son."

Carrie bit down on her lip. Whatever those pictures had triggered in Cal—a memory, a feeling—it was nothing good. She was desperate to know but she was also afraid. To push him again so soon could succeed in doing more damage than good.

"A few more days," she said, feeling suddenly tired. "Give us that at least. Jesus, the press is still outside our house."

Detective Turner glanced through the window at Cal. "I'll talk to the boss, see what she says. But remember, we're on the same side here, Carrie. We want to help Cal, not hurt him."

He walked away. Carrie stared after him.

Feeling miserable, she slipped inside the car. Cal was sitting with his head bowed and Rex the dinosaur clutched in his hands.

"Come on," she said. "Let's go home. Hopefully Dylan hasn't killed anyone."

She started the engine and drove away from the station, anxiety mounting as she wondered what had happened to her son.

22

TREVITHICK ROW WAS SITUATED HALFWAY down the east side of the cove. Unlike the rest of the town's architecture, this street was made up of fifties style housing, built to replace a terrace of cottages that had been ravaged by a fire. When viewing the town from the beach, Trevithick Row stuck out like a hangnail.

Carrie liked these houses, with their clean lines and spacious rooms. She peered up at them as Dylan pulled the car into the kerb.

It was a short journey from their home. A five-minute walk, maybe eight with Melissa. But Carrie hadn't wanted to subject Cal to prying eyes.

Now, as the car engine puttered into silence, she checked the street. It was empty. Unbuckling her seatbelt, she hopped out of the car. She knocked on the back-passenger window. Cal looked up and she smiled at him, then beckoned for him to get out. He did so, slowly, cautiously, as Dylan helped Melissa onto the pavement.

Up ahead, the front door of a whitewashed house opened.

"Nana Joy!" Melissa cried, and went stampeding into the small but meticulously-kept garden.

Carrie had always thought it strange that Melissa insisted on calling Dylan's mother Nana Joy. It wasn't as if she'd met her other grandmother to need to differentiate between the two. Surely just *Nana* would do.

"Well, hello my sweet angel," Joy said, planting a kiss on Melissa's forehead. She was a small, birdlike woman with a nest of short, greying hair and bundles of nervous energy. "No school on a Wednesday?"

Melissa threw her arms around her grandmother's neck and scrambled into her arms.

"Don't worry, she'll be going back soon," Dylan said, peeling Melissa from Joy and setting her back on the ground. "And go easy on your Nana. Her bones are old, you don't want to break them."

He kissed his mother on the cheek as she slapped him playfully on the arm.

"I'm not dead yet," she laughed. "And you're not too old for a good spanking."

Her eyes moved beyond Dylan, resting on Carrie and Cal, who were still hanging back by the garden gate.

"Hello, Carrie," she said, smiling.

Carrie turned and gave Cal an encouraging nod. He hovered outside for a second more, then gradually moved up beside her.

"This is Dylan's mother, Joy," Carrie explained, nodding to the woman in the doorway.

Cal glanced in Joy's direction for the briefest of moments before returning his gaze to the garden path.

Carrie hooked her arm in his and gave him a gentle tug. "Come on. Let's go say hello."

She could feel the tension in his muscles as they walked towards the house. When they reached the door, she gave Joy a brief hug.

"Well," Joy said, her voice trembling with nerves as she gazed at the boy on the path. "I'm very pleased to meet you, Cal."

Without warning, she threw her arms around his neck and pulled him close.

"Oh, my boy!" she cried. "What a miracle!"

Carrie watched as Cal grew rigid with his arms planted by his sides, his eyes growing large and round. She smiled to herself. Only ten days ago he wouldn't have entertained a stranger being within a metre of him.

Joy released him from her embrace.

"Sorry," she said, smiling at Carrie.

"It's fine." Carrie nudged Cal's shoulder. "Nana Joy can get emotional."

Dylan's mother laughed. "Come on, then. Let's see if I have something nice to eat."

The interior of the house was light and airy, the furnishings simple yet comfortable. Melissa had already positioned herself on the living room floor with her toys, while Dylan spoke to his father, Gary. The two looked very much alike, one an older, greyer version of the other. As always, the topic of conversation had already moved onto the current state of the fishing industry, and both men were shaking their heads.

Cal's introduction to Gary was slightly more reserved.

"Hello, young man," Gary said, extending a hand, his eyes everywhere but the boy in front of him.

"Shake his hand," Carrie said, when all she wanted to do was tell Gary to give his step-grandson a big hug.

Cal was motionless, staring at Gary's open hand. After what seemed like minutes, Gary retracted his hand and slid it into his pocket. They were quiet then. The air in the room felt thick and gloopy.

"I'll make some tea," Joy said.

Carrie nodded. "I'll give you a hand if you like."

"Nonsense, you sit down and get comfortable." Joy paused, linking and interlinking her fingers. "Cal, would you like some tea?"

Cal didn't answer. His attention was focused on a corner of the room, where a fluffy white cat sat in a green armchair.

"Cal? Joy asked you a question," Carrie said.

Ignoring her, Cal padded across the room. He crouched down, until his face was square with the animal's. The cat glared at him through wary, yellow eyes.

"Cal, please answer your grandmother." Dylan watched him, a frown wrinkling his forehead.

Joy flapped a hand. "He doesn't have to call me that."

It was as if Cal couldn't hear them. He cocked his head, watching the cat. To Carrie's surprise, he reached out a hand and began stroking its head. It was the first physical contact she'd seen him offer. The cat began to purr loudly. It pushed its head against his hand.

"Cal," Dylan said. "Please, don't ignore me."

"He'll have juice," Carrie said to Joy.

"Her name is Daisy," Joy said, watching Cal. "You must have a gift because usually, she hates strangers."

Cal continued to stroke the cat's head.

Carrie glanced at Dylan, who returned her stare with annoyance, as if Cal's obliviousness was somehow her fault.

"I'll put the kettle on," Joy said.

"I want to help!" Melissa jumped up from the floor, where she'd already begun drawing in her sketchbook, and ran over to her grandmother.

Joy's shoulder's loosened. "You do? Well then, you'd better come with me."

Taking Melissa's hand, Joy headed out of the living room towards the kitchen. More silence fell. The only sounds were the rolling vibrations of Daisy's purrs.

"When are you off to sea, then?" Gary asked Dylan, breaking the quiet.

"Tomorrow."

"You'll be glad to get back on the boat. It's been a while."

Their conversation resumed.

Carrie stood in the middle of the living room, her heart skipping with excitement as she watched Cal. This was good progress; Cal was voluntarily reaching out and showing emotion.

She had been worried about today. But except from ignoring everyone in the room, Cal was doing okay. It would be a strange experience for Gary and Joy, too. Usually, grandparents got to know their grandchildren from birth. But there were plenty of loving step-grandparents out there. This was no different. Except that Cal had vanished from the world for seven years.

An hour later, the atmosphere had become more relaxed. As usual, Melissa was taking up much of the attention.

Cal remained seated in the armchair, his arms folded across his chest. Carrie tried to involve him in Melissa's games, but each time he shook his head and returned his gaze to the cat, who was now curled into a ball on the carpet and dozing in the afternoon sunlight.

Melissa was making quite a show, singing songs she'd learned at school, before getting her parents and grandparents involved in a game in which they had to guess the animal she was pretending to be.

Every so often, as the adults laughed and clapped at her antics, Carrie noticed her glancing in Cal's direction, a slight, triumphant smile on her lips.

"Now, guess this one," Melissa said, her head swivelling from adult to adult. Carrie was convinced that one day, her daughter would either become a movie star or would be running the country.

Bringing her hands up to her chest, Melissa began to flap her arms and skip around the room.

"A chicken?" Nana Joy suggested, The girl shook her head.

Carrie smiled. "An emu?"

Melissa came to a standstill and beamed at her captive audience. "That's right! Now, try this one."

She hunched her shoulders and raised her hands to chest height, then curled her fingers into claws. She scrunched up her face, wrinkling her nose and brow. Her lips curled back, revealing her teeth, and she let out an almighty roar.

"Goodness!" Joy said, laughing. "Aren't we the little actress?"

Melissa stomped around the room, roaring and snarling.

"I've got it, you're a bear," Dylan said, grinning at his daughter, his eyes sparkling with pride.

Melissa shook her head as she snarled and stamped her feet.

Gary raised a finger. "An angry kangaroo?"

Laughter rippled around the room. Melissa threw her arms in the air. "No, silly Grandpa," she said, staring at the adults as if they were incomprehensibly stupid. "I'm a dinosaurus-rex!"

"I think you mean Tyrannosaurus rex," Grandpa Gary said.

Melissa shook her head from side to side. "No, dinosaurus-rex! Like this one."

She deliberately stared at Cal, who was watching her with narrowed eyes. Carrie drew in a sharp breath as Melissa pulled out Cal's toy dinosaur.

Before she could stop him, Cal was on his feet, his eyes as dark as thunder. He lunged forward. Melissa shrieked as he twisted her wrist with one hand and took back the dinosaur with the other.

Dylan flew towards them. "Cal, no!"

Cal retreated, his dinosaur clutched in his fist as Melissa wailed in pain.

Carrie jumped up. "Dylan, take it easy."

Dylan ignored her. He stabbed a finger in Cal's face. Cal flinched and began to tremble.

"Don't you ever do that again!" Veins popped at the centre of Dylan's forehead. "You want to pick on someone, you pick on me."

Carrie felt the anger unleash inside her. "That's enough, Dylan!"

Nana Joy moved to the middle of the room, where Melissa was slumped and weeping.

"Now, let's all calm down," she said, wrapping an arm around her granddaughter. "What's done is done. Perhaps you could say sorry to your sister, Cal?"

Cal's eyes were trained on Dylan's. His face was deathly pale.

"Dylan," Carrie said again, this time more forcefully.

Gary stood in the corner of the room, watching the scene unfold through dark and serious eyes.

Dylan straightened and took a step back.

Cal turned and bolted from the room. The front door opened and slammed shut.

"Great," Carrie said, shooting Dylan a glare. She moved over to the door.

"Your daughter is upset," Dylan said.

Carrie froze. Melissa was now hugging her grandmother and sobbing into her chest. From the window, she could see Cal had reached the garden gate.

She turned back to Dylan.

"So is yours," she said.

Then, she went after Cal. She reached the garden gate, just as he was about to go through. He whirled around as she drew near. For a second, she thought he was going to run. But he stood still, his shoulders heaving up and down, his fingers turning white as they squeezed the dinosaur in his fist.

"Look at me," Carrie said, keeping her voice low but firm. When Cal refused to look up, she said: "I'm not going to get angry with you. Please, look at me."

Slowly, Cal lifted his head.

She could see the shame in his eyes. He knew he'd done wrong.

"Melissa shouldn't have taken your toy. But that doesn't mean you can hurt her. It's not how we do things in this family, Cal. We talk about things. If there's a problem, we try and fix it. Melissa's young. She's four years old. You can't hurt her like that. Or anyone else."

Cal lowered his head. His shoulders sagged.

Carrie took a step closer. "I know this is hard. I know this is confusing. But everyone's trying, Cal. Melissa isn't used to being . . . She's not used to having a brother. But she *will* get used to it. And soon, she'll love you just as much as I love you. It's going to take a little time, that's all."

She stared at her son, feeling his pain, his confusion, and his fear emanating from every pore.

Dylan's reaction had spoken volumes. He was afraid of Cal. Afraid that Cal might be a danger to Melissa. The realisation hurt Carrie like an arrow in her chest. She stared at her son, seven years of guilt bearing down on her.

"Cal?" His eyes met hers, just for a second. "I love you."

And then she did something she had been wanting to do since her son had returned to her. She threw her arms around his neck and pulled him into an embrace. She felt his body turn to stone. She heard air fly from his lungs. But he did not fight her. He did not pull away.

"Everything is going to be fine," she said in his ear. "We're all going to be just fine."

Letting him go, she brushed a hand against the side of his face and smiled. Cal stared at her with sad eyes, then glanced back at the house. Dylan stood in the living room window with Melissa cradled in his arms. Both were glaring at Carrie.

"Do you want to go back inside?"

Cal shook his head.

"I'll take you home, then. But Cal, even if you can't say it right now, you need to find a way to apologise to your sister."

Cal's dark eyes narrowed. He looked back at the living room window. Slowly, he nodded.

"Okay," Carrie said. Dylan had retreated and had been replaced by Gary, whose expression told Carrie everything she needed to know. "Go wait in the car."

23

THE REST of the day had been strained. When Dylan returned home with Melissa, Cal retreated to his room and refused to come out. Carrie tried repeatedly to persuade him to come downstairs for dinner. Giving up, she took a plate of food up to his room, where she found him lying on his stomach beneath the bed and poring over his old comics that she'd held onto.

Conversation with Dylan was stilted. They avoided the subject of Cal's behaviour until they'd said goodnight to both children. In the living room, the discussion quickly turned into an argument, punctuated by hushed, angry voices.

"We don't know what we're dealing with," Dylan said, pouring whiskey into a tumbler. "What if he hurts Melissa again? What if we're not there to protect her?"

"*Protect* her? You're talking about my son as if he's some sort of monster," Carrie snapped. "I would never put our daughter in a position where she could get hurt. Today was unfortunate. But I talked to Cal. He knows what he did was wrong."

"How do you know that? How can you be so sure?"

"Because he's my son."

Dylan was quiet, staring into the amber liquid in his glass. "Perhaps I shouldn't go tomorrow."

Pouring herself a glass of red wine, Carrie shook her head. "He's not a dangerous animal, Dylan. He's not going to kill us in our sleep. He's a sixteen-year-old boy who's been through hell. He needs time to adjust, just like the doctors said. We all do."

"And in the meantime? How do we make sure Melissa doesn't get hurt again?"

"We keep a close eye. We get them involved in play together. We make sure Melissa doesn't take any more of his things."

"You're saying today was *her* fault?" Dylan swigged his whiskey and winced at the burn.

Carrie clenched her jaw. Sometimes Dylan was impossible. And so was she. She let out a frustrated breath and gulped her wine.

"What I'm saying is sometimes siblings fight. One minute they're best friends, the next mortal enemies. And around it goes. They're going to fall out. That's what kids do." She wasn't sure she was helping to ease Dylan's mind. "He's not going to hurt her. We'll be fine for a few days. Then you'll be back. Next week, Cal starts his therapy sessions. In a month's time, we'll all be one big happy family."

"What about the police? They're going to want answers soon enough. Tess, too."

"And so do I," Carrie said. "But if we push Cal now, he may never talk again. I won't let that happen. It's difficult, but we need to wait until he's ready."

They were quiet, the ticking of the wall clock the only sound.

Dylan drained his glass. He stood. "I think Melissa should go back to school tomorrow. She's had enough time off."

"Fine."

He hovered, the anger in his eyes fading, until all that was left was sadness. "I want everyone to be safe, Carrie, that's all. I want everyone to be happy. Cal, too."

"I know." Carrie avoided his gaze.

Dylan announced he was going to bed. He needed to be up at three to meet the crew and catch the tide.

"I love you," he said. "I love our family. And I'll learn to love Cal. I need time, that's all. We all do."

He kissed her head and left the room.

Carrie sat for a while longer, a confusing mix of anger and guilt giving her a headache. She drained her glass of wine and poured another. She could understand Dylan's concerns. But Cal was not his son. He didn't know him like she did. Cal had once wept uncontrollably after accidentally treading on a snail. He wasn't violent by nature. He was a kind and sensitive boy who loved people and animals. Who would do anything to help anyone.

But that was before, a voice whispered in her mind. *Who knows what's happened to him since. Or what he's become.*

Carrie sat up, alarmed by the thought.

No, Cal was a good boy. Whatever trauma he'd experienced, they would work through it together. Mother and son. And she would prove to Dylan that he was wrong about Cal.

That Melissa was safe. They all were.

24

Quiet had settled over Devil's Cove. Above the rooftops, a vast blanket of stars shimmered. The ocean was calm. The beach was still. Even the music and voices seeping from The Shack was subdued tonight.

Grady Spencer shut his garden gate and with Caliban by his side, set off for their final walk before bedtime. As he passed by Rose Trewartha's house, he glanced at the upstairs window. The curtains were open, light spilling out. It was the girl's room, Natalie Tremaine.

The one whose parents had been caught extinguishing cigarettes on her back.

Grady smiled to himself. It hadn't been difficult to find out about her, even when she'd refused to answer his own questions. All he'd had to do was take Caliban for his walks and eavesdrop on conversations. The people of Devil's Cove liked to talk. Especially about a curious creature like Natalie Tremaine.

And she was a curious creature. Cutting her hair off like that. Keeping herself to herself. She interested him. Perhaps he'd invite her over to drink tea with a lonely old man.

Moving on, Grady passed by the Pengelly house. All the windows were lit up. They didn't like the dark in that house anymore, oh no. Because it was filled with nightmares and horrors and things that could make a person's hair turn white. Grady smiled. The Pengellys knew all about what lay in the dark.

Memories of the journalist crept into his mind. That idiot thought he'd worked everything out. Well, Grady had shown him he hadn't learned a thing. And now, he would always be in the dark.

Snickering at the irony, the old man picked up his pace, tapping his cane along the pavement. Reaching the end of the road, he headed downhill. It wasn't his usual route, but this evening he'd felt a yearning to see the boy. The house had been quiet since he'd been gone. Except for when he'd made the journalist scream.

As he walked, Grady wondered if he should do something about the idiot's car. Perhaps he would just leave it to rust. He hadn't gone near it, so they wouldn't find his fingerprints. And no one would suspect a frail old man living alone of heinous acts.

Even if they did, there wasn't much left of the journalist to find. Caliban had unwittingly seen to that.

His thoughts returned to the boy and a black hole opened inside his chest. Despair crawled out to poison him. Grady stumbled to a halt. Caliban pulled on his leash and emitted a strangled whine. His house was empty without the boy. He'd had to find more papers, more things to fill it with. It was those idiots at the farm. They'd tried to take him away. Tried to make him theirs. And in the confusion, the boy had vanished.

Now he was back with his mother. Back where he didn't belong. Because the boy was his. He had kept him these last seven years. Fed him. Beat him. Once, he'd almost killed him. But he'd let him live. Because the boy was his to do with what he wanted. Carrie had lost ownership of him that day on the beach.

"Mine," Grady said through clenched teeth. "All mine."

Tugging on Caliban's leash, he set off again. The gradient of the hill pained his knees as he descended into the cove. But he didn't care. Because he was going to see him. He was going to get him back.

Maybe not tonight. There wasn't enough time to think of a plan. But soon, he would find a way to lure him back to his home. Back to his cage, where he slept next to Caliban like a good dog.

He ran a tongue over his lips as he turned onto Clarence Row, where cottages were shrouded in darkness. But there was a light on in the Killigrews' living room.

His breaths growing more ragged by the second, Grady came closer. The curtains were half open. He strained to see inside, hoping for a glimpse of the boy. The hole in his chest grew wider. Deeper. It was Carrie. She was sitting alone. She was crying.

Pathetic, Grady thought. *Ungrateful!* She had her boy back. What did she have to be sad about? Well, he would give her something to feel sad about soon. He was going to take his boy back. She would never see him again.

You'll cry then, he thought, bringing a smile to his lips.

He looked into the darkness of the upstairs windows and a whimper escaped his lips. He was lonely without him. Yes, Caliban gave him companionship but it was not the same. Because you couldn't teach an old dog new tricks and Caliban was getting on in his years. The boy was young, though. He could be taught all kinds of tricks. To fetch. To beg. To play dead. Perhaps even to hunt.

The old man lingered by the garden gate, his lips twisting cruelly as he watched Carrie dry her face with the back of a sleeve then empty her wineglass.

Tapping his cane on the pavement, Grady Spencer walked on. He would get him back. Sooner rather than later. One way or another.

And if he wouldn't come, or if they tried to stop him, he'd make sure the boy belonged to no one.

Not even to him.

25

Margaret Telford woke in the early morning light with a troubled feeling. Something was not right. She glanced across her bedroom, taking in the colourful quilt draped across the bottom of her bed, and the framed prints of flowers adorning the walls. It took just a few seconds to realise what was wrong.

She glanced at the door, at the gap beneath. Alfie was not there.

Usually, he was like clockwork, climbing the stairs to sit outside her door and enthusiastically wag his tail. She could always hear him upon waking, his aged, laboured panting loud enough to reach her ears. But today the house was unusually quiet.

"Alfie?"

She waited for him to bark a reply, or to playfully scratch at the door. But there was nothing. Only a flutter of anxiety in her chest.

Pulling back the sheets, Margaret swung her legs over the side of the bed and slipped her puffy feet inside a pair of slippers. Slowly, she stood. Her knees creaked painfully and she hovered for a moment, swaying from side to side, waiting for the discomfort to lessen.

"Alfie, here boy," she called.

When Alfie failed to reply this time, she pulled an old blue robe over her nightdress and shuffled to the door.

He was not outside. She looked along the small landing. Sometimes he could be found in the bathroom, attempting to drink from the toilet. There was no sign of him anywhere.

Making her way to the top of the staircase, Margaret gripped the rail and called for him again. The silence of the cottage was unsettling. Alfie was getting on now. The stairs were becoming harder for him. Just as they were for her.

Perhaps he couldn't manage them today. Perhaps he had tried and given up, returning to his basket in the kitchen. There had been a lot of excitement in the last week and a half. Which reminded her: Carrie Killigrew had still not stopped by to thank Margaret for saving her son's life.

Not that she had dragged him from the ocean for gratitude. But her arms and knees had been suffering ever since. And since Callum's identity had been revealed to the press, she'd had to fend off a barrage of reporters all wanting to ask her questions, when all she wanted was to be left alone, thank you very much.

Gripping the rail, Margaret hauled herself downstairs and poked her head around the living room door. It was dark and shadowy, the curtains still closed.

Alfie was nowhere to be seen.

Margaret made her way through the narrow hall and headed to the kitchen. Nothing seemed out of place. It was as she had left it; surfaces clean, dishes dried and put away in cupboards, flagstone floor mopped and sparkling. The only thing out of the ordinary was Alfie's basket.

It was empty.

Margaret shook her head in confusion. She had checked every room in the house. Where else could he be? She turned a full circle. Her eyes rested on the kitchen door.

Unless Alfie had learned to unlock doors and take himself for a walk, he had to be in here somewhere.

He couldn't have just disappeared into thin air.

Margaret began to panic. Something was very wrong. For a second, she wondered if it was her mind. A quick glance to a photograph on the refrigerator door confirmed that it wasn't. She stared at the image of Alfie, taken on the lawn just last month.

Surely he couldn't be outside…

Moving across the flagstones, she grasped the handle of the back door. To her surprise, the door swung open.

She had locked it last night before she'd gone to bed. The same as she did every night.

And yet the door was unlocked, the bolts drawn back.

Margaret frowned. She wasn't often forgetful, even at her age. Perhaps there was something wrong with her mind after all.

"Decrepit old fool," she said, scolding herself. She was lucky she hadn't been burgled in the night.

Pulling the door open to its fullest extent, she stepped outside. A breeze was blowing up from the ocean, chilling the morning air.

"Alfie? Are you out here?"

Folding her arms across her stomach, Margaret peered across the overgrown lawn at the pile of junk lying in the far corner. Perhaps Carrie Killigrew could show some gratitude by sending young Callum over to help clear up that mess. When he was well enough, of course. What a strange thing it was, that she was even thinking his name. The boy had died. Now he was alive. It was a miracle.

But where in the world was Alfie? Margaret turned. Shifting her gaze to the right. Her blood turned to ice.

There was a brown, hessian sack sitting beneath the kitchen window. Margaret stared at it, her chest rising and falling.

What was it? Where had it come from? It certainly didn't belong to her.

Shuffling forward, Margaret took a closer look.

She froze. Her hands flew up to her mouth.

A dark, wet patch stained the side of the sack. It looked very much like blood.

"Dear Lord," Margaret whispered into her fingers. Her heart pounded so hard she began to feel dizzy.

She squeezed her eyes shut, then opened them again.

"Alfie, where are you?" she cried.

The sack sat motionless, taunting her. She should call the police. Whatever lay inside the sack, it couldn't be anything good.

It couldn't be...

A horrifying image tore through her mind.

"Oh, Alfie!"

Margaret hurried back to the house, hobbling up the step and returning to the kitchen. She pulled open a drawer, grabbed the sharpest knife she could find, and returned to the garden.

She stood in front of the sack, unable to breathe, her heart smashing against her ribcage.

"Please, God," she whispered. "Please, don't let it be him."

Bending down, she fumbled with the thin cord that was knotted around the neck of the sack. She began to cut.

The cord was strong, making hard work for her arthritic hands. She whimpered as she moved the knife back and forth, slicing through the twine. It fell away.

Margaret dropped the knife to the ground.

She stared back at the house, then across the fence. Perhaps she should call her neighbour, Larry. Perhaps he could look inside the sack for her.

But she knew Larry would still be asleep.

Bile rising in her throat, Margaret closed her eyes and pulled open the neck of the sack.

She whispered a prayer, drew in another breath, then opened her eyes again.

It was dark in there. Too dark to see.

She opened the neck of the sack wider.

She stared up at the sky, at the clouds. She lowered her eyes.

What she saw inside forced a scream from her throat so shrill that the neighbours' dogs began to bark in a frantic chorus.

The world turned red, then yellow, then white.

Margaret Telford tumbled into darkness.

26

ROSE TREWARTHA WAS a stout woman in her mid-fifties with a round, ruddy face and a smile that could light up the darkest void. She sat at Carrie's kitchen table, soft hands clasped around a mug of tea, as Carrie glossed over the events of the past two weeks.

When she'd finished talking, Carrie felt drained and empty. She glanced through the doorway, out into the hall. The sounds of early morning cartoons drifted out from the living room. Cal had barely touched his breakfast. He seemed exhausted, as if he'd been awake all night. Sleeping under the bed couldn't be good for his health. She had to find a way to get him onto the mattress.

Carrie returned her attention to her friend.

"Thanks for taking Melissa to school," she said with a smile. "I should have taken her myself but I didn't want to leave Cal alone, not yet. And I'm not sure he's ready for all those staring faces. It's been bad enough with the press. Thank God they've finally gone."

"Don't you worry your head about it," Rose said, in her thick country accent. "That little bird can talk the hind legs off a donkey! Didn't pause for breath the whole way there. Seemed glad to be back with her friends, too."

Carrie reached a hand across the table and Rose squeezed it. "I'm so glad you're here. I've hardly seen a soul since Cal came back. And now Dylan's gone to sea . . ."

Tears formed at the corners of her eyes. She willed them away.

Dylan had left in the early hours while it was still dark. He'd showered and dressed, then wrapped himself around her until it was time to leave. She had pretended to be asleep, even when he'd kissed her cheek and whispered goodbye.

"You're looking tired, bird," Rose said, her smile fading. "You've got a lot on your plate right now. Are you managing?"

"I'm fine," Carrie said. "It's a lot, but we're working through it."

Rose squeezed her hand again. "I know when something is wrong, Carrie Killigrew. Ever since you were a little girl, those hardened eyes could fool everyone else but me."

Carrie felt the fight leave her body. Her shoulders sagged. She couldn't say it. She couldn't admit that she was failing her family.

"I forgot the sugar," she whispered and tried to stand.

Rose held fast. She raised an eyebrow.

They were quiet for a moment longer.

Carrie let it out. "It's Dylan. He thinks Cal could be dangerous."

"Why would he think something like that?"

She told Rose about the incident at Dylan's parents. About Cal's strange habit of sleeping under the bed and his animalistic behaviour at the dinner table. As Carrie talked, Rose's eyebrows knitted together in a concerned frown.

"Dylan didn't want to leave today," Carrie said. "He's worried Cal will hurt Melissa again. Clearly, he doesn't think I can cope on my own."

The two women sat in quiet contemplation.

"Here's the problem." Rose said at last, staring at Carrie with an expression falling somewhere between concerned parent and Victorian headmistress. "Maybe you *can't* cope on your own."

Before Carrie could protest, Rose held up a hand.

"What I'm saying is, it's a lot to take on. And you don't have to cope on your own, no matter how much you insist on playing the martyr. You have a husband who loves you very much. And yes, he's going to struggle at first—his family of three has become four, and through no choice of his own. But Dylan loves you. He *will* come through for you. You need to give him a chance. Stop building a wall around you and Cal. And Dylan's not the only one you can rely on either. You have Gary and Joy."

Carrie snorted. "After yesterday, I'm sure they think Cal's some sort of freak."

"Nonsense. What about Kye? Does he know his son is alive?"

"I've talked to his parents. He's somewhere in Dubai, working. I've told them they'll need to wait to see Cal. I don't want to over-whelm him."

Rose picked up her mug. "And your parents?"

"What about them?"

"Don't you think they'd like to see their grandson again?"

Carrie was quiet, unhappy memories flooding her mind.

"You haven't told them, have you?" Rose said, staring at her.

"I'm sure they're having the time of their lives sailing around the world. I wouldn't want to spoil it for them."

"Nonsense!" The irritation in Rose's voice made Carrie feel like a child. "No matter your feelings about your parents, they have a right to know their grandson is alive. And if you don't tell them, all it's going to take is for them to switch on the world news, or for a friend to see Cal's face on the television and ask them all about it. And then, they're going to wonder why their daughter hasn't told them their grandson is alive."

Carrie's anger spilled from her mouth. "When I thought Cal was dead, when I believed he was never coming back to me, their response was to pack up and leave. They left me on my own to deal with the loss of my son. I have no obligation to them."

She leaned back, her chest tight and heavy. Rose nodded. She sipped more tea. "You feel abandoned by them."

"That's putting it mildly."

"Tell me it's none of my business, Carrie, but as a friend of your mother's—and of the family's—I agree your parents made some bad choices back then. But grief causes people to behave in surprising ways. It can twist perceptions. It can stop people from seeing beyond their own pain. I'm not excusing the choices they made, but don't you think this is a chance to make things right with them?" She leaned forward. "If you don't tell them about Cal and they find out some other way, those bridges could be burned forever."

Both women were quiet for a moment, staring off into space. Rose was right, of course, but at the same time Carrie knew she had every right to be angry with her parents. They had abandoned her. Left her behind like an unwanted dog in a vacated house.

"You can't keep pushing everyone away," Rose said, her voice low and soft. "You've been doing it for seven years. Let people help. Let us take some of the burden. And give your family time. Melissa will come to love having a big brother. And Dylan will soon call Cal his son. But it's only going to work if you stop treating everyone as an obstacle."

She reached a hand across the table. Carrie took it in her own.

"You have your son back. Isn't that a miracle?" A smile lit up Rose's face. But as quickly as the smile had appeared, it faded. "Now, if only we could say the same for poor Tess Pengelly."

Carrie's body tensed. She returned her hand to her lap.

"What is it?" Rose asked.

"Tess came by demanding to talk to Cal. She's convinced he was with Noah. That he knows where to find him."

"And what do you think?"

"I don't know. We won't know anything until Cal talks."

"He still hasn't?"

Carrie lowered her head. "I'm starting to worry he never will. That whatever's been done to him, it's damaged him for good."

A tear slipped from her eye. She let it sail down her cheek and hang off her chin.

"Perhaps it might help if he could get out and see more than these four walls," Rose said. "Perhaps he needs to be with some people his own age. He used to be friends with Jago, didn't he? And I know my Nat is a fearsome looking beast, especially now she's decided to chop all that hair off, but she's a teddy bear, really. Of course, she'd die if she heard me say such a thing."

"I don't know. It's too early."

"You can't keep him locked up forever, Carrie. Don't make him a prisoner of this house."

Leaning back in her chair, Carrie gazed out into the hall. It was true that Cal was becoming more restless. Only this morning, he'd been unable to sit still and had moved back and forth from sofa to window, staring at the road outside.

"You're afraid he'll disappear again," Rose said. "That you'll lose him if you let him out of your sight."

Another tear escaped Carrie's eye. "I need to know what happened to him. I need him to talk so the police can catch the bastard who took him from me. I need to know I won't wake up tomorrow to find him gone."

"Time," Rose said. "What you need is time."

She patted Carrie's hand then finished her tea.

"I best be off. I'm making pasties for supper tonight. They're Nat's favourite."

"You spoil that girl," Carrie said, drying her face.

"Well, no one else is going to," Rose said.

Carrie stood and the women embraced.

"Thank you," Carrie whispered.

Rose smiled. "Don't be daft. I'll be back later with that little scallywag of yours, if she don't talk me to death first!"

Waving a hand, Rose said goodbye and left through the back door. Now alone, Carrie mulled over their conversation, glancing at the phone on the kitchen wall. Her mother's mobile number was scrawled in an old address book shoved at the back of a drawer.

She'd deleted it from her own mobile phone. It was childish, she knew, but it had felt good at the time.

She chewed on her lip for a minute. Was she ready to have that conversation with her parents?

Maybe. Maybe not.

Rose was right, she supposed. She would have to make the call soon or risk irreparable damage. And as much as she was still angry at her parents, the thought of losing them all together was one she didn't want to haunt the rest of her days.

Later, she thought. *I'll do it later.*

She wandered into the hall, heading for the living room.

Cal was at the window again. He turned when she entered, staring at her with dull eyes.

"How are you doing?" Carrie asked. "Want to watch something together?"

He shook his head and returned his gaze to the window. His chest heaved up and down as he expelled a long, sad breath of air.

"Something to eat, then?"

Carrie leaned against the door jamb. Her heart felt unbearably heavy. Rose's words echoed in her mind.

"How about meeting an old friend?" she said.

Cal turned. The dullness in his eyes lit up.

Slowly, he nodded.

27

CARRIE HAD CALLED Jago around noon, asking if he would like to see Cal. Now, he stood on her doorstep, crackling with nervous energy as he waited to be let in.

It had taken him three attempts to convince Nat she could not come along. She was curious to meet Cal, to be involved, but this afternoon was not about making friends. It was about discovering if Cal had been with Noah.

The door opened and Carrie greeted him. He had always liked Carrie. Even if she had distanced herself from his mum, he still held a fondness for her that had carried over from his childhood. And unlike most of the people in Devil's Cove, now that he was a young man, Carrie treated him as such.

"How are you?" she asked, pausing to peer into the street as she welcomed him in.

Jago shrugged. "Fine."

"And your mum?"

Jago thought back over the last few days. The news of Cal's return had shattered his mother. All the worry, all the pain and grief of these last two months had finally consumed her. She'd returned home from the Killigrew house in a strange, distant daze. Since then, she'd been doped up on diazepam and shut away in her room. Jago had cooked for her but she'd barely eaten. She was giving up; he knew it with unfettered certainty. She was beginning to accept that Noah was dead.

Jago had enough hope for them both. He was going to find out what Cal knew if it killed him.

"Mum's fine," he said.

Carrie's face grew serious. "Will you tell her I'm sorry about the other day? It was bad timing, that's all."

Jago nodded. His eyes wandered to the open living room door and a jolt of nerves shot through his body. He could sense Cal was in there. Waiting for him.

Carrie placed a hand on his arm. He tensed.

"Do you want to go say hi to a long-lost friend?"

"Sure."

"There's just one thing before you do. Please, don't ask him about where he's been. And I know it's tempting, but you can't ask him about Noah, either. He's not ready. He doesn't even know you have a brother." She paused. "It's okay to talk about before though. Some old memories might help him."

Nodding, Jago slipped his bag from his shoulder.

The curtains of the living room were half open. The television was switched on, the volume turned all the way up. Cal sat crossed-legged on the carpet half a metre away from the screen.

He didn't look up, even when Carrie cleared her throat.

"Cal, there's someone here to meet you."

Cal was transfixed, images from the screen flickering in his pupils. It was only when Carrie picked up the remote control from the armchair and hit the power button that Cal glanced away from the screen and noticed Jago.

Jago stared back. It was a strange sensation, like looking into the eyes of a ghost. But that was exactly how Jago felt. Even if this ghost had grown older. He couldn't quite recall the exact memory of when he'd last seen Cal, but it would have been just days before he'd supposedly drowned.

If their mothers hadn't been friends, he suspected their own friendship wouldn't have developed. But as children, thrown together during holiday times and weekends, their friendship had bloomed into something solid and trustworthy; two boys exploring caves and woodland, and digging holes in the backyard for no other reason than to make a muddy mess.

Now, Jago felt those seven missing years stretching out between him and Cal like an ocean. He looked the same, kind of. Obviously older. But there was something else about him that Jago couldn't quite grasp. Something in his eyes that was deeply unsettling.

It didn't feel like two old friends meeting after years apart. It felt like two strangers meeting for the first time.

"Cal, this is Jago," Carrie said. She glanced in Jago's direction. "The two of you were friends when you were children. Do you remember?"

Jago felt Cal's eyes upon him. It was a strange sensation, as if Cal could see through flesh and bone. But if there was any recognition there, it didn't show.

"Hey," Jago nodded, lifting a hand. "Long time, no see."

Cal continued to stare.

Carrie let out a strange noise, halfway between a sigh and apologetic laughter.

"Don't you remember, Cal?" she pressed. "The two of you spent so much time together."

She turned to Jago, nodding. Apparently, it was his turn to say something. He stepped closer. Cal leaned back slightly but remained seated, cross-legged on the carpet.

"Maybe this will jog your memory," Jago said. Digging into his bag, he pulled out an old photograph album. He inched closer, showing it to Cal.

"Pictures?" Carrie asked.

"I went through Mum's old photos after you called. Found this album. Most of the pictures are from when… From just before." Jago stared at the album and hunched his shoulders. "I thought it might help."

"That's very thoughtful." Carrie sat down on the left side of the couch and patted the space beside her. "Let's take a look," she said to Cal, who was still staring at Jago with his strange, dark eyes.

Slowly, he got up and sat next to his mother, wrapping his arms around his wiry frame. Jago hovered, staring at mother and son. This was not part of the plan. He had hoped they would be left alone.

"Come on," Carrie smiled. "He won't bite."

Moving over to the couch, Jago perched himself on the end seat next to Cal. Opening the album, he angled it so everyone could see.

"It's just a few pictures," he said.

The first was of Jago and Cal, aged ten and nine, standing on the beach in wetsuits, damp hair plastered across their brows. Jago looked up to see Carrie's face turn pale. He quickly turned the page, revealing images taken one Halloween. Jago was dressed as a werewolf. Cal as a zombie. The picture seemed ironic to Jago, considering Cal had recently come back from the dead.

Carrie startled him by laughing. "Oh, I remember this! You boys ate so many sweets you both had to take the next day off from school."

Jago smiled, remembering. He could still feel the pain in his stomach now. Beside him, Cal stared blankly at the picture.

Jago turned the page. A heavy ache began deep in his chest as his eyes fell on one particular photograph. It was a snapshot of both the Killigrew and Pengelly families, enjoying a picnic up at Briar Wood. A young Cal sat at a picnic bench, cuddled into his mother's side. Tess sat opposite, beaming at the camera, while Jago stood next to his father, helping him light the barbecue.

Cal stared at the picture. A line appeared at the centre of his forehead.

"Do you miss your dad?" Carrie said to Jago.

He stared at the picture of his father, uncomfortable feelings churning in his stomach.

"I'm sorry. That was a stupid question. Of course you do."

Jago remained silent. He went to turn the page but Cal reached out a hand to stop him. He looked up, meeting Jago's gaze. Something stirred in his eyes. He glanced back at the picture then withdrew his hand. Had it been recognition?

The next few pages contained more images of Cal and Jago from a time when the world was in balance and little boys hadn't vanished. So much had changed since then. Not just Cal's disappearance and reappearance; not just the loss of Noah. But a change in family dynamics. And a shift in beliefs.

Jago had once been a happy, smiling child, but now he was a sullen, morose young man. He had been that way a long time before Noah had vanished from the backyard.

They were reaching the end of the album. He glanced across at Carrie, his knee jiggling up and down. He had to get Cal alone or his whole reason for visiting would be meaningless.

"Carrie, do you think I could have some water?"

Like a statue brought to life, Carrie blinked and shook her head. "Of course. I'm sorry, where are my manners? We have juice if you prefer? Or tea?"

"Water is fine. Thanks."

Carrie stood. "Cal? You want water?"

Cal stared up at her. He nodded once before returning his attention to the photo album.

Jago watched as Carrie made her way to the door, where she hovered for a moment, as if unsure about leaving them alone.

"I'll just be in the kitchen," she said.

When she was gone, Jago leaned back and took a long, observational look at Cal.

Cal stared right back.

"This is weird," Jago said. "Can't you talk at all?"

A pained expression flickered across Cal's face. He turned away.

"Sorry, buddy. I didn't mean to hurt your feelings. It's been a long time, hasn't it?" Jago hesitated, wondering if he should ask the next question. *Fuck it.* "Cal, where the hell have you been?"

Cal turned back to him, his eyes growing dark and shiny.

"Did someone take you?" he pressed. "Where have they been keeping you all this time? How did you get away?"

He watched as Cal's mouth opened and his chest began to heave up and down. His large, frightened eyes remained fixed on Jago, who glanced at the open living room door. He reached for his bag. "There's another picture I want to show you," he breathed, keeping his voice low as he pulled out a rolled-up poster. "I have a brother. His name is Noah. He's four years old. He disappeared two months ago. No one can find him. Not the police. Not me."

He checked the door again then unravelled the poster.

Noah's beautiful smiling face stared up, a mop of blond hair hanging over blue eyes so mesmerising that anyone who gazed into them instantly fell in love.

Jago paused, looking up from his brother's face, ignoring the pain tearing at his heart.

"Do you recognise him?" he asked Cal. "Where you were, where you've been . . . was he there, too?"

Cal stared at the poster. He reached out with searching fingers and touched Noah's face.

"You know him, don't you?" Jago said, his pulse racing. "You've seen him before."

Cal's eyes grew impossibly dark. His jaw clenched.

"Tell me, Cal. Please. Where's my brother?"

A strange sound came from the back of Cal's throat. Something like a sob cut off by a choke. His fingers began to tremble on the paper, making Noah's face blur.

"Please, Cal," Jago whispered. Desperation clawed at him as his eyes shot back to the living room door. "You're the only one who can help me find him."

Cal shook his head, freeing tears.

Jago leaned into him. "Who took him? Is he here somewhere in the cove?"

Now Cal's whole body trembled. A strangled whimper gurgled in his throat as Jago grabbed his arm. He recognised Noah. Jago felt it in his blood, in his bones. He held the poster closer to Cal's face.

"Please, Cal. Tell me. Is Noah . . . Is he . . ." He couldn't say it. Not out loud. Because voicing such a terrible thought might make it true. *Is Noah dead?*

Cal shook his head, over and over. He pulled away and let out a piercing, drawn out wail. Jago's eyes flew to the door. He quickly rolled up the poster and stuffed it into his bag, just as Carrie came running in from the kitchen.

"What happened?" she said, setting two glasses of water down on the coffee table. She rushed forward, kneeling in front of Cal, who was now rocking back and forth, his hands clasped over his ears and tears splashing onto his lap.

Carrie glared at Jago. "What happened?" she repeated.

Jago stared from mother to son. "I don't know. One minute we were looking at pictures, the next he started freaking out."

Cal's face twisted into a silent scream.

"It's okay, I've got you," Carrie soothed, rubbing his arms. "I'm right here. I've got you."

Jago clutched the photograph album as he watched Carrie comfort her son, moving her hands from his arms to his shoulders and back down again.

"I didn't mean to upset him," he said. "Maybe I should go."

Carrie nodded. Her eyes flicked in his direction.

Standing, Jago threw the album into his bag. Not knowing what else to say, he nodded goodbye and headed for the door.

"Jago?" Carrie wore a strange expression on her face, as if she sensed he'd been up to no good.

"Yes?"

"You will come by again, won't you?" She glanced at Cal as she continued to rub his shoulders. "It's overwhelming for him, that's all. He just needs some time."

Jago hesitated. He nodded. "Sure."

He let himself out, almost running from the house. When he'd reached the road, he allowed himself a few unsteady breaths.

Cal had recognised Noah. The only way that could be possible was if he and Noah had been held together. But Cal's reaction was deeply troubling.

He had been terrified.

Reaching the end of the road, Jago took a left and headed back up the hill. Horrible images taunted his mind and he fought to expel them. Someone had taken Cal. Years later, that same person had taken Noah. Somehow, Cal had managed to escape. But Noah hadn't. Jago walked on, a sick feeling of dread threatening to bring him to his knees.

He froze and slowly turned to view Devil's Cove.

He would tear this town apart to find his brother. And if Cal refused to help, he would tear him apart, too.

28

By the time Jago strolled up to his house, Nat had already smoked two cigarettes. She'd had a bad day at college, with Sierra Davis giving her more grief about her cropped hair. Well, screw her, she thought. There were more urgent things to worry about than the opinion of some brainless, superficial idiot. So why couldn't she get that brainless, superficial idiot out of her head?

Sierra was not the only person who'd irritated her today. She'd been desperate to come along and meet Cal. Her curiosity was piqued but it was more than that. Jago's old friend had returned.

How long would it be before they became best friends again? Where would that leave her?

Jago stopped outside his garden gate, nodding in her direction. She walked up to him and they perched on the garden wall.

"So, how was it?" she asked.

Jago was quiet as he pulled out his tobacco pouch and began to roll a cigarette. "It was weird," he said. "The last time I saw Cal we were kids. Now he's a teenager. But it's more than that. There's something not right about him."

"You mean apart from being alive when he should be dead?"

"It's the way he stares at you, like he's still a little kid. And the whole not talking thing is creepy." He lit his cigarette and inhaled deeply. "There's something else. I showed him Noah's picture. He started freaking out. He recognised him, I know it. But it shouldn't be possible because Noah was born after Cal disappeared."

"Maybe Carrie showed him a picture."

"She told me she hadn't mentioned Noah yet. She said he wasn't ready."

Nat heaved her shoulders. "I take it Carrie was out of the room when you showed him?"

"She was in the kitchen." Jago took another drag on the cigarette. "The only way he could recognise Noah is if he's been with him."

Goosebumps teased the surface of Nat's skin. There could be any number of reasons explaining why Cal had recognised Noah's picture. There were posters with his face on them all over town. His picture had been in the newspapers again within the last few days, the press speculating a connection between the boys' disappearances.

Or perhaps Cal hadn't recognised Noah at all and Jago was seeing what he wanted to see. She glanced down the street. Something else was troubling her and she wondered if telling Jago about it would only fire his suspicion. If she didn't tell him, he would find out anyway and she might not be there to act as his voice of reason.

"Did you hear about Margaret Telford?" she said, flicking her finished cigarette into the distance.

Jago sat up. "What about her?"

"The police have been to her house today."

"Why?"

"Not sure. Rose told me when I got home. Apparently one of Margaret's neighbours heard screaming."

Jago stared at her, his eyes growing wide. "I wonder what that's about."

Shrugging, Nat ran her fingers over her scalp. She could see by

Jago's lined expression that he was already connecting the two events. It was strange, though, she agreed, that the person who saved Cal's life should be heard screaming at the top of her lungs.

"What are you going to do about Cal?" she asked.

Jago's face turned serious. "Carrie's asked me to come back and visit him. I'll wait till we're alone again and this time, I'll press him harder."

"You think that's a good idea? If Carrie finds out what you're doing, she'll go ballistic. She'll stop you from seeing him again. Besides, don't you think Cal's probably traumatised enough without you making it worse?"

Anger flashed in Jago's eyes.

"Worse?" he said. "What if he knows exactly where to find my brother? What if waiting for Cal to tell us in his own time means it'll be too late? I'm not taking that chance."

Nat stared at the ground.

"I'm just saying . . ." she muttered. When she looked up again, Jago was shaking his head as if she were some ignorant child who had no idea what she was talking about. But she knew more about trauma than most people in this stupid town.

Sucking in a breath, Nat held it for a second then let it go, expelling her anger.

"Just be careful," she said.

Jago said nothing. His eyes were fixed further down the road, on a dark blue Renault.

The car had been there for a few days. Nat had noticed it while hanging out of her bedroom window, smoking cigarettes after Rose had retired for the night. She didn't think it belonged to any of the neighbours.

Nat watched as Jago jumped down and paced towards the car. Slipping off the wall, she followed behind.

"Whose is it?" she asked, peering through the driver window. She grimaced as she noticed a wad of bloody tissue sitting in the passenger seat. Next to her, Jago grew very still. He glanced both ways along the road, then tried the driver door. It was locked.

"Remember that journalist from the other night? The one who told me about Cal? This is his car. It's been here since Sunday."

Nat cupped her hands to her face as she peered in. "Why would he leave it here?"

"The last I saw him was when I laid him out on the garden path. He wouldn't have just wandered off. It doesn't make sense."

The two were quiet, staring into the car interior.

Nat shivered. She met Jago's gaze.

Strange things were happening in Devil's Cove. Any event out of the ordinary should have torn away the boredom of small town life. But all Nat felt as she stepped away from the car, was a creeping sense of unease.

29

RAIN ROLLED in on Friday morning, turning the ocean muddy grey. With it came a damp chill that sank into the bones of the cove's inhabitants. Carrie had been up since 6 a.m., distracting her anxious thoughts with housework. She'd left the children to sleep while she'd prepared breakfast. Now, at a little after seven, she returned upstairs with an empty laundry basket. Stopping at the top of the landing, she cocked her head. Melissa's sing-song voice floated out from her bedroom. Smiling, Carrie pushed open the door. She stopped still.

Melissa was in the centre of the room, surrounded by toys. Facing her, with a handful of Lego bricks, was Cal.

"Good morning," Carrie said from the doorway. Her children looked up briefly before returning to their play. Carrie watched them for a short while, a warmth spreading through her stomach. Stepping into the room, she carefully circled them and began stripping Melissa's bed of sheets.

Cal had made some kind of vehicle while Melissa had crafted a small building, on top of which she'd placed a toy figure.

"Help me!" she cried in a cartoon voice. "My house is on fire!"

Her gaze turned to Cal, who picked up the vehicle and turned it over.

"*Cal!* You have to rescue me," Melissa whined.

Carrie waited. Her heart danced with delight as Cal placed the vehicle back on the carpet and pushed it towards the house.

"I hate to break up your play," she said, after a minute more of watching, "but it's almost time to get ready for school."

Melissa scrunched up her face. "But I want to play with Cal."

"I'm very happy to hear that, sweet pea. You can play with Cal all you want. But later."

"Why do I have to go to school and Cal stays home?"

"You know why. Now, up you get," Carrie said.

She hadn't given much thought to Cal's education. She wasn't sure where to begin. He had missed seven years of schooling. She had no idea of his abilities. It was something she would need to discuss with that social worker. Whatever her name was.

But not yet. Cal had been home for less than a week.

He was watching her, the toy vehicle forgotten. Carrie smiled at him. For the briefest of moments, he smiled back.

"Breakfast will be on the table in ten minutes," she said, buzzing with joy.

Leaving Melissa to grumble, she carried the basket of dirty sheets into Cal's room. Her wide, happy grin was quickly wiped away. There was an unpleasant smell. The stench of stale air, sweat, and something else she couldn't define.

Wrinkling her nose, Carrie dumped the basket on the bed and wrenched open the curtains. A row of toy figures, including Rex the dinosaur, stared at her from the window ledge. She smiled as she opened the window and sucked in the morning air and rain.

"Boys," she muttered. Why did they always smell so bad? Cal had not slept in his bed again. It was becoming a habit. Wherever he had been all this time, had he been forced to sleep on the ground? She longed to ask him. For him to tell her everything so she could strip it from his memory and wash it clean like dirty sheets.

She looked out at the rain. She would be taking Cal into town today for the first time. Cove Crafts had been sitting unopened for days now. She'd missed the last week of business, which meant even less money to tide them over the winter months. And now she had the thankless task of packing up the stock and storing it away until spring. She would get Cal to help her but she would keep him in the storeroom, away from prying eyes.

A change of scene would be good for him, she thought, hearing yesterday's conversation with Rose in her head. Meeting with Jago hadn't gone as well as she'd expected, although she had her suspicions that Jago had said something to upset Cal while she'd been out of the room. But it was a start, at least. Perhaps today would be another step forward.

Movement below pulled her from her thoughts. Her neighbour, Dottie Penpol, stood just outside the garden gate, wearing a raincoat and a scarf wrapped around her head. She peered at the house with wide, curious eyes.

"Can I help you with something, Dottie?"

"Goodness, Carrie. You scared me out of my skin!" Startled, the elderly woman shot a hand up to her chest. "Everyone fine in there?"

"Oh yes, we're all doing very well, thank you." Carrie watched her through narrow eyes. She was still annoyed with Dottie for talking to the press.

"And that boy of yours, is he well?"

"He's just fine."

"It must have been such a shock to find out he was alive!" Dottie said, arching an eyebrow. "Where has he been all this time?"

"I don't know."

"You don't know? Well, how can that be?"

Dottie waited, open-mouthed, for Carrie to explain. When she didn't, she clamped her jaw shut.

"Well, it's a miracle. A true blessing," she said, finally. "The Lord really does move in mysterious ways."

Tell that to Tess Pengelly, Carrie thought. "You be sure to have a nice day now, Dottie. You don't want to stand there for too much longer or you'll catch a cold."

The elderly woman pursed her lips, as her eyes wandered to the living room window.

"Quite," she said, then took a step closer. "By the way, did you hear about Margaret Telford?"

Carrie felt a chill creep in through the window.

"Margaret Telford? What happened?"

"The police were at her house yesterday. And those funny men in white suits. Larry Bolitho said they were out in her yard examining something."

"Examining what, exactly?"

Dottie shook her head. "No idea. But Larry reckons whatever it was, it was something unpleasant. Well, I best be off. Mabel's having a last day sale on postcards."

Carrie waved as her neighbour trundled off. She turned to face the room. Anxiety washed over her as she wondered what had been found in Margaret Telford's garden. She had yet to thank the woman for finding Cal. Perhaps she'd call her later today.

She moved to the bed and began pulling off the sheets, even though they'd not been slept in. Perhaps she should stay home with Cal, after all. The shop could wait another day.

But it would be another day Cal had to stay locked up inside. It would be another day to wait for life to return to normal.

The bed stripped, she hooked the basket under her hip and headed for the door. She stopped and tilted her head, sniffing the air. What was that smell?

She would take Cal to the shop. She would cancel Rose and drive Melissa to school herself. The sooner life returned to normal, the better.

30

THE CONTINUING rain allowed Carrie the excuse of driving down to the sea front, where she parked the car on a side street and hurried Cal into an alleyway and through the rear entrance of Cove Crafts.

In just that short distance, she'd seen Cal change from observant to alert, his head swivelling on his shoulders as he absorbed his surroundings.

Once inside, Carrie made some tea for them both then showed Cal how to build the flat pack boxes that the shop's stock would be stored in over the winter season. Leaving him to work in the store-room, she moved to the shop floor, where she logged onto a desktop computer and began the laborious task of stock checking.

Occasionally, she would look to the back of the shop, or out into the town square, where a handful of shoppers moved from store to store. At first, Carrie thought she'd managed to avoid a full inquisition by the cove's inhabitants thanks to the bad weather keeping them at home. But as the morning progressed, the rain dried up. Then, every ten minutes or so, someone would notice her at the counter and peer through the glass in search of the enigmatic, returned-from-the-grave, Cal Anderson. One or two even ignored the *Closed* sign and came inside, only to find Carrie alone.

If they'd ventured a little further, they would have found Cal, methodically building boxes and stopping occasionally to examine a mermaid figurine or miniature ship's wheel from the shelves of excess stock. But Carrie had not allowed them to get that far.

Lunchtime arrived. Carrie returned to the storeroom where Cal had built four neat towers of boxes and was sitting on a chair in the corner, poring over a book of local history. The current page showed an old illustration of smugglers carrying crates of rum from the beach, where a wrecked ship had run aground.

"When you were little all you wanted to be was a pirate," she said, startling him.

Cal stared at her before returning his attention to the book.

Is that where you were? Off sailing the seas in search of buried treasure? Carrie watched him for a moment, revelling in the sight of her son.

"Lunchtime," she said, crossing the room to the small refrigerator. "I made ham sandwiches."

Cal turned the pages of the book, his brow wrinkled with concentration. Removing the sandwiches, Carrie put them on plates and poured out two glasses of orange juice. The picnic table in the small courtyard was still wet, so they remained in the storeroom.

"Cal? Are you going to eat?" She waited for him to respond. When he didn't, she drummed her fingers against the top of her thigh. "Cal? Please, don't ignore me."

The slightest of smiles rippled across Cal's lips. Closing the book, he stood up.

Then he froze.

He turned his head in the direction of the shop.

Carrie followed his gaze. "What is it?"

Brushing past, she motioned for him to stay, then entered the shop floor.

"Is someone there?" she called out.

A small Yorkshire Terrier appeared in the aisle and snarled at her. Ignoring it, she reached the counter to find a figure peering down at the computer screen.

"Hello, Mr Spencer," she said, sidestepping Caliban, who had scampered in front of her to issue a warning yap. "I'm sorry but we're closed. Until spring. How are you keeping?"

Even bent over his stick Grady was a formidable figure; one Carrie wasn't particularly fond of. It wasn't that she had personal reasons to dislike him. It was his nature, she supposed. She didn't like the way he looked at people, as if he deemed himself superior. She didn't like the way he always had something bad to say about his fellow townsfolk. He could dress it up as being a lonely old man, but Grady Spencer was a misanthrope of the highest degree. The kind that not only hated people but actively went out of his way to let them know.

Tapping his stick on the floor, Grady turned away from the computer.

"Oh, you know. I keep myself to myself, don't I?" he said, flashing her a shrewd look before casting his eyes over the store. Beside him, Caliban sniffed the air and let out a yap. "That boy of yours turned up again, I see. Where is he, then?"

Carrie arched an eyebrow. At least the old man wasn't pretending to be interested in her wares.

"Actually, he's in the storeroom, keeping a low profile. Which is exactly how I'd like to keep things for now. Let's call it a settling in period. I'm sure you understand, Mr Spencer."

"Doesn't make a difference to me." Grady's eyes drifted back to Carrie, hungry and expecting. "Has he said anything? About where he's been?"

"Not yet. But I'm sure once he's feeling better, he'll tell us exactly where he's been and who did this to him."

That was all she was giving the old man.

Grady nodded. For a moment, his gaze lingered on the back of the shop. At his feet, Caliban continued to sniff the air and growl. "You think someone took your boy, then?"

"I don't think. I know. There can't be any other explanation."

"Maybe he wandered off."

"For seven years?"

"Maybe he didn't much like it where he was." The old man sneered, his lips twisting at the edges.

Clenching her hands by her sides, Carrie forced a smile. *Gnarly old bastard.*

"Well, he seems happy enough now. If you'll excuse me, I need to get on with closing up."

"Don't mind me," Grady said, waving a knotted hand. "Husband away, is he?"

Carrie looked up to see a strange smile ripple across the old man's lips. "He'll be back on Sunday."

She turned away, pretending to work on the computer. When she looked up again, Grady was by the front door and staring in the direction of the storeroom.

"Did you hear about Margaret Telford?" he said, his gaze sliding back to her.

"I heard the police came around." Carrie didn't want to spend another second talking to the man, but she was curious about what had happened.

"Dog's dead," Grady said, with a half-smile. "Found pieces of him in the backyard. So I heard."

Carrie drew in a shocked breath. "My God, poor Margaret."

The old man glanced down at Caliban, who was busy wagging his tail and whining, his nose pointed at the back of the shop. "Terrible thing to happen after finding your son, don't you think?"

"Do they know who did it?"

"Someone with a grudge against her, I imagine."

Grady smiled. He pulled open the door.

"Come," he barked at Caliban, who scampered back to his master's side.

As soon as she was alone, Carrie crossed the floor and locked the door. She leaned against it for a second, horrified by what Grady had told her. Poor Margaret, she thought, and wondered again who could have done something so horrific.

Her face pale and waxy, she returned to the storeroom.

Cal was not where she had left him.

Panicking, she spun around.

"Cal? Where are you?"

She moved to the back door and pulled it open. The small yard was empty. She returned to the storeroom and was about to grab her keys and head into the alley behind the shop, when she heard a sharp intake of breath.

She turned her head to the corner of the room, where Cal had wedged himself beneath the shelves, and was sitting with his knees pulled up to his chin. He was deathly pale. His body quivered like an autumn leaf.

"Cal, what is it?" Carrie rushed forward onto her knees.

He stared at her and shook his head.

"Talk to me. What's wrong."

She reached out a hand. Cal flinched.

"Won't you tell me?" Carrie said. "Please, Cal. Can't you try to say something? Even just a word?"

Cal pushed back against the wall and balled his hands into tight fists. Carrie's phone began to ring.

She sat back. "I'm sorry. I just want to help, that's all. I just want you to be happy."

She pulled her phone from her pocket as Cal continued to glare. Melissa's school was calling.

"Good afternoon, Mrs Killigrew. This is Valerie Taylor, the school receptionist. Mrs White would very much like to see you when you collect Melissa this afternoon. There's been an incident."

Carrie's heart thumped a little faster. "An incident? Is Melissa all right?"

"Oh no, it's nothing like that," the receptionist said. "Melissa is fine. But Mrs White would like to see you as a matter of urgency."

Carrie turned to see Cal still crammed into the corner of the storeroom, watching her. "What's this about?"

"We'll see you at the end of the day," the receptionist said. She hung up before Carrie could question her further.

Lines of worry creased Carrie's brow. The beginnings of a headache began to manifest at the top of her skull. She looked up at Cal then back at her phone screen. Grady Spencer's words echoed in her mind.

She stood.

"Come out of there, Cal," she said softly. "Everything's fine."

Her words sounded as empty as the surrounding boxes.

31

PORTH AN JOWL PRIMARY SCHOOL was situated at the very top of the cove, just past Briar Wood and opposite the caravan park. It was a small Victorian building with an even smaller playground, where less than a hundred young students spent their lunch hour chasing each other while collecting new bruises and grazes. Now, the playground was a hive of voices as parents arrived to collect their children.

Carrie pulled up on the road outside and switched off the car engine. A few heads turned in her direction, more interested in her passenger than they were in her.

Cal had spent the short drive with his face turned to the window. It had taken Carrie almost fifteen minutes to convince him to come out from under the shelves and even longer to leave the shop. Once inside the car, his agitation had lessened, the hum of the engine and the changing view acting like sedatives. At the sight of the crowd, Cal pulled away from the window.

"Maybe you should stay here," she told him. "Unless you want to come inside with me."

Panic returning, Cal shook his head.

Carrie stroked his hand, feeling tendons tensing beneath his skin. "I'll leave the radio on but don't touch anything. And if anyone tries to speak to you, ignore them."

She punched the button on the stereo and pop music began to filter through the speakers. Cal cocked his head, listening to the tune.

"You'll be okay?" She didn't feel comfortable leaving him, but the alternative would be even more stressful.

Cal nodded. He pressed the button on the stereo, changing the channel.

Stepping out of the car, Carrie closed the door. At the school gates, she stopped and glanced back at the car, then pushed the remote lock button on the car key. Cal's head snapped to the left, startled by the click of the locks. He peered through the window, touching the glass with his fingertips.

"Five minutes," Carrie mouthed, spreading her fingers.

Pushing past the other adults and children, she headed for the main building. Someone called hello to her, but she ignored them, hurrying through the doors and away from the staring faces.

As she entered the reception office, she wondered if she'd been right to leave Cal alone in the car. His behaviour in the store had worried her. What had he been so afraid of?

She reached the reception desk, where Valerie Taylor sat behind a glass partition, talking with another parent. Carrie waited, staring out the window into the playground, watching the other parents and children walk away hand in hand. Had Cal overheard Grady Spencer talking about Margaret Telford's poor dog? Was that what had upset him?

She shuddered as she turned back to the desk. It would have taken a very sick individual to mutilate an animal in the way Grady had described. The murder of Margaret's dog could not be a coincidence. It was almost as if someone had wanted to punish Margaret. But for what? For saving Cal's life?

"Good afternoon, Mrs Killigrew. You're here to see Mrs White?" Valerie said, interrupting her thoughts.

Carrie nodded. "I can't be long. Cal is waiting in the car."

"Of course. I'll take you through, then I'll fetch Melissa. She's in with the after-school club."

Carrie was led along a long corridor, its walls adorned with artwork and writing done by the children. Valerie was silent, leaving her to grow increasingly disturbed by the thoughts churning her mind.

She stopped in her tracks, growing suddenly pale.

What if whoever had taken Cal was responsible for killing poor Alfie? That would surely mean Cal's abductor lived in the cove. Did that also mean Cal had been kept hidden away all these years just metres away from her? The thought had crossed her mind more than once since his return, but she had dismissed it. Because that would mean it was entirely possible she knew her son's abductor.

"Mrs Killigrew? Carrie? Are you all right?" Valerie had stopped outside the headteacher's office door.

"I'm fine."

Looking unconvinced, the receptionist knocked and waited until a woman's voice instructed them to enter.

Elsa White was tall and gaunt, dressed in a tweed jacket and skirt, her white hair pulled back in a tight bun. She had been the headteacher at Porth an Jowl Primary School for what seemed like forever, even when Carrie had attended. Her hair had grown whiter, her face thinner, but not much else had changed.

Also present was Laura Rhodda, Melissa's teacher, who stood and smiled nervously as Carrie entered. She was younger than Carrie, perhaps in her late twenties. She was not from the cove.

"It's nice to see you, Carrie," Elsa White said, her voice soft yet firm. "Please, sit down."

The three women sat for a moment, silence pervading the room.

"I can't be long," Carrie said. "I've left Cal in the car."

"Of course." Elsa's face softened a little. "How is he?"

"Getting there. The doctors say it will take a little while." Carrie shifted on the chair, crossing her legs.

"It was such a tragedy when he disappeared," the headteacher said. "Callum was always such a bright, kind boy. I'm so glad he's come back to you."

Carrie smiled and nodded. She turned her attention to Laura Rhodda, who was busy staring at the desk. "Melissa was involved in some sort of incident?"

The warmth in Elsa's face quickly faded. She glanced sideways at Laura.

"Mrs Killigrew," the teacher began, her voice soft and unsure.

"Mrs Killigrew?" Carrie laughed. "This must be bad if you're addressing me as *Mrs Killigrew*."

A pained look passed over the teacher's face. "Carrie... It's nothing too serious, I hope. But something I—*we* thought you should see."

For the first time, Carrie noticed a roll of paper clutched in the teacher's hands.

"This morning in art class, I asked the children to draw a picture of their family. I asked them to think about what their family meant to them. I'm afraid that Melissa drew something rather disturbing."

Carrie stared at the roll of paper, her mouth running dry.

"Oh?"

Elsa nodded at Laura. Slowly, she unrolled the paper and flattened it out on the desk.

Carrie leaned forward.

"As you can see, it's rather gruesome," Laura said.

Carrie's eyes bulged in her head. Her jaw dropped open.

"Holy shit!"

Melissa had drawn a picture of the Killigrews' house and garden. She had taken pains to colour each flower in the garden, and to draw the pattern of the curtains in the living room and bedroom windows. But it was the people she'd drawn that were causing so much concern.

Two figures lay in the garden, their heads severed from their bodies and red crayon smears soaking the ground. Outside the garden gate, three figures wore happy smiles as they danced away, heading towards a figure that filled Carrie with horror. It was much larger than the others, made up of dark scribbled lines, with a twisted, monstrous face and horns sprouting from its head.

Carrie stared at the picture, her face draining of colour. She looked up, trying to force words out of her throat.

"Why would she draw this?" she managed to say.

Elsa White clasped her hands together. "We were hoping you could tell us. It's very much out of character for Melissa to draw something so...colourful, shall we say?"

Carrie's gaze was pulled back to the drawing. *Colourful* was not a word she would have used to describe such horrors.

"Do you think it could be a reaction to Callum's return?" Elsa suggested. "Perhaps it's her mind's way of expressing how she's feeling."

"I want to see her. I want to see her now."

"She should be right outside."

Elsa stood and went to the door. The receptionist, Valerie, stood on the other side, her hand wrapped around Melissa's, whose eyes were large and round. They grew wet as she saw her mother. Her lower lip began to tremble.

"It's okay, sweet pea," Carrie said, reaching out a hand and helping Melissa into the chair next to her. "You're not in trouble. We just need to talk about something, that's all."

"Do you know why we had to call your mummy today?" Elsa asked her.

Melissa shook her head and stared at her knees.

"Sweet pea," Carrie began. She picked up the drawing and was immediately drawn to that terrible, demonic figure. "Do you remember drawing this in art class today?" Melissa peered at the drawing with large, sorrowful eyes. "Do you want to tell me why you drew a picture like this?" The little girl shrugged and pushed her lower lip out even further. "It's okay. Remember, you're not in trouble. We're just talking. Do you want to tell me who's in the picture?"

Another shrug. Carrie pointed to the headless bodies on the floor. "Is this Mummy and Daddy?"

Melissa glanced at her teacher, then at Mrs White. She nodded.

Carrie stared down at her own lifeless, headless corpse. She pointed to the three smiling figures who were running away. "And who is this?"

Melissa was silent, her small face lined with worry. She reached out her index finger. This is me," she whispered, pointing to the smallest stick figure with a nest of wavy hair. Her finger moved to the figure on the right of the trio, who was much bigger than the others. "This is Cal."

"And who's this?" Carrie pointed to the smaller figure in the middle and saw that her hand was trembling. A horrible feeling of dread had seized her. She knew the answer before Melissa could speak his name.

"That's Noah," her daughter said.

Carrie glanced over the desk at Elsa White, whose face was a myriad of concerned lines. Beside her, Laura Rhodda looked scared to death. Carrie pointed to the final, monstrous figure on the page. "And this?"

Melissa looked up with frightened eyes. She stared at the picture again and withdrew her hand to her lap.

"It's okay, sweetie. You can tell me."

Melissa shook her head.

Elsa White leaned to one side. "Perhaps you could be so good, Miss Rhodda, and wait outside with Melissa?"

It took a moment for the teacher to peel her alarmed gaze from the little girl. She crossed the room and held the door open.

"I won't be long," Carrie said, stroking her daughter's hand.

She watched as Melissa was ferried outside.

"Are you all right?" Elsa asked, when they were alone.

Carrie shook her head. "It's not every day you learn your four-year-old daughter wants you dead."

"I'm sure she wants nothing of the sort, Carrie. I'm sure it's merely a reaction to having to make room for Cal. She's been an only child her entire life. She's never had to share you or her father. The drawing is her mind's way of dealing with all those confused feelings."

Carrie stared at the picture. Something about it didn't make sense. Why was she running away with Cal, smiling and happy, if she resented him being here?

And what about Noah? His presence in the picture disturbed her far more than her own severed head resting in a flower bed. But what chilled her the most was that dark, horned figure.

"I suppose everything's changed for her," she said. "For us all."

Elsa White was silent for a moment, her hands clasped together on the desk. "You know, Carrie, we do have a school counsellor visiting us once a week. Perhaps Melissa would benefit from a little time with him? It would be non-invasive, just play and talk. He may be able to help Melissa understand the changes that are happening around her right now."

Carrie leaned back, shaking her head. "I don't know…"

Dull pain throbbed at the base of her skull. Cal's return was never going to be easy, she knew that. And dealing with whatever was going on inside his head was stressful enough. But having both of her children in therapy? She was beginning to feel a lot like a shitty mother.

"I'll tell you what," Elsa said, her face softening. "Take the weekend to think about it. Having Melissa talk to a professional could make things a little easier for you. A little less on your plate to deal with."

Carrie let out a deep, trembling breath. She nodded.

"Good. And perhaps Melissa will be open to further discussion at home, away from her terrible headteacher." Elsa smiled wryly, then leaned forward and took a closer look at the picture. "It's strange she drew Noah Pengelly, isn't it?"

Carrie stared at the three figures running away, gleeful smiles on their faces. When Noah had disappeared, Melissa had been curious to know what had happened to her friend. Gradually, as the months faded, so had her interest in Noah.

Or so Carrie had thought.

"Can I take this?" she asked, rolling up the picture.

Elsa White nodded her head. "Of course. Although it's not quite one for the refrigerator door, is it?"

Carrie stood.

"Come see me first thing Monday morning," the headteacher said, shaking her hand.

The playground was almost empty as Carrie and Melissa walked silently back to the car. Carrie's mind flashed with images of Melissa's drawing. Her headache grew worse.

Cal was in the front passenger seat, his expressionless face watching as they drew near.

"I want Cal to sit in the back with me!" Melissa said, pulling away from Carrie and running to the car.

As she came closer, Cal trained his eyes on her. He smiled.

Carrie slowed down. She watched Cal climb out and open the rear passenger door. Melissa clambered in and he followed her, slamming the door behind him.

By the time Carrie had walked around to the driver side, both children were wearing their seat belts. They stared at her as she climbed in. In the rear-view mirror, Carrie saw them turn to each other and smile. She should have been happy. But all she felt was a quiet, unsettling anxiety. She glanced down at the rolled up picture on her lap.

"Let's go home," she said.

32

Detective Turner stood on the garden path, a grim expression on his face, as Carrie pulled up outside the house. In the back seat of the car, Melissa was busy showing Cal a story book she'd brought home from school. Cal looked up and saw the police officer. His eyes narrowed.

"Take your sister inside," Carrie said, passing her house keys to him. "I'll be there in a second." Climbing out, she helped Melissa onto the pavement.

Detective Turner came up to the gate.

"This is a surprise," Carrie said, as she ferried the children into the garden.

Detective Turner stood to one side.

"Sorry to drop by unannounced," he said. He locked eyes with Cal as he passed by. "How are you, young man?"

Cal said nothing as he took Melissa by the hand and walked her to the front door.

Once they had disappeared inside, Carrie folded her arms across her chest and leaned against the gate post. "Judging by the look on your face, I'm guessing this isn't a social call."

"I'm afraid not," Turner said. "It's been requested that I try to talk to Cal again."

"I thought we agreed he wasn't ready yet. And what about the intermediary?"

"There's been a development. DCI Marsh is keen we try and get Cal talking sooner rather than later."

"You mean Margaret Telford's dog?"

Turner stared at her open-mouthed.

"It's a small town. You know how quickly news spreads."

The detective was quiet for a moment. He glanced up at the neighbouring houses. "Can we go inside and speak?"

"I'd rather not. I don't want my children hearing about how that poor animal was hacked into pieces. Do you know who did it?"

"Not yet. It's part of the reason I'd like to talk to Cal."

"Why? You're not suggesting he had anything to do with it?"

"Of course not. But it's hard to believe the attack was just a coincidence."

Carrie tightened her grip around her ribcage. Her eyes moved to the house. Cal was in the living room window, watching them.

"What are you saying, Detective? That whoever took Cal killed Margaret's dog? That means it would have to be someone local. Someone we know."

"It's too early to say anything yet," Turner said. "But if Cal could talk to us, or communicate what's happened to him, it would really help us out."

Cal was still standing at the window, his expression stony. He wasn't going to talk to the detective. He wouldn't even talk to his own mother. Besides, she still had to get to the bottom of Melissa's disturbing picture.

"I'm sorry, Detective Turner, but this isn't a good time," Carrie said. "Perhaps you can talk to the intermediary and arrange something with her. Give Cal another day or two. We're making progress but I don't want to risk everything by trying to force him to speak."

Turner frowned and dug his hands inside his pockets. Noticing

Cal, he turned his body slightly, so that his back was facing the window.

"I'll see what I can do. But it needs to be soon, Carrie. The powers that be aren't going to wait forever. We're drawing a blank. People want answers. Answers we can't give them right now."

"And by people, you mean Tess Pengelly," Carrie said, feeling miserable.

Detective Turner shook his head. "I mean people. If word is out about Margaret Telford's dog, then it won't be long before your friends and neighbours start drawing conclusions of their own. The last thing we need is for people to panic. It's not going to help either investigation."

Carrie glanced over Turner's shoulder. What would happen when the inhabitants of the cove started making connections. Would they point fingers at Cal? At her?

They'd already formed their opinions about Carrie seven years ago. She didn't care what people said about her behind closed doors. But she cared what they said about her son. All she wanted was for him to return to a normal life. To be welcomed back by the community. Not ostracised. Not feared.

"There's something else," Turner said, dropping his voice down low. "This afternoon, a local newspaper reported one of their journalists missing."

An icy sliver slipped down the back of Carrie's neck. "Really? Who is it?"

"Scott Triggs. He wrote some deeply unpleasant things about the Pengellys back when Noah disappeared. He called the paper on Sunday evening, telling them to hold the front page for an exclusive story. Somehow, he'd figured out Cal's identity ahead of our press conference. He called in, said he'd have the story and an exclusive photo within an hour. They didn't hear from him again." The detective leaned forward. "Did he come to your house last Sunday?"

Shit. Did she mention that Dylan had gone after Triggs? That there'd been a scuffle and he'd smashed the journalist's camera? She

had no real idea what had happened out there, or where the journalist had disappeared to.

"He was taking pictures of us through the kitchen window,"
Carrie said. "Dylan chased him away. We didn't see him after that. I
don't remember seeing him the next day when the rest of the press
arrived. But he'd stopped me out in the street a few days earlier,
trying to get me to admit Cal was alive. I ignored him." Her mind
raced. First Margaret Telford's dog. Now this damn journalist. She
stared up at the detective. "What's going on here?"

Deep lines spread across Turner's face. "We don't know yet.
Which is why we need to talk to your son."

Carrie expelled an unsteady breath.

"Let me talk to him," she said. "I'll try tonight."

"I'd rather—"

"I'll try tonight," Carrie repeated.

The detective nodded. "Okay. If you learn anything, you'll call
me right away?"

"Of course."

Glancing back at Cal one last time, Detective let himself
through the garden gate.

"I'll contact the intermediary," he said. "Just in case."

Carrie watched him climb into his car, start the engine, and pull
away. She waited until he had reached the end of the street and
headed left, disappearing from view.

When she could no longer hear the hum of the car engine, she
turned and walked to the door. Cal was still watching her from the
window.

With trembling fingers, and her mind overwhelmed with worry,
Carrie pushed open the door and stepped inside.

33

As the evening drew in, a dark, ominous mood fell over the Killigrew house. Carrie sat at one end of the kitchen table, with her children on either side. She did not engage them in conversation but instead lost herself in worried thoughts as she picked at her meal. Occasionally, her eyes moved from son to daughter, scrutinising them. More than once, the children's gazes met across the table. Carrie felt pangs of envy.

With dinner over and the children sent off to the living room, Carrie busied herself with cleaning up. As she loaded the dishwasher, her thoughts flicked from Melissa's disturbing drawing to Margaret Telford's butchered dog to the missing journalist.

As she returned cutlery to the drawer with a clatter, she pictured the horribly deformed figure that Melissa had drawn. Who was he? Something wasn't right. She didn't care about theories of attention seeking or Melissa expressing feelings of neglect. Something was wrong with that picture, way beyond the blood.

The kitchen now clean and tidy, Carrie moved into the hall.

Laughter floated out from the living room. It was Melissa's

laughter. Carrie pressed her ear to the closed door and listened. As if Melissa could sense her mother on the other side, she fell silent.

Carrie opened the door.

They were sitting on the living room carpet, Melissa opposite Cal, a battalion of toys scattered between them. As Carrie entered, her children looked up. Their smiles faded.

"Are you guys having fun?" she asked, stepping forward.

Cal and Melissa stared at each other with stony expressions.

"What were you laughing about?"

Melissa shrugged her shoulders then turned back to Cal.

A stab of irritation pierced Carrie's already grim mood. "Well, it's time for bed, Melissa. "Perhaps the two of you could tidy up this mess first."

She watched as her children turned away from her, their faces pulled into scowls. Slowly, they began to pick up toys and return them to the large toy box in the corner.

When they were done, Carrie nodded to the stairs.

"Say goodnight to your brother, Melissa. Cal, you can watch television for a little while."

Leaving him in the living room, Carrie took Melissa by the hand and wordlessly led her up to the bathroom.

The silence continued as her daughter brushed her teeth and dressed in her pyjamas. Now tucked up in bed, Carrie stared at Melissa's gloomy expression.

"What is it, sweet pea?"

Nothing. Not even a shrug.

"Are you worried about the talk we had with Mrs White?"

Pushing her lower lip out and narrowing her eyes, Melissa turned away.

"Remember what I said—you're not in trouble. We were just talking about the picture you drew."

Melissa shot her a sideways glare.

"Sweet pea, why did you draw Noah?"

Her daughter swung her shoulders from side to side. Picking up a stuffed rabbit, she hugged it to her chest.

"Have you been thinking about Noah lately?"

"Yes."

"You miss him?"

Sealing her lips together, Melissa looked away. She nodded.

Carrie took her daughter's hand and kissed it. She was beginning to wonder if Elsa White had been correct.

Melissa's whole world had changed. A boy she'd known had disappeared and was now probably dead. Another boy who was *supposed* to be dead had barged his way into her family and shoved her to one side.

Carrie reached out and stroked the girl's head.

"I know things are tough right now. But it will get easier, I promise. But drawing pictures like that... Are you angry with Mummy and Daddy?"

She watched as Melissa shook her head then returned her gaze to the stuffed rabbit.

"What about the monster in your picture? Is it from a bad dream?"

Melissa shook her head again.

"Something you just made up?"

When Melissa spoke, her voice was barely a whisper. "Not supposed to talk about the bad man."

"The bad man? That's the monster from your picture?"

Melissa nodded. Her frown grew deeper.

"Why can't you talk about him?"

"Not allowed to."

"It's just a picture. He can't hurt you because he's not real."

"Yes, he is," Melissa said.

"No, he's not. Monsters aren't real."

"He *is* real!" Melissa suddenly bellowed. Tears slipped from her eyes as she clutched her rabbit. "Cal says not supposed to talk about the bad man or he'll come and get me."

Goosebumps crawled over Carrie's skin.

"Sweet pea, that's not true," she said. "Cal can't speak. You know that."

"Yes, he can!" Melissa wailed. "He talks to me all the time."

Carrie froze. Her heart hammered in her chest. She placed trembling hands on her daughter's shoulders.

"Cal talks to you?"

Melissa nodded. She wiped away tears and stuck out her lower lip again.

"What does he talk about?"

"Not supposed to say."

Nausea churned Carrie's stomach. Surely it was a lie. It had to be. So why did she believe every word her daughter was saying?

"Melissa, please. It's very important you tell me. What has Cal told you?"

Silence. Melissa turned away.

"Has he talked about Noah?"

Now, Melissa began to sob. Her shoulders shook as tears ran down her face in streams.

"I want Daddy!" she wept. "I want to go to sleep!"

Pulling her daughter to her chest, Carrie embraced her.

"Daddy will be home on Sunday," she whispered. She turned to face the open bedroom door. Television sounds floated up. She kissed the top of Melissa's head. "No one is going to hurt you, sweet pea. No one."

Cal was sitting cross-legged in front of the television as an action film exploded across the screen. Carrie stood in the doorway, watching him. He knew she was there. Every few seconds she saw his eyes flick in her direction before returning to the television.

Moving into the room, she sat down next to him and put a hand on his shoulder. He flinched.

"I need to talk to you," Carrie said.

Cal ignored her and flipped the button on the remote.

Taking it from him, she switched off the television. Cal furrowed his brow.

Slowly, Carrie unrolled Melissa's picture.

"Do you see this? Do you see what Melissa drew?"

Cal's eyes begrudgingly moved over the sketch.

Carrie pointed to the three children running from the house. "Melissa says this is you, this is her, and this is a boy called Noah. He's Jago's little brother and he's been missing for a while. Have you heard about him?"

She watched as Cal focused on where she was pointing. His eyes seemed to grow darker.

"The police have looked all over but they can't find him. No one can." She leaned in closer. "Do you know where he is?"

There was something in Cal's eyes. Something black and impenetrable. He turned his head and stared at the blank television screen. "What about this character?" She pointed to the demonic figure. In the dim light of the living room, he looked even more terrifying. "Melissa called him the bad man."

Cal's eyes wandered back to the picture. She couldn't be sure in this light, but his face seemed to grow a shade paler. He turned away again, his breaths audible.

Carrie put the picture down on the carpet and flattened it out.

"Cal, I want to help you," she said, watching as he stared down at Melissa's drawing. "I know it's difficult. I know you don't want to think about it, but I need you to try. If Noah was with you... If he's still alive..."

Cal's fingers curled over his palms and dug into the flesh.

"I want to help," Carrie said again. "Can you tell me who did this to you? Where they've kept you all this time? If you can't tell me, can you show me?"

She stood and grabbed one of Melissa's sketch books from the side. She held out a pencil.

Cal glared at it.

"If you know where Noah is, you can tell me. Write it down. Do you remember how to write?" She could feel frustration bubbling inside her as Cal remained unmoving. He turned his head away from the pen and paper. His face drew up into a scowl.

"Please," Carrie said, resting a hand on his knee. Her voice trembled. Tears welled in her eyes. "I know you speak to Melissa. I know you've told her things. And I just—"

Without warning, Cal batted her hand from his knee and jumped up. He headed for the door.

"Sit down!" Her voice was loud and angry, startling them both.

Cal bowed his head. He remained standing.

"Sit down," Carrie said again, this time in a soft, guilty tone.

Cal stayed, rooted to the ground.

"Why can you talk to Melissa but not to me?" They were not the words she'd intended. She looked up at him, her eyes begging. "Please, Cal. Please, talk to me."

But Cal did not talk to her. Instead, he left the room.

She heard his footsteps thunder on the stairs. She heard his bedroom door slam shut. She heard Melissa, startled and awake, call out for her.

Ignoring her daughter's cries, Carrie brought her hands to her face. She squeezed her eyes shut. Tears came. She let them run down her face and drip on the empty sketch paper.

After a minute, she stopped crying, dried her face, and cleared her throat. Melissa's drawing caught her eye. The bad man stared at her, his glowing eyes burning into her skin.

Cal was not going to tell her what she wanted to know. Nor was Melissa. But perhaps she would tell her father.

Suddenly, Carrie wanted nothing more than for Dylan to come home. To be wrapped in his arms. She thought about contacting him on the satellite phone then changed her mind. He wasn't due back for another forty-eight hours. Telling him everything now would leave him trapped on a boat and worrying about his family.

And he would turn against Cal. He would make her send him away.

Upstairs, Melissa had fallen silent. Carrie got to her feet.

As soon as Dylan was home, she would get him to talk to their daughter. Until then, she was on her own.

Picking up Melissa's drawing, she stared at it for a while longer. Dread crept beneath her skin. Making her way to the kitchen, she pulled open a drawer and hid the picture inside. She locked the back door, slid the bolt across, and pocketed the key. Then she moved from room to room, ensuring all the windows were locked and the curtains were closed. Finally, she locked the front door and removed the key. She would think about calling Detective Turner in the morning. Until then, no one was getting in or out of her house.

34

NAT'S HEAD felt as if someone had opened it up with a pickaxe. She'd been awake for thirty seconds, had no idea what time it was, and was vaguely aware of a buzzing somewhere near her right ear.

Last night, she'd downed half a bottle of cheap whiskey stolen from Jack Dawkin's shop. She felt bad for stealing it, but what choice did she have? She was still six months away from being legally able to buy alcohol, and thanks to her youthful looks, no fake ID in the world was ever going to convince Jack to take her money. Besides, Jack overpriced everything. If they didn't use those damned security contraptions at the supermarket, she would steal from there. At least they'd be able to afford losing a bottle or two.

It was risky stealing from Jack. His shop was small and cramped, making it easy to get caught. She'd only stolen from him once before. The guilt had stopped her from doing it again, until last night.

She supposed she could, like any other underage kid in town, persuade someone old enough to buy the booze for her. But that meant having more friends than Jago. He'd been in a mood last night and hadn't wanted to see her, leaving her no choice but to slip a whiskey bottle into the inside pocket of her military jacket before paying for her tobacco at the counter.

Now, after a night of knocking back whiskey and listening to punk music at a damaging volume through her headphones, she found herself regretting stealing the booze in the first place.

Nat groaned as she scrabbled for her phone and opened an eye to see who was calling.

"What time is it?" she mumbled.

Jago's low tones mumbled into her ear. "Nine-thirty. You sound like shit."

"It's Saturday morning. Why are you calling so early?"

"Have you seen the police outside?"

"What? Wait a second."

Nat pushed herself up onto an elbow and grimaced as the pounding in her head intensified. Dragging herself out of bed, she stumbled to the window and pulled back the curtains. A patrol car was parked outside. A few metres along, the journalist's car was being loaded onto the back of a tow truck.

"What's going on?" she said into the phone.

"I don't know. But if they talk to you, you can't tell them what I did."

Nat looked around for her tobacco pouch and papers. "So, you punched him. He deserved it."

"What if I was the last person to see him? It won't look good."

"That's a little dramatic, isn't it?"

"Just keep it to yourself."

Tobacco located, she tucked the phone between her ear and her shoulder, and began rolling a cigarette. "Fine. What are your plans for today?"

"I'm searching the hotel. Want to come with me?"

"Maybe. But it seems like a waste of time. The police already searched it."

"That was two months ago. Besides, they're under-resourced because of the cuts. Maybe they didn't search the whole place."

"There's no chance Noah could have climbed the hotel gates; they're two metres tall. And they're the only way in."

"Whoever abducted him could have helped him over."

Hearing the desperation in Jago's words, Nat softened her voice. "If someone had taken him up there, don't you think the police would have found him? Besides, the whole place is boarded up. Come on, Jago. Noah's not up there. He can't be. And if you really thought he was up at the hotel, wouldn't you have searched the place already?"

Silence. The cigarette rolled, Nat licked the gum and sealed it shut. She sighed.

"There's a window at the back," Jago said at last, his voice cold and distant. "The board is loose. Some of the kids from town go up there to hang out. He could have got in the same way."

Nat shook her head. Jago's reasoning was becoming more ridiculous by the second. Tucking the cigarette behind her ear, she bent down to search for her military boots. The pain in her head grew sharp and nauseating.

"I thought you were going to speak to Cal again," she said. "It sounds like a safer idea than wading through used condoms and junkie needles."

"I'll talk to him later. When Carrie lets me."

"She must be so weirded out with her dead son walking around like that."

Jago was silent again. Guilt pulled at Nat's conscience. She supposed if it were her little brother who was missing, she would go searching places he couldn't be in, too. The alternative was to give up hope.

"Look, I'll check with Rose and see if I can come with you," she said, letting out a heavy breath. "Margaret Telford's dead dog has made her all twitchy, and now that the police are outside I'm anticipating a full curfew, effective immediately."

"Whatever," Jago said. "I'll be heading up there as soon as the police are gone. Let me know."

Nat slipped her feet into her boots and scanned the floor for her jacket. "Sure thing, Mister Monotone. I need to smoke a cigarette then throw up. See you later."

Jago huffed a sigh into her ear.

She hung up and let the phone fall to the bed. Sometimes, she felt like murdering Jago in his sleep.

Giving up on finding her jacket, she pulled a black hooded top over her head, grabbed a lighter from the bedside table, and stumbled downstairs.

Her attire looked out of place in Rose's cottage, which was rustic perfection, kitted out with a whole farmyard of porcelain animals and soft furnishings in floral print.

Nat hated every inch of it. But she loved Rose, who was kind and caring; much more than her parents had ever been.

She found her in the kitchen, staring worriedly through the window into the back garden.

"Have you seen the cops outside?"

Rose jumped. Her hand shot to her chest.

"I've just had an officer on the doorstep," she said. "They wanted to know if we'd seen some journalist hanging around. Apparently, he's missing."

"Oh?"

Rose turned back to the window. "He's not the only one."

"What is it?" Nat asked, as she moved further into the room. The smell of coffee hung in the air, tantalising her hungover taste buds. A fresh pot sat on the side, next to a mug that already contained milk and sugar.

Rose shook her head. When she turned around again, her round face had grown two shades paler.

"I can't find Honey," she said. "I've looked all over the house."

Nat poured hot black coffee into the mug and stirred the liquid with a teaspoon. She glanced up. "She'll be around somewhere. She only ever goes outside to take care of business. She's probably asleep under a cushion somewhere."

"No, I've looked. She's not in your room?"

"Honey doesn't go upstairs. Besides, she's not allowed in my room."

"What about last night? You made sure she was in when you locked up before bed, didn't you?"

"Of course."

The truth was Nat had been so drunk when she'd last gone outside for a cigarette, she couldn't remember where the damn cat had been.

Having stirred her coffee, she picked up the mug and took a sip. It was hot and glorious. Instantly, the hammering in her head receded a little. But now she felt another sensation. Guilt.

Had she accidentally locked Honey outside? Sometimes the cat did follow her outside when she went for a smoke.

"She'll be around somewhere," she said. "I'll smoke this, then I'll help you find her."

Rose glanced at the cigarette in Nat's hand. "Those things will kill you."

"So will those curtains," Nat muttered, glancing at the windows.

"You're not seeing Jago today?"

"Maybe. He wants me to go on another one of his searches."

"Where to this time?"

Nat raised an eyebrow. Sometimes it was safer to lie. "The woods again, I think."

Rose thrust a hand on her hip and stared through the window. "I don't know, Nat. The whole cove doesn't feel safe today. I asked that policeman about Margaret Telford's dog but he couldn't tell me a thing. Said they're still looking into it. I don't like the idea of you wandering off."

"I'm almost eighteen. I'll be fine."

"The last thing I need is social workers coming around, telling me I'm not doing my job. That I'm not taking care of you."

Nat took another sip of coffee.

Rose stared at her for a long time, worry lines ageing her skin. "I could do with your help looking for Honey. That awful business with poor Margaret has got me worried out of my mind."

"Cats wander sometimes."

"Not my Honey."

Guilt pressed down on Nat's shoulders as she brushed past Rose. "I'll ask the neighbours if they've seen her. Once I've smoked this and drank a gallon of coffee."

"You were boozing again last night, weren't you?" Rose said, shaking her head. "I wish you wouldn't."

Nat pulled open the kitchen door. Fresh air rushed in, making her feel a little better. "Come on, Rose. Even you were young once."

Rose wagged a finger at her. "You have a shower before you go and bother the neighbours. Or they'll smell you coming."

Giving the woman a military style salute, Nat stepped outside and sparked up her cigarette. The lawn was choked with weeds. She'd promised Rose several weeks ago that she'd mow it. She'd get around to it one day.

Puffing on the cigarette, she glanced at the tall wooden fence that separated their garden from Grady Spencer's. Perhaps Honey had found her way to the other side and was now stuck.

"Damn cat," she muttered and took another sip of coffee.

Uneasiness returned to her as she thought about the police outside. What had happened to that journalist? To Margaret Telford's dog?

She wasn't sure if she wanted to find out.

35

CARRIE WOKE WITH A START, pulling herself from a nightmare. She'd been running through the streets of the cove, calling for Cal, already knowing she'd lost him forever. Turning over, she reached out for Dylan. It took her a second to remember he was still at sea. After all these years, it still took her a second.

Blinking the sleep away, she checked the time and was startled to see it was almost ten. Memories of last night's confrontation with Cal played on her mind. He could talk. He hadn't admitted it but the look in his eyes had told her Melissa had spoken the truth. And the truth felt like a hundred bee stings.

Hauling herself out of bed, Carrie threw on one of Dylan's sweaters and grabbed the door keys from the side. Out in the hall, a voice stopped her in her tracks.

"Mummy?"

Melissa sat on her bedroom floor in her usual position. Her typical morning cheer was absent.

"Morning, sweet pea. What's up?"

Melissa put down the doll she'd been playing with and folded her arms. Her eyes glistened. "Are you mad with me and Cal?"

Guilt squeezed Carrie's lungs. It took a few seconds to think of the right words. "I'm not mad. I'm worried."

But this only confused Melissa further. Her forehead wrinkled. Her eyes moved off to the side.

Carrie moved further into the room and crouched down. She stared at her daughter for a long time, then ran a hand through her long hair.

"I want you both to be safe," she said. "If there's a bad man that wants to hurt you, I need to know who he is. I need to tell Detective Turner all about him, so he can stop him from hurting anyone."

Melissa picked up her doll and wrapped its hair around her fingers.

"If you don't want to tell me, maybe you can speak to Daddy when he comes home tomorrow," Carrie said. She slid a finger beneath Melissa's chin and gently guided her face upward. "You can tell us anything, sweet pea. Even if you're scared or worried that someone will hurt you. We'll always make sure you're safe."

Melissa blinked. She let out a long sigh through her nostrils. "I want Daddy to come home now."

Carrie felt a sting in her heart. She forced a smile to her lips and stroked her daughter's cheek. "You know I love you, don't you?"

Melissa avoided her gaze. She nodded then picked up another of her toys.

Leaving her daughter to play, Carrie returned to the landing. It was beginning to feel a lot like her family was falling apart. She walked a few steps to Cal's room and paused outside, wondering if she could take another rejection. But wasn't that part of being a parent? Sometimes you just had to take your children's feelings on the chin.

Knocking softly on the door, she entered Cal's room. She wrinkled her nose. That bad smell was still there, despite her having aired the room yesterday. She would need to have a conversation about personal hygiene.

Carrie turned to the bed. She gasped. Cal was not lying under it in his usual position. He was on his side on the mattress, the bedsheets draped over him, his back to the room. He was asleep.

Carrie watched the gentle rise and fall of his ribcage. The pain she felt in her heart lessened.

"Cal?" she whispered.

He didn't stir. She stood for another minute, watching her son sleep in his bed. It was a simple yet wonderful sight.

But she needed him awake. She needed to ask him again about the bad man. About Noah Pengelly.

Detective Turner would soon be expecting a phone call. She would have to tell him about Melissa's drawing. About the fact that Cal had been speaking to his sister. And once the police had learned he could talk, they would expect him to tell them everything he knew.

And if he refused? What then? It would seem very much like he was hiding something.

Carrie stared at his sleeping form. *Are you hiding something, Cal? Why are you hiding it from me?*

Leaving him alone, she drifted downstairs. She would delay Detective Turner until Dylan returned home. Once he'd convinced Melissa to talk to him, they'd speak to the detective together. Hopefully, Cal would cooperate. If he didn't want to talk, they could use visual aids, or pencil and paper like the intermediary had suggested.

If he still refused then they would have to find another way. Noah Pengelly was still out there somewhere. Whether alive or dead, he deserved to be found. And now, more than ever, Carrie sensed that Cal knew where to find him.

Melissa's drawing felt like proof.

36

NAT STOOD on Grady Spencer's doorstep, listening to the chime of the doorbell fading as she cast an eye over his overgrown garden. The police had cleared out ten minutes ago, taking the journalist's car with them. She'd thought it was their presence making her feel uneasy, but now they were gone she felt no better.

Perhaps, beneath her hangover, she was genuinely worried about Honey. After all, Devil's Cove was a small town. What if the sicko who'd murdered Margaret Telford's dog was still hiding out here somewhere?

She could hear Grady's dog, Caliban, yapping inside the house. She had never liked the animal, despite its cool name. Still, she didn't hate it enough to do what had been done to the other poor mutt.

Nat pressed the doorbell again. Perhaps Honey wasn't the cause of the bad feeling. Perhaps it was because she'd had to call Jago and tell him she couldn't help search the hotel. He hadn't said much but his tone had spoken volumes. He was out there looking for his little brother. Meanwhile, she was here looking for a stupid cat.

Jago was her best friend. Her only friend. But he was more like the brother she'd never had. And her heart wasn't as cold and dead as people thought. She felt Jago's pain as if it were her own. She felt his worry. His loss. She wanted to help him find Noah. She wanted to help him find his brother alive.

The scrape of locks being drawn back distracted her from her thoughts.

The door opened a crack. Grady Spencer stared at her with a suspicious eye. At his ankles, Caliban emitted an irritating growl.

"Good morning Mr Spencer, it's Nat from next door," she said, then wondered why she was introducing herself. Grady Spencer knew exactly who she was. He'd certainly asked enough probing questions about her past. Not that she'd answered any of them.

Grady pulled the door open wider. Over his shoulder, Nat saw the stacks and towers of a hoarder's kingdom. She'd never had reason to enter the old man's house and now, seeing what lay inside, she hoped she never would.

"Ah, young Natalie," Grady said. His lips parted to reveal broken yellow teeth. "To what do I owe the pleasure on this fine Saturday morning?"

His laughter was liquid and rasping. Nat tried very hard to hide her disgust.

"I'm looking for Honey. Rose's cat? She's missing."

Grady arched his eyebrows and wiped his mouth with a papery, lined hand. "Your cat, you say? Well, no, I haven't seen any cat. Saw the police, mind you. Gone now, have they?"

Nat nodded.

"Had one of them knocking on my door asking questions, too. Told him I never heard about no journalist."

Grady watched Nat closely, making her feel uncomfortable. She didn't know much about him. To her, he was simply the old man from next door, who liked to know everyone's business. And he was a little creepy. She suspected that living alone, he was also deeply lonely. But it wasn't her responsibility to keep him company. That's what families were for. Unless your family was made up of uncaring assholes.

"Well, thank you," she said. "If you do happen to see her, could you let Rose know?"

"Worried, is she?"

"She's pretty attached to that cat."

Grady looked over Nat's shoulder, into the street beyond. "Well, she has a right to be worried. Especially after what happened to Margaret Telford's dog. You hear about that?"

Nat nodded.

"Terrible business," Grady said. "Hacked to pieces, it was. And the police aren't doing much about it. Mind you, they've got bigger fish to fry with that Pengelly boy still missing."

A horrible image of Honey flashed in Nat's mind. She pushed it away. "Well, like I said…"

She turned to leave. Grady's hand shot out and grasped her wrist. "Perhaps she's got into my backyard. Take a look if you want."

Nat stared down at the old man's fingers. He released his grip.

She didn't want to go searching around Grady Spencer's yard, thank you very much. But now she couldn't shake the image of Honey's mutilated body from her mind.

She glanced across at Rose's cottage and heaved her shoulders. She would take a quick look. Then she would call Jago and tell him she'd changed her mind.

She turned back to Grady and nodded.

"Just go around the side of the house, there," the old man said, pointing. Nat followed the path with her eyes, watching it disappear around the corner. "There's all sorts of places for her to hide out there. Be careful, mind. That yard could do with a good tidy up. If I was ten years younger, I could do it myself. But not now, not with these old bones."

He stared at Nat with expectant eyes.

Nat smiled politely. There was no way in hell she was going to be spending her day clearing up the old man's junk.

"I'll just take a quick look," she said.

"Take all the time you need."

She felt Grady's eyes on her back as she turned and rounded the corner of the house.

Getting to the backyard was like negotiating an assault course made up of old refrigerators, broken furniture, and trash. When she had weaved her way through, she discovered that the backyard was no better.

"So, this is where old appliances go to die."

Grady Spencer had created his own junkyard, complete with maze-like paths running through it all. There had to be the contents of an entire home here, cast out and left to rust.

Where did she begin? There was no way she was heading into that mess. There were probably rats. Definitely disease. A myriad of accidents waiting to happen. Instead, she stood at the corner of the house with her arms wrapped around her chest and called for Honey.

She waited for an answer. When none came, she called again.

"Here, Honey! Here, cat!" She squeezed her ribcage and took a step forward. That was as far as she was going. She called once more and was answered by silence. "Damn stupid animal."

Honey was a fussy creature. There was no way she'd be hiding in that infested scrapheap. Wrinkling her nose, Nat turned and faced the back of the house. The paint on the window frames was cracked and peeling. She could see curtains through the dirty glass, all yellowed and stained, as if they'd never been washed. There was an iron grille in the ground. Through it, she could just make out a small basement window.

That bad feeling returned to her. It was like butterfly wings flapping in the pit of her stomach. Moving quickly, she returned to the front of the house, where Grady Spencer still stood in the doorway, with Caliban now resting beside his feet.

"No luck?" He stared at her with intense eyes.

Nat shook her head. "Thanks, anyway. I'm sure she'll show up."

"You could have a quick look inside," Grady said. "I leave the windows open. Sometimes cats come in."

"I should probably get back…"

"There's all kinds of hiding places in there. And old Caliban here is useless when it comes to chasing moggies out." He stared at her, hopefully.

Again, Nat glanced over his shoulder into the cluttered hall. If the inside of the house was anything like the backyard, it wouldn't be just a quick look. It could take hours.

Something in her gut told her to stay outside, to turn around and return home. But if Honey was in there, if she was trapped somehow, Rose would never forgive her if she found out Nat had turned around and given up.

She glanced over the fence at Rose's cottage. She could hear her calling Honey's name. Guilt lured Nat to Grady's front door. This is your own stupid fault, she told herself.

Five minutes. That was all she was giving Honey. Then the stupid cat was on her own.

Grady was staring at her, his yellow smile splitting his face. He stepped to one side.

"Well come in. Don't be shy."

Looking back at the street behind, Nat felt the flutter in her stomach grow more intense.

She was being ridiculous. Grady Spencer was an old man who couldn't hurt a fly. He was lonely, that was all. Loneliness made people do odd things, like turn their homes into mazes of junk.

A chill ran down the length of Nat's spine. She shook it off as she stepped inside Grady Spencer's house.

It returned the moment she saw him close the door behind them. There was a musty smell in here. Like the windows hadn't been opened in years. But hadn't Grady just told her he kept them open?

Nat stared down the length of the hall, eyeing the piles of junk.

"I'll show you around, shall I?" Grady said.

He shuffled past her, a curious expression on his face.

Reluctantly, she followed behind.

37

THE MERMAID HOTEL watched over the cove like a battle-weary sentinel; its upper levels blackened with soot. What had been a thriving hub for holidaymakers was now an eyesore that was slowly crumbling into the sea.

Jago scrambled over the rusting gates and landed heavily on his feet. The nearest houses were just a hundred metres away, and although a small copse of trees blocked their view of the hotel, he found himself glancing over his shoulder. Satisfied he hadn't been seen, he pushed forward, his boots crushing the weeds that sprouted from cracks in the forecourt.

As he moved, his thoughts turned to Scott Triggs. Something wasn't right. People didn't just leave their cars behind and disappear into the ether.

Not when they were about to land a front-page story.

The journalist's disappearance and the murder of Margaret Telford's dog had to be connected. But how?

The hotel loomed over him. Staring at its boarded-up windows, he skirted the once grand entrance steps and turned the corner.

The rear garden had been an elegantly landscaped space filled with swathes of hardy shrubs; one of the few plant types capable of surviving the salty air and coastal winds. Now abandoned, the garden was a strangled mass of grass and weeds, fenced off by eroded iron railings.

With his back to the hotel, Jago stopped to take in the view. Beyond the garden, was an endless expanse of charcoal sky and green ocean. Gulls flapped overhead. A ship sailed in the distance, a speck on the horizon.

As much as he hated living in Devil's Cove, he could never complain about the view.

He turned back to the hotel, taking in its charred upper floors before lowering his gaze to the ground floor and locating the kitchen window.

The wooden board came away easily. The glass had been knocked out a long time ago, providing easy access for bored youths looking for a secret hideout away from their banal lives. As far as he knew, few kids came up here now; as fun as it was to get wasted or laid, falling to their deaths in a collapsing building was not as appealing.

Leaning the board against the wall, Jago hoisted himself up and swung his legs through in one fluid movement.

Planting his feet on the floor, he dusted himself off and looked around. The hotel kitchen had once been filled with industrial sized cookers and refrigerators, and a horde of kitchen staff racing to prepare fine cuisine. Now, its contents were gone, the empty space filled with dust and dirt, littered with empty beer cans and bottles.

With just one window of light, the room was cast in long shadows. Someone had been here recently, after all. Sets of footprints were stamped in the dust, and led away from the window.

Jago walked from one end of the room to the other, inspecting the graffiti tags on the walls and wrinkling his nose at a long ago used condom hanging from a nail.

Someone had removed the inner door that led to the restaurant. He was greeted by more darkness as he walked through.

Pulling his mobile phone from his pocket, he selected 'flashlight mode'. A white beam shot out, illuminating the space around him.

The emptiness of the restaurant felt vast. A few tables remained, covered in thick dust. Black mould sprouted from a stack of chairs in the corner.

A memory sprang to Jago's mind. He had visited the Mermaid Hotel in its former glory only once, shortly before the fire. He had been twelve years old. His mother had just discovered she was pregnant with Noah. His father, who had finally quit the booze months before, had insisted on taking his family for a celebratory dinner.

His mother had dressed in a glamorous blue gown, and she had joked that soon she would be as glamorous as a potato sack. Both he and his father had put on shirts and ties.

He remembered his parents both ordering lobster and laughing as they struggled to get to the meat. He remembered looking around the grand room, admiring the sparkling crystals of the ornate chandeliers, and the glow of candlelight, and how all the smartly attired serving staff had smiled and treated them like royalty.

A week later, his father was dead.

Caught up in bad storms, a fishing trawler had sent out a Mayday call. By the time Jago's father and the rest of the lifeboat crew had reached the trawler, the storm had grown with terrifying intensity. No one had come home that night. Not the fishermen. Not the crew trying to rescue them. It had been the biggest tragedy to hit the cove since the loss of Cal Anderson.

Holding his phone out ahead of him, Jago moved swiftly through the restaurant. Several pairs of footprints led to a set of double doors. Pulling them open, he found himself within a short, dusty corridor.

He walked on. His heart rate was up. His breaths were quick and shallow. He would never admit it aloud, but the darkness of the hotel scared him. A few seconds later, he stood at the centre of the hotel's reception area, turning a full circle as he cut through the shadows with the phone light. Dust layered the front desk. Behind it, an empty key rack lay on its side.

On his left, another set of double doors, the glass long ago smashed, had once served as the hotel's main entrance. Cracks of light sneaked around the edge of the boards. On his right, lift doors were sealed behind padlocked iron grilles. A once grand staircase, its carpet now rotting, climbed upward.

Jago tested the bottom step with his foot. Only the ground floor windows had been sealed, which meant there was light up there. That would make his search easier. It would make him less afraid.

Satisfied the steps would hold, Jago began to climb. He wondered, as he always did, if today was the day he would find Noah.

As he reached the landing of the next floor, the voice that had been taunting him since his brother's disappearance whispered in his ear. *You don't really expect to find him alive, do you? Give up, you idiot! You're searching for a corpse.*

He continued to climb the steps, making his way to the upper floors. Noah was alive. He might not be here at the hotel, but there could be evidence that pointed to his whereabouts. A clue to who had taken him. And someone *had* taken him. He'd been sure of it before, but ever since showing Cal his brother's picture, Jago was utterly convinced.

Someone had taken his brother and Cal knew who. Because the same person had taken *him*.

Noah's dead, the voice whispered. *You really think he was taken to be kept as a pet? They took him and did terrible things to him. They killed him and laughed while they did it.*

Jago reached the landing of the fourth floor. A long corridor stretched out before him. At the far end, light spilled in through the window, illuminating dusty carpet. There were no footprints up here.

The fire had begun on the top floor, caused by an electrical fault in one of the guest rooms. Its occupants had burned to death while they'd slept. Fortunately, the holiday season had only just begun and the hotel had been almost empty. There were no other casualties. But the top floor had been decimated, the floor beneath it severely damaged.

Except for the scorched ceiling where the paintwork had bubbled, the floor where Jago now stood had had a lucky escape.

The hotel owner, an outsider from out of the county, had failed to renew his insurance. He'd lost the Mermaid Hotel and all its contents. The bank had repeatedly tried to sell the hotel grounds but no one wanted to buy a burned-out building on a cliff's edge, overlooking a place that spent half the year as a ghost town.

Walking the length of the corridor, Jago turned a hundred and eighty degrees. He began his search.

The first door was unlocked. The room inside looked much like the rest of the hotel. Furniture had been removed or destroyed. Dust lay in thick drifts. Trails of rodent paw prints disappeared into holes in the walls.

He made quick work of checking the room. The bathroom was dark and shadowy. Out of curiosity, he tried the tap. Nothing came out.

Returning to the main bedroom, he stared out the window. The beach was far below, the town to his right. Was Noah down there, hidden away in someone's home? Or had he been taken away from the cove? If that were true, finding him would be almost impossible. But Cal had been found on the beach. Right down there.

Would Noah resurface, too? Would Jago need to wait seven years for it to happen?

He's dead. You should have been there taking care of him, not out getting wasted.

The next room was locked. Instinctively, he knocked on the door. "Noah?"

Silence smothered him. He pressed against the wood. It felt weak and rotten. He rammed his shoulder into it. The lock flew away and clattered on the floor. The door hit the wall and bounced back.

The room was empty. Jago moved on to the next, then the next, finding only dust and disappointment. Once he was done, he headed to the floor below.

Frustration started to set in. If Nat had been here, they'd be able to cover the hotel in half the time. He felt a twinge of guilt. He still couldn't understand how a cat's whereabouts were more important than his brother's, but he understood Nat's loyalty to Rose. The woman had given her a home. She had loved her when her parents hadn't given a shit.

This floor was identical to the one upstairs. Except there were footprints, recently made, moving up and down the corridor.

Jago tried the first few rooms, coming across signs that people had been here—empty beer cans, cigarette butts, a hypodermic needle, abandoned underwear—but all were covered in months of dust.

His eyes returned to the footprints in the corridor. Whoever had made them had travelled the same route several times. Jago followed them, coming to the last door on the left.

Blood rushing in his ears, he pushed it open.

Like the others, the room was void of furniture. But unlike the others, much of the dust had been disturbed. And there were more footprints.

Jago placed his foot next to one. It was slightly smaller than his, but not small enough to belong to a child.

He moved further into the room. Then froze.

In the corner, lined up in rows on top of an old stool, was a battalion of small, plastic figures. Soldiers, animals, monsters, and spacemen. An old Marvel comic book lay on the floor—Spider-man Vs. Venom.

There was something else, next to it. Something white and long.

Jago drew closer and crouched down. At first, he wasn't sure what he was looking at. Then, as he reached out a hand to pluck it up, he saw the blood and recoiled in horror.

It was the severed tail of an animal. Jago was almost certain it belonged to a cat.

38

As HE SHOWED Nat into his living room, Grady Spencer felt the thud inside his chest increase to an almost audible level. Beads of perspiration formed at his temples and he wiped them away. He did not want to alert the girl to his intentions. Not yet. She already looked wary, her large green eyes looking about his home as if she'd walked into an abattoir. The irony was that she had.

"Go ahead," he told her, pushing open the living room door and standing to one side. "Take a look."

He watched as Nat took a cautious step inside. He knew the place was a mess. With piles of papers and boxes of junk, he rarely went in there now. But they were all his things and he couldn't let go of them. They made up his home. His kingdom.

As the girl took a cautious step inside the room, Grady's hands twitched. How he longed to reach out and touch her skin. For his fingers to wrap around her scrawny neck and squeeze.

For now, he stood, exaggerating his wheezing breath; the facade of a weak, diminishing old man, masking the surprising strength he still had.

Nat looked around the room, her face strange and pale. She was disgusted, he could tell.

His home frightened her. That pleased him.

"I don't think Honey's in here," Nat said. She looked to him for a second, meeting his gaze, and he saw that her pupils had dilated.

Grady's heartbeat sped up a little. "No matter. There are plenty of other nooks and crannies to explore."

He turned and headed further down the hall. He paused, looking over his shoulder to see if she was following.

Nat stepped back into the hall. But she didn't follow. Instead, she turned to face the front door.

"This way." Grady moved down to the next door, with Caliban trotting alongside. "I'm afraid this room is a little more cluttered than the last. But you'll forgive an old man's lonely attachments."

She was hesitating. She was going to leave. Grady clenched a frustrated fist. But then Nat moved towards him and, avoiding his hungry stare, slipped into the dining room.

"What is all this stuff?" she asked, her eyes widening at the maze of junk that was piled up to the ceiling.

Grady shrugged. "Bits and pieces."

He needed to think fast. The cat was not here. The house was locked up like a fortress. The only way a living creature could enter was if Grady had lured it in himself.

"At school, are you?" he asked, adopting a conversational tone. Perhaps that was the way. Distract her. Make her feel relaxed.

Nat ventured further into the room, staring up at the towers of junk with a look of morbid curiosity. She thought he was a freak. Grady smiled to himself.

"College," Nat replied. "It's my final year. Then I'm out of this place."

The old man raised an eyebrow. "Big plans, eh? And where are you going, young lady? Off to London, are you?"

"Maybe. Maybe not. I might travel for a bit."

"I thought you young women were all about going to university these days. Educating yourselves so you can be better than us men."

"Not better. Equal," Nat said, picking up an old newspaper from a large pile. She eyed it curiously. "And I can't afford university. No parents means no help. No one gets through university these days without it."

"No family, eh?"

"None worth talking about." Nat glanced at him for a second. She took another step into the room, carefully inching her way around the towers of junk, mesmerised by the old man's collection of strange treasures.

"And what about young master Pengelly," Grady said, shuffling forward. He'd managed to calm his heartbeat a little. Which was good because he was becoming breathless, his mind unfocused. "What's his plan for the future?"

"How should I know?"

"I see the two of you together. Thought you were a pair."

The girl stared at him again, this time her eyes narrowing with disapproval. "People need to stop thinking that."

Laughter, cracked and rasping, escaped Grady's lips. "Young love, eh? Best to let go of it, if you ask me. That boy won't be going anywhere. He's stuck in this place, just like his mother."

Deep creases appeared across Nat's brow. She had suddenly lost interest in the room's contents and was looking at the open door.

"I suppose they're no closer to finding that boy, are they?" Grady stepped to the right, blocking the exit.

"No, they're not. Which is why me and Jago are looking for him."

Grady arched his eyebrows. This was a new development.

"Playing detectives, are we? Think you can do a better job than the police?"

Nat was silent, but he saw a flash of irritation in her eyes. He asked her the question he'd been wanting to ask since she'd showed up on his doorstep.

"What about that other lad? Carrie Killigrew's boy. Met him, have you?"

Her eyes were fixed on the space beyond his shoulder. She shook her head. "Jago's been to see him. They used to be friends."

"Has he, now? Said anything, did he? About where he's been hiding all this time?"

"Jago said Cal couldn't speak. Some sort of mutism caused by PTSD."

"Really? Now isn't that a strange kettle of fish! So, no one knows what happened to him?"

"Looks that way."

She was looking over his shoulder again, her eyes round and anxious. Grady stepped aside and saw anxiety turn to relief.

His mind raced as he tried to think of ways to make her stay. Perhaps he should offer her something to drink. He could drug her like he'd intended to drug that journalist prick before he'd had to bash in his head. He didn't want to hurt this girl like that. Not yet.

"You want some tea?" he offered as they re-entered the hall. "Don't have any coffee. Hate the stuff."

Nat took a step towards the front door. "I should probably go. I really don't think Honey is here."

"But we haven't checked upstairs yet."

"Honey doesn't do stairs. Even at home."

He was going to lose her. If he couldn't drug her, he would have to subdue her another way. And the only other way he knew was violence. It had worked with the journalist, but he had surprised him. He could already tell that this girl had a sharp mind and trusted nobody. Which instantly made her a tricky target. But all the more intriguing for it.

He wanted her. If he let her go now, he would not get a second chance. But if he used violence there was the risk she would fight him. And there was enough pain and anger in her eyes to know that she would not hold back. Which meant there was a chance she might get away. And then it would all be over.

Grady cursed his old bones. He was stronger than most his age, yes. But he was a shadow of the man he used to be. He needed to be clever with his violence. He needed to rely on surprise.

"You know," he said, shifting his weight and smiling down at Caliban, "there's a chance your moggy could have got into the basement. I leave the window open down there to keep it aired. The damp's no good for my old bones, you see. Cats often sneak in that way."

He watched the girl like a fisherman watching his line, waiting for the fish to take the bait. Nat's expression remained adamant: she was leaving.

"Might be worth checking," he continued. "Only it's not particularly safe. Lots of things lying around a cat might get trapped in. Or worse…"

A flicker of something that looked like guilt passed over the girl's face. Her gaze travelled beyond him, along the hall. Nat let out a heavy sigh. She nodded. Grady almost squealed with delight. "This way. The door's right here."

Beckoning her with a hand, he shuffled further along the hall, towards a locked door on the left. Turning the key, he pulled it open.

Darkness stared back at them.

Grady reached in and flipped the light switch. A dull, orange glow illuminated the shadows, revealing stone steps leading down to a second door, which was painted a deep red.

Nat shuffled forward. Resting a hand on the door jamb, she leaned over and peered down into the basement.

Grady watched as she wrinkled her nose. He often forgot about the bad smells that floated up from there. He'd grown quite used to them over the years.

He stepped back, watching Nat hover in the centre of the doorway, one hand clutching the jamb, one hand pressed against the door. She was changing her mind.

"Maybe give her a call," Grady said.

He glanced down to his right, where an amber glass paper-weight rested on a pile of old books. He picked it up, feeling its heftiness in his hand. Used correctly at the right angle, with enough force, it could smash a skull in.

Or it could simply knock a person unconscious.

Doing it while she stood at the top of the basement stairs presented a risk. If he couldn't catch her in time, she would go tumbling down, spilling her precious brain. And he wanted her perfect. He wanted her intact. To begin with.

He waited as Nat called the cat. She sounded embarrassed, he thought. Or perhaps it was fear he could hear.

"I don't think she's down there," she said.

Grady moved up behind her. The paperweight felt good in his hand. "Maybe she can't hear you. Maybe you need to get closer."

He was near enough to smell the scent of her skin mingled with cigarettes and coffee.

His heart throbbed uncontrollably as he tightened his grip on the paperweight. Ready to strike.

Sensing his closeness, Nat turned her head.

From somewhere in her jacket, a phone began to ring.

"Excuse me," she said, her voice small and breathless as she ducked around him and pressed the phone to her ear.

It was too late. The excitement that had taken control of him burst like a bubble. If he were to strike now there would be a fight. One that he would most likely lose. Despairing, Grady dumped the paperweight back on top of the books. He glanced miserably down at Caliban, who let out a pitying whine.

"What was that? The line's bad," the girl was saying. "Are you at the hotel? Jago? Hello?"

All he wanted now was for the whore to leave his house and never return. She'd dirtied his rooms with her stink. He felt violated.

Hanging up, she slipped the phone into her pocket and shot Grady a nervous stare.

"I have to go," she said.

Grady had already lost interest. The girl was just meat again. Indistinguishable from the rest of the carcasses in the cove.

A black, cavernous hole opened inside him. Unable to hide his disappointment, he grunted.

"Thanks for letting me look," Nat said.

He made no move to let her out. Instead, he stood and watched her hurry down the hall and slip through the front door. Beside his feet, Caliban let out another soft whine and nudged his foot.

Grady smiled down at the dog.

"Come on, boy. Let's see what Daddy can find you to eat."

Returning to the basement door, he reached for the stair rail and began to descend the steps.

Caliban followed behind, his tail wagging with excitement.

39

NAT FOUND Jago sitting on the seafront railings and smoking furiously. Rose had not been happy about her heading out to meet him, but she hadn't tried to stop her.

"Just be careful," she'd said. "And keep an eye out for Honey."

Nat had neglected to tell Rose about her unsettling experience inside Grady Spencer's house. What was there to tell? A bad feeling was not evidence of anything. But he'd been right behind her. She'd felt his breath on the back of her neck. And the old bastard had lied about the windows always being open. They had all been shut.

Perhaps loneliness had turned him into a horny old perv. Or perhaps there was something else there. Something darker. Either way, for now, she kept her thoughts about Grady Spencer to herself.

Upon seeing Nat, Jago slipped down from the railings and began to walk. She caught up with him, grabbing his arm.

"What is it? What did you find?"

He stared at her, flashing one of his perplexing looks that drove her insane—a pained expression somewhere between *leave me alone* and *please make it all go away.*

She snatched his cigarette and used it to light her own.

"You're the one who called me," she said when he still didn't reply. "Stop being such a freak."

"I found a tail," Jago said, his complexion growing paler. "A severed tail."

Nat choked on cigarette smoke. "What kind of animal?"

Jago turned away. She punched his arm.

"I—I don't know," he mumbled.

Fuck.

"It was in one of the upstairs rooms, along with some toys," Jago said.

"It's probably someone from town. You said people used to hang out up there for kicks."

"People our age don't play with toy soldiers. And I don't think the kids in town cut up animals for fun."

A breeze blew in from the ocean as they continued to walk along the promenade. On the beach, a handful of people walked their dogs. Nat looked over her shoulder, up at the Mermaid Hotel. Was it Honey's tail Jago had found? Had she suffered the same fate as Margaret Telford's dog?

"You should go to the police," she said. "Tell them what you saw. It could be a lead."

"Maybe."

"What do you mean, maybe? This is important, Jago. Even if it's nothing to do with Noah, some psycho's going around mutilating animals."

"Two animals."

"That we know of." Nat said. "Most serial killers start with the torture and mutilation of animals. It's like training. They begin with something small and easy—birds, rats. Then, when they're feeling more confident, they move on to larger animals. And when they get bored of animals, that's when they start on people."

Jago stared at her with wild eyes.

"It's true. I've read a lot of books about serial killers," she said.

"Career goal?"

"Just trying to understand why people hurt other people." Nat flicked the ash from her cigarette and watched it sail away onto the sand below. "I mean it, Jago. You need to go to the police."

"Or what? You will?"

They walked on in silence. Above them, clouds churned and darkened. Rain was on the way.

"It's Cal," Jago said at last.

Nat shook her head. "Why would he do that to Margaret's dog after she saved his life? It doesn't make sense."

"There's something wrong about him, Nat. Why hasn't he told anyone what happened? If someone abducted him all those years ago, why hasn't he given their name to the police? Why hasn't he told anyone a damn thing?"

"It's called post-traumatic stress. Jesus, give him a break. You have no idea what he's been through."

Jago ground to a halt. "He recognised Noah's picture. It means they were together." He let his cigarette slip from his fingers and crushed it beneath his boot. "I need to see him again. He needs to tell me where my brother is. And if he won't, I'll beat it out of him."

"What you need to do is talk to the police," Nat said. She didn't like the way Jago was looking at her, or the words that were coming out of his mouth. "It's their job to find out what Cal knows."

"You mean like how it was their job to find my little brother?"

Anger flashed in Jago's eyes.

"Maybe this can help them," Nat said, looking away. "They don't have any leads. You know that. We've been searching for weeks. We haven't found a single thing. Until now. Please, Jago. Think of Noah. We're not going to find him by ourselves."

Jago clenched his jaw. The vein at the centre of his forehead began to pulse.

"Get over yourself," she said. "It's the right thing to do."

Slowly, Jago took a step back.

"You're right," he said. "*We're* not going to find Noah. I am."

He turned to leave. Nat moved quickly, blocking his path.

"Do you think Carrie's going to stand by and let you beat up her son? You're going to get yourself arrested. Then the police won't listen to anything you have to say."

"You need to move."

He was glaring at her, his eyes burning with anger in a way she'd never seen. But she stood her ground.

"This isn't you, Jago. You don't hurt people."

"Maybe it's time to start."

He stepped to the side. Nat jumped in front of him. Colour rushed to Jago's face. He leaned in, clamping his teeth together.

"What do you care anyway?" he hissed. "It's not like you give a shit about anyone."

The words were like a punch to Nat's gut. She winced. "I'm standing in your way because I *do* give a shit."

"The only thing you give a shit about is making yourself the most ostracised person in town because God forbid what might happen if you actually let someone care about you. Maybe that dead heart of yours might actually start beating."

He glared at her, his complexion flushing to a deep scarlet. But he wasn't just angry now, she could see. He was embarrassed. He turned away, planting his gaze firmly on the hotel.

"Come with me, don't come with me. I don't care anymore."

This time, when Jago stepped to the side, Nat remained still. She watched him stalk across Cove Road, heading back into town. Tears brimmed in her eyes. Invisible hands pressed down on her chest. But she did not call out for him. She did not beg him to come back. Turning on her heels, she stared across the beach at the dark sea. She felt completely alone. More than that, she felt afraid.

Something terrible was happening in this town. She could sense it like a darkness, seeping up from the pavement and into her feet, working its way through her veins.

"Screw you, Jago," she said.

Giving the hotel one last glance, she headed back home.

40

AN OMINOUS MOOD stalked the Killigrew household, moving from room to room. In the kitchen, Carrie stood in front of the work top, pushing her fists into a large ball of dough. She had been overjoyed to see Cal asleep in his bed, but now she was consumed by misery. Cal could speak. But he didn't want to speak to her.

At the kitchen table, Melissa sat alone, kneading her own piece of dough. She had wanted to play with Cal but Carrie had insisted she helped with the bread. She couldn't allow her children to be alone together, not until she knew what had been said between them. Melissa had responded by sitting in self-imposed silence while shooting angry glares across the kitchen.

In the living room, Cal sat on the couch and watched television. He flicked from channel to channel, watching but not really watching. Occasionally, he glanced at the open door and a deep crease burrowed into his brow.

The dough was ready. Carrie dumped it in a mixing bowl and covered it with a towel. "Are you done?" she asked Melissa, who wordlessly held out her piece of dough. Carrie placed it inside a smaller bowl and covered it with another towel. "We need to put this somewhere warm so it can rise."

Melissa shrugged her shoulders.

"You're not talking to me, either?" Carrie watched her daughter turn away. "Fine. Suit yourself."

Opening the pantry, she placed both bowls of dough inside, then began clearing up the floury kitchen worktop.

The sound of the doorbell chimed through the hall. Melissa looked up.

Pulling off her apron, Carrie draped it over a chair.

"Wait here," she said

Melissa stuck out her lower lip.

As she made her way to the front door, Carrie glanced into the living room. Cal was standing up, his eyes fixed on the living room window.

The bell rang again. Someone started hammering on the door.

Frowning, Carrie peered through the peephole.

"Jago . . ."

The last time she'd seen him angry was when he'd lost at a game of musical chairs on his tenth birthday. But the anger she saw on his face now was much darker and deeper.

She opened the door a few inches. "What is it? What happened?"

Jago glared at her as if she were the cause of all his fury. Then he looked over her shoulder and his eyes lit up like lightning strikes.

"I need to see Cal," he said.

Carrie turned around. Cal was standing in the hall, watching Jago. "Why?"

"I need to talk to him." He moved forward.

Carrie blocked his way. "I think you better talk to me first. What's going on?"

Jago pressed his lips together. He was staring at Cal now with an intensity that scared her.

"If you can't talk to me, Jago, you'd better turn around and go because whatever's on your mind, I don't like the way you're looking at my son."

Jago's angry gaze met hers. For a second, she thought he was going to barge past.

"I found something," he said, at last. "Up at the hotel."

"What were you doing up there?"

"Looking for Noah."

Carrie glanced back at Cal, who hadn't moved an inch. "What did you find?"

"You don't want to know." The fury in his eyes wavered and was replaced with horror. He lowered his head. "Please, Carrie. I'm not here to cause trouble. I just need to ask some questions."

For a long moment, they stood facing each other as Carrie tried to read his thoughts. Some of the anger had left him. Whatever he'd seen up at the hotel had left a mark. And as wary as Carrie was about letting Jago into her home in such a volatile mood, she found herself desperate to know what had happened. She looked over her shoulder at Cal, who stared right back.

She opened the door wider. "No trouble. I mean it."

Jago held up his hands.

Standing aside to let him in, she closed the door then pointed to the living room. Jago headed for it, eyeing Cal as he passed by.

"Give me a minute," Carrie said, touching Cal's arm. Melissa appeared from the kitchen and Carrie held up a hand. "Stay there."

She followed Jago into the living room, where she found him pacing up and down in front of the television.

"Now, do you want to tell me what the hell's going on?" Carrie said, crossing her arms over her chest.

Sucking in a breath, Jago told her what he'd found. The toys. The comic book. The bloody, severed tail that he thought belonged to Rose's cat, Honey.

Carrie listened with mounting horror. Every few seconds or so, she checked the doorway. She could see Cal's shadow on the floor. He was listening to every word.

"I think whoever killed Margaret's dog has been hiding out at the hotel," Jago said.

"What does that have to do with Cal?" Carrie was disturbed by what he'd told her. She glanced back at the door. "Because if you're thinking he has something to do with this, you're wrong. He's barely left the house since he came home. And any time he's been outside, he's been with me."

Jago looked disappointed.

Was that why he was here? Because he believed Cal had killed Margaret's dog? Was that what the people of Porth an Jowl were thinking, too? The very thought of it made Carrie feel sick to her stomach. But the toy figures Jago had found—she couldn't get them out of her head.

"How could you even believe that?" she whispered. "You're supposed to be Cal's friend."

Jago stared at the floor. "That was a long time ago."

"Then why are you here, Jago?"

He looked up, his eyes two black pools. "I want to know where my little brother is. I want to know if he's still alive."

His shoulders drooped. For a second, those black pools became glistening and watery.

Carrie felt pain emanating from him like radiation. It was nauseating.

Jago's expression hardened once more.

"I showed him Noah's picture," he said, defiantly. "The last time I was here. When you were in the kitchen."

Carrie's pity turned to anger. She'd been right to be suspicious, after all. "You promised me, Jago. You told me you weren't going to do that."

"I had no choice. Cal recognised him. He recognised Noah."

Confusion swept over Carrie. She was furious with Jago for breaking her trust and upsetting Cal, but she was also angry at herself. All she'd wanted was for Cal to forget everything that had happened and resume a normal life. For them to be a family again.

Deep down, she'd known that Cal could lead them to Noah. She'd felt it as if she knew where to find him herself. But it hadn't stopped her from wishing him to forget. It hadn't stopped her from wishing for her family's happiness over Noah's life.

"Cal," she said, her voice shaking.

He appeared in the doorway with hunched shoulders and his fingers pressed into his thighs.

"Do you know something? Do you know where we can find Noah?"

For a moment, she thought he was going to run upstairs. But to her surprise, he stepped into the room.

"I know it's hard for you," Carrie said. "I know it's scary, but can you answer one question? Just one question, that's all."

She glanced at Jago, who slipped off his backpack and pulled out a roll of posters. He held one up. Noah's smiling face stared out.

"Was my brother with you?" he said, no longer able to mask the desperation in his voice.

Cal stared at the poster. His jaw clenched.

"Please, Cal," Carrie said. "Try to think. He's four years old. He vanished two months ago."

"Jesus Christ, why can't you just tell us?" Jago suddenly snapped. He thrust the poster forward. "Is my brother dead?"

Carrie shot him a look, silencing him. She took another step closer to her son. "We just want to know where we can find him. So he can be free like you."

Cal stepped back. His eyes were fixed on Jago, like a mouse watching a snake.

"Please, Cal," Carrie could feel Jago's anger seeping into her. Infecting her. She tried to expel it. "Please, talk to me."

Before she could register what was happening, Jago threw his bag down and launched himself across the room. Carrie watched open-mouthed as he grabbed Cal by the front of his T-shirt and pushed him into the hall and up against the stair rail.

"Enough of this shit," he snarled, his face inches from Cal's. "Tell me where my brother is or so help me God…"

"Jago, stop!"

Carrie flew at them.

Jago raised a fist and aimed it at Cal's face.

"Where is my brother?" he roared.

Everything seemed to slow down. Jago drew back his fist, ready to strike. Carrie ploughed forward, making a grab for his arm.

Cal's lips curled back over his teeth in a vicious sneer. Then he lunged at Jago's neck.

Teeth sank into flesh. There was a terrible scream.

Carrie was flung to the side as Jago crashed onto his back. Cal was on top of him, his jaws clamped to his neck. Jago thrashed his arms and legs. He screamed in agony. He brought his fists up and pummelled Cal in the ribs.

"Cal, stop!" Carrie shrieked.

But he would not stop. He was a wild animal, his eyes rolling in their sockets, oblivious to Jago's blows.

Carrie scrambled to her feet. "Cal, please!"

She brought her hand up and slapped him hard across the back of his head.

Startled, Cal released his grip on Jago's neck and rolled off him. He crouched back on his haunches and glared at Carrie. Blood smeared his lips and jaw. His eyes were wild, primal. Barely human.

Jago kicked his feet against the floor, pushing himself away from Cal.

Swooping down, Carrie helped him to sit up. There were teeth marks on his neck, raw and bloody. They were Cal's teeth marks. Her son's.

Carrie was frozen in a shock-induced paralysis. Her eyes swung from the wound on Jago's neck to her son's bloody mouth and back again, not quite comprehending what she was seeing.

A small shape hovered in the kitchen doorway.

Melissa looked up with wide, terrified eyes. Tears streamed down her face.

Carrie shook herself free.

"Stay in the kitchen, sweet pea! Everything's okay."

But nothing was okay. Even a four-year-old could see that.

Cal had gone into some sort of trance. He remained crouched up against the stairs, blood and saliva dripping from his chin, his eyes distant and glassy.

Melissa was still hovering at the end of the hall, her shoulders shivering with every sob.

"Please, baby. Go in the kitchen. I'll be right there."

A groan made Carrie look down. Jago was pushed up against the wall, blood oozing down his neck.

"Let me help you," she said, one eye on Cal. She was afraid of him. Afraid of her own son. What if he pounced again? What if he went after Melissa?

Jago pulled away from her. Using the wall, he pushed himself to his feet. A bloody hand clamped across his neck, he stumbled past Carrie.

"Jago, please wait!"

He threw open the door, letting in the late afternoon light. He turned to face her, his skin ashen.

"If my brother dies, it will be your fault," he choked. "You've let a monster into your home."

Before Carrie could say another word, Jago fled from the house.

Panic gripped her. The neighbours would see him running down the street, a bloody bite mark tattooed on his neck. They would know where he was running from. And it would be over for Cal—he would never be welcome in the cove.

If she went after Jago, if she persuaded him to come back, she could talk to him. Calm him down. Make sure he didn't tell anyone about what Cal had done.

Behind her, Cal was still on his haunches, blood smeared across his mouth. This was not her son. Her son was good and kind and had so much love to give. The boy in her hallway was a feral beast.

Slowly, Carrie shut the front door. Melissa hadn't moved, although she'd stopped crying.

"Go upstairs," Carrie said to Cal. "Go and wash your face. Then go to your room and stay there."

Cal didn't move. He was still in a trance, like a lion after a kill.

"Now!" Carrie bellowed. She shoved her hands into her pockets, preventing them from lashing out.

Cal blinked as if he'd just woken up. Wiping a hand across his mouth, he stared at his bloody fingers. Confusion rippled across his face. He stood. Without making eye contact, he turned and made his way upstairs.

Carrie heard him close the bathroom door. She heard running water. Then she clamped her hands over her mouth and collapsed against the door.

"Mummy?"

Her heart was beating so hard it hurt. She couldn't think straight. What had been done to her son? The water shut off. A second later, the bathroom door opened. She heard Cal's footsteps, soft and deliberate, on the upstairs landing. His bedroom door closed.

Carrie glanced down and saw splashes of Jago's blood on the floorboards. A bloody handprint smeared the wall.

"Mummy, I don't like Cal anymore."

She looked up. Melissa was tiny and fragile. Carrie imagined a dog snatching up a rag doll in its powerful jaws and shaking it furiously from side to side. She propelled herself through the hall and swept her daughter up in her arms.

"It's going to be all right. You're going for a sleepover at Nana Joy's."

Taking her into the kitchen, she set her down at the table, then grabbed the phone from the wall.

"Is Cal coming, too?"

"No, he's staying right here."

"But what if the bad man gets me?"

Carrie's fingers hovered over the telephone keypad. If there was a time for Melissa to talk it was now. The phone still clutched in her hand, she crouched down beside her daughter and looked up into her frightened eyes.

"Why did you draw Noah in your picture?"

Melissa's lower lip began to tremble.

"Please, sweet pea. Don't you want to see Noah again? Has Cal said anything about him? Anything at all?"

Now, Melissa began to cry. She nodded.

Carrie held onto the table as the room began to spin. She resisted the urge to fly upstairs and shake answers from her son.

"What does Cal say about Noah?" she whispered.

"He goes to see him," Melissa sobbed, rubbing her eye with a fist.

"But that isn't true. Cal has been here all the time. We're always together."

"At night time," her daughter wept. "He goes when we're sleeping."

She couldn't breathe. A deafening rush of blood in her ears buried Melissa's weeping. Carrie stood. The room swayed. She moved away from the table, turning her back to the room.

With trembling fingers, she dialled Joy Killigrew's number.

41

By the time Jago stumbled into his kitchen, the side of his neck was a swollen mass of blood and bruise. Pain shot through his tendons to the top of his skull as he tore open the freezer door and pulled out a tray of ice.

He looked around for a clean towel. Dirty dishes filled the sink. Food crumbs covered the surfaces and the floor. Grabbing a towel from the oven handle, he smashed the tray against the worktop to loosen its contents, then set about fashioning an ice pack. He pressed it to his neck. Fiery pain ripped through him. He winced, sucking in air between his teeth, and waited for the pain to subside.

He was furious. And at the same time filled with despair. Images of Cal flashed in his mind. He was barely human. Beyond saving. The Cal he knew was dead. Did it mean that Noah was dead, too?

A deep, wrenching emptiness tore open his stomach. To never see his brother again would break him. Noah had been the heart and soul of the Pengelly family. He had been hope and happiness, proof that even in the darkest hours, light could prevail.

Now that light was gone. And with it, Jago's final shred of hope.

"What happened to you?"

His mother stood in the doorway, dressed in three-day old clothes. Her hair was lank and greasy. The circles under her eyes were like black holes. It was as if Noah had been the air she breathed and now she was dying.

It made Jago furious. Because he was her son, too. And he was still here. Still alive.

"I'm fine," he said through clenched teeth.

"Let me help you." Tess swayed on her feet. She came closer, bringing with her the stench of booze. She reached out a hand. Jago slid away. They were opposing magnetic forces, unable to touch.

"Jago . . ." his mother began.

"I said I'm fine." He hung his head and stared at the floor. "Just go to bed, Mum."

He turned and went upstairs, anger punctuating every step. He had a good mind to go back to the Killigrews' house. He could take a knife, some sort of weapon. Then Cal would see just how brightly his anger burned.

Entering his bedroom, he slumped down at his desk. The ice pack was beginning to melt. Blood and water trickled beneath his T-shirt. He stared into space for the longest time, his heart thumping, his breaths growing thin and shallow.

"My brother is going to die," he whispered to the room.

It whispered back. *Your brother has been dead for months.*

A tear escaped from Jago's eye. Panicking, he swept it away. He hadn't shed a single tear since Noah had vanished. To do so would be to accept his brother was lost. Until now, he had believed Noah would one day be found.

A second tear spilled down his cheek.

"No," he hissed. "Stop it."

But the tears wouldn't stop. He flipped open his laptop and hit a button. Loud rock music blared from its speakers, drowning out his sobs. In his pocket, his phone began to vibrate. He pulled it out, staring through blurred vision.

Fresh flames of anger ignited. Carrie was calling him.

"Leave me alone," he breathed. He wiped away more tears.

Perhaps Nat was right. Perhaps he should call the police. The evidence he'd found at the hotel might be enough to bring Cal in. Especially if they found fingerprints, DNA, anything that connected him to the mutilated animals. He would be sectioned and carted off to a psychiatric ward, locked up for years.

Jago had lost his brother. Now, he'd make sure Carrie lost her son for good. Because it was *her* fault, wasn't it? If she'd kept her eyes on Cal that day, none of this would be happening. Jago was certain of it. Noah would be downstairs right now, cutting shapes out of Play-Doh. His mother would be sober, the house filled with light. Perhaps even his father would be alive.

It seemed to Jago that Cal's disappearance had left a black cloud hanging over Devil's Cove that rained down a torrent of misfortune.

He should have listened to Nat. Yet again he'd let his temper choose the wrong path. He had the detective's card somewhere. Making the call might not bring Noah back, but it would hurt the Killigrews. And that would satisfy him for now.

Over the music, he heard his mother knock on the locked door. He watched as the handle moved up and down.

Where had he put the detective's card? He sifted through the crap on his desk then scanned the floor. A blue light brought his attention back to the desk. He'd received a text message.

A message from Carrie Killigrew. What did she possibly have to say that could make things better? He stared at the screen, his finger hovering over the delete tab. But a voice, rising from his unconscious, pleaded with him to stop.

He opened the message.

Give me until tomorrow. I know how to find your brother. Please trust me.

"Bullshit," he spat, staring at the words. And yet, he could not bring himself to delete them.

He sat, reading the message over and over, the music so loud it hurt his ears.

I know how to find your brother.

Was it true? Or was it a ploy to stop him from contacting the police? Perhaps it was both.

He leaned back in the chair, his neck throbbing, not knowing what to believe. Hope returned to him. But he was terrified. Because to hope meant to believe, and if he discovered Carrie was lying to him, there was no telling what his rage could make him do.

Suddenly, he didn't trust himself to be alone. And there was just one person whom he felt safe enough to be around.

Turning down the music, Jago dialled Nat's number.

She picked up after seven rings.

"You're a prick," she said. "And an asshole."

"I know, and I'm sorry. But I need you."

The line went quiet, long enough for Jago to wonder if she'd hung up.

"You're a complete loser, too. And you suck."

Jago found himself smiling. "Yes, I do."

"I'm glad we've got that straight. I feel better already. I'll be over in five."

He waited for Nat to hang up, then opened Carrie's text message. He clung onto his hope with white knuckles.

42

QUIET SETTLED like mist over Carrie's house. Gary Killigrew had collected Melissa three hours ago, but not before Carrie had cleaned up the blood. Gary had been concerned, wanting to know why both Carrie and his granddaughter had seemed so distressed. She had promised to have answers for him tomorrow.

As Gary had led Melissa away, she had turned and stared at Carrie with a tear-stained face.

"I love you, sweet pea," Carrie had said.

"Love you, too."

Cal had not come out of his room and had ignored her calls to the dinner table. Instead, Carrie had made a plate of sandwiches and left them outside his door. She'd hovered, tempted to go in there and confront him. But she'd learned by now that confrontation only pushed him further away. And she didn't want to push him away.

She wanted to follow him.

The chiming of the hall clock broke the silence. It was 11 PM. Carrie locked the front door but left the key in the lock. If Cal was leaving, there was only one way he could go. Switching off the lights, she headed upstairs. The plate of sandwiches was still sitting outside Cal's door, the bread turning stale. Guilt tugged at her mind. She shook it off. She was doing this for his own good. So they could all move on.

"I'm going to bed now," she called into the silence. "We'll talk in the morning."

She waited for a response, knowing it would never come.

In her bedroom, she switched on the corner lamp, kicked off her shoes, and climbed onto the bed. Pulling her knees up, she turned to face the door.

As she waited, her thoughts turned to Jago. He hadn't replied to her text message. And yet the police hadn't showed up either. Carrie could only imagine he'd granted her wish. That he had pinned his last shred of hope on her.

She would not let him down. She would find Noah. She'd find him tonight.

And then things would be better. The Pengellys would have their boy back. She would make sure Cal received the help he needed. Whether that would be here at home, or out of the county, she was still undecided. But it was not a decision to make on her own. She knew that now. When Dylan came home tomorrow, they would sit down and have a serious discussion. They would make a choice that was right for everyone.

For now, Carrie focused on her breathing and stared at the bedroom door.

An hour passed. Her eyelids grew heavy. Soon, she was struggling to stay awake. Perhaps he had somehow sensed her plan. Perhaps he had spent his energy attacking Jago and was now asleep. Perhaps he was curled up under the bed, terrified by the things he'd done. Suddenly, Carrie wanted nothing more than to go to him. To climb under the bed with him and pull him into her arms.

No matter what had happened, Cal was still her son. And she loved him.

From the hall, she heard the squeak of a door handle turning.

Her eyes snapped open. She reached for the lamp, switched it off, and slipped beneath the sheets.

Her bedroom door opened.

She could sense him hovering in the doorway. She could hear his breathing, could smell his musty scent.

He stood for a long time, watching her. He was testing her, she realised. Checking to see if she really was asleep. Carrie slowed her breathing, willed her heart to beat silently.

The door closed again. She heard footsteps on the landing, then on the stairs.

Carrie moved quickly, slipping out of bed and into her shoes. She pressed her ear against the door and listened. A second later, she heard the sharp click of a key turning in a lock. The front door creaked open. Silence followed. Carrie held her breath. There was a soft thud as Cal closed the front door behind him.

She wasted no time, clearing the landing and the stairs in seconds. She grabbed the bag she'd left hanging on the stair rail, waited a few seconds more, then pulled open the front door.

The night was dark, the air chilled by the changing season. Carrie tiptoed to the garden gate. She ducked down. Cal stalked through the street like a cat. He moved quickly, weaving in between the cars until he came to the end and headed left on Cove Road, disappearing from view.

Carrie counted to five then took off after him. He was heading uphill, growing smaller by the second. Carrie kept her distance as she followed behind. She watched him cross over to the other side and vanish into shadows. For a moment, she thought she'd lost him. Then he resurfaced near the top, pausing to stare down at the cove.

Carrie ducked behind a car and waited. When she looked up again, Cal was gone.

Strangely, she was not worried. It was as if she could sense him. As if the umbilical cord was still attached, pulling her to him. She had lost him for seven years. She wouldn't lose him again.

She got going, her legs complaining as the hill got steeper. Finally, she reached the top. Catching her breath, she turned and looked over the cove.

The sky glittered with stars. The sea was black and still. A bright beam swept through the dark, emanating from the lighthouse up at Desperation Point. Even when surrounded by horror, there was always beauty to be found.

Carrie shifted her gaze to the left, where the hotel lay in shadows in the distance, looming like a monolith over Devil's Cove.

That was where she would find him. She could sense it. Could feel him pulling on the cord, reeling her in.

Stepping off Cove Road, Carrie hurried past a small row of houses, heading for the tree-lined lane that would take her to the Mermaid Hotel.

43

CARRIE STOOD in front of the Mermaid Hotel, looking up at the chained front doors and wincing in the darkness. Climbing over the gate had been more difficult than she'd anticipated. Perhaps in her twenties she would have vaulted over with the grace of a gymnast. But she had landed badly as she'd jumped down and now her right ankle throbbed.

She'd heard about kids coming up here to smoke weed and make out. There had to be a way inside. Somewhere they wouldn't be seen from the cove.

Hobbling, she turned and headed to the rear of the hotel. The garden was hidden in shadows. Beyond, the ocean and sky were indistinguishable from each other, creating an endless black void that Carrie found terrifying.

Pulling a small pocket torch from her bag, she pointed it at the ground and flicked the switch. A bright beam of light balled up. She directed it at the bottom row of windows. The board had been removed from one of them.

Carrie stared into the rectangle of darkness as cold crept beneath her clothes. She limped forward.

Throwing the bag through first, she clamped the torch between her teeth and hoisted herself up. Once inside, she slung the bag over her shoulder and waved the torch beam around the gutted kitchen.

Sets of dusty footprints led through a set of double doors on the far end. Her pulse racing, Carrie followed them into the once grand restaurant.

Quickening her pace, she cut through the room and found herself in a long corridor. She pointed the torch in both directions. Her heart jumped. The footprints diverged in two directions. Some led towards the front of the building. Others trailed in the opposite direction.

Carrie looked both ways, gripped by terror. She was standing in pitch darkness in an abandoned hotel, not knowing who or what might be lying in wait.

That wasn't entirely true. Her son was here somewhere, hiding in the shadows.

"Cal," she whispered, trying to push away her fear. "Your mother's here. Everything's going to be okay."

But which direction should she take?

She thought back to that afternoon. Jago had told her he'd made his gruesome discovery in one of the upstairs rooms.

She took a step towards the front of the hotel, just as a deep, resonating boom filled her ears.

Carrie spun on her heels, splashing light on the walls. She held her breath and listened. The sound did not come again. Her heart in her throat, she traced the myriad footsteps trailing along the corridor. Did they belong to Cal?

Only one way to find out.

Carrie turned and headed away from the front of the hotel. Now, the only sounds she heard were the shuffling of her feet and her quick, frightened breaths.

The footprints went on, passing several closed doors, until they reached the end of the corridor and stopped in front of a large metal door.

She pointed the torch, illuminating a sign on the wall.

BASEMENT.

"Oh, great," she whispered. She'd seen one too many horror flicks to know nothing good ever came from exploring the basement.

Again, she was aware of the danger she'd put herself in. She should have called Detective Turner hours ago. But it was too late for that now. Cal was down there somewhere. She could sense him again, tugging on the invisible umbilical cord. He was down there, and he was going to lead her to Noah.

With shaking fingers, Carrie reached for the handle and opened the door. It was heavy and she grunted as she pulled it back. That was the noise she'd heard: the basement door slamming shut.

A flight of stone steps was illuminated in the torch beam. She leaned forward and looked down.

Fear stole her breath.

Even if it was just Cal down there, she wasn't about to head into the basement without some sort of protection.

Spinning around, she scanned the floor. A broken chair leg lay in the shadows.

Scooping it up, Carrie turned back to the basement steps. She checked that the door could be opened from the inside. Then she waited for the pounding in her ears to quieten.

"Okay," she whispered.

Chair leg in one hand, torch in the other, she stepped forward. The door swung shut behind her. She leaned back, stopping it from slamming shut, letting the catch rest against the jamb.

Satisfied she had a way out, she turned back to the darkness. The torch beam flickered. She shook the torch and the beam corrected itself.

Slowly, Carrie descended into the basement.

44

AT FIRST, Carrie was too terrified to move. She stood at the foot of the basement steps, trying to see beyond the edges of the torch beam. It would be easy to turn back; to take the steps two at a time and run from the hotel. But she would be leaving Cal behind. Leaving Noah.

She willed her legs to move forward. They did, slowly at first, making her shuffle like one of the zombies from those stupid films Dylan would persuade her to watch with him.

Oh, Dylan. How she longed for him to be by her side right now. The truth, she feared, was that when Dylan returned home tomorrow, they might never watch a stupid film together again.

Carrie crept forward. Smells assaulted her: rotting timber, mould, rust. And something else, sharp and putrid, like spoiled meat.

Wrinkling her nose, Carrie swung the torch beam from side to side. She was in a large room filled with old furniture and broken wine racks. Empty barrels lay on their sides, decaying and covered in mildew. Several open doorways led off into more darkness.

If the basement covered the same floor area as the hotel above,

Carrie was standing at the mouth of a rabbit warren; a labyrinth in which she could easily get lost. Perhaps never find her way out again.

She turned on her heels, noting the position of the stairs, mentally mapping out her path. She swung back around. Which doorway did she take?

She pointed the torch beam into the first on the right, revealing another, smaller room. Water ran down its mossy walls. More wine racks lay inside, broken and rotting.

A quick check of the next doorway revealed a similar picture. Carrie pointed the torch at a doorway in the north wall. A long corridor revealed itself. She stared into the darkness beyond.

Was Cal down there? She strained to hear above the drips and splashes of water.

She advanced, the chair leg gripped tightly in her fist. There were more storage rooms on both sides. Most were empty. A few contained further remnants of the hotel's old furnishings.

As Carrie crept further along the corridor, the air grew thinner and more pungent. The sweet, acrid smell she could not place grew stronger. Her heart pounded. Fear made it hard to breathe.

But she had to keep going. Noah's life depended on it.

New sounds reached her ears. Scrabbling and scratching. Carrie cocked her head. The sounds grew louder.

Something clambered over her feet.

Carrie yelped. She spun around, pointing the torch at the empty ground. Whatever it was had scurried away.

Again, she thought about turning back. Then she heard more sounds coming from up ahead.

She could hear footsteps. Human footsteps.

Pressing the torch to her chest, Carrie plunged herself into darkness. It was Cal. It had to be. But what if it was someone else?

Carrie stood completely still, listening to the footsteps move further away. Then they were gone. Whomever they belonged to had disappeared.

She felt the walls close in on her and the air rush from her lungs. She had to go on. Whether that was Cal up there or someone else, she had no choice but to go on. Pushing one foot in front of the other and keeping the torch pointed to the ground, Carrie forced herself along the corridor.

Something glistened in the light. It was sand, she realised, and wondered how it had found its way into the hotel basement.

The corridor was coming to an end. The terrible stench grew stronger. And now Carrie knew where she had smelled it before.

In Cal's room.

Terrified, she inched ahead. Torch light rebounded off the wall up ahead.

"Cal?" she whispered. "Are you here?"

She walked another metre into the chamber. Then froze.

The torch trembled uncontrollably in her hand, making the light shudder and shake.

"Oh, my God."

The room was filled with piles of old furniture: tables, chairs and sofas all stinking and rotting and covered in black mould. But they were not the cause of Carrie's horror.

It was the things on the table by the wall.

Animal parts—a severed cat leg, a bloody ear of an unidentified creature, the head of a fox missing its eyes—were laid out in a neat, deliberate row. Something else had been placed behind them.

The chair leg dropped from Carrie's hand and clattered to the ground. She stumbled forward, almost tripping.

It was a child's stuffed animal. A blue bear with a missing eye. Carrie recognised it instantly. She had seen it countless times in the last two months, broadcast on television news bulletins and clutched in the arms of a little boy whose beautiful, smiling face peered out from fading posters around town.

The blue bear belonged to Noah. It was caked in old, dried blood. Nausea erupted in Carrie's stomach and shot up to her throat.

"Oh, God. No . . ."

Very carefully, she lifted Noah's blue bear and turned it over. It had been his favourite. A gift from his father, purchased the day Tess had discovered she was pregnant. And now, here it was, in a place no child should ever have to see, soaked in blood.

And there was something else. If Carrie had any reason to doubt Noah was dead, it was quickly extinguished upon seeing what the bear had been perched on. A human skull. A child's skull.

Clutching the bear to her chest, Carrie stumbled back.

Something was happening to her. Reality was slipping away.

Was this where Cal had been coming at night? To see Noah. Down here in the darkness and decay of the basement.

She was going to be sick. She staggered away, the bear still clutched in her hand.

Confusion overwhelmed Carrie. She fell to her knees. She needed to vomit. To expel these horrific thoughts and feelings. But they would not leave her body. They were hers to keep.

How would she tell Jago? Tess? How could she explain to them what she had found? How could she ever look her son in the eye again, knowing where he had been coming each night?

How could she—

Someone was watching her. She could feel their eyes burning into her back. Slowly, Carrie got to her feet. She turned, pointing the torch at a space behind.

Cal stood in the light, his skin as pale as bones. His dark, black eyes glistening and fathomless.

Carrie pressed the bear to her chest.

"Cal?"

Sadness emanated from him in waves, threatening to knock her to the ground.

"Cal, baby?"

He shook his head. Tears spilled down his face. He pointed a finger at the corridor from which Carrie had entered. He was telling her to leave.

"I can't," Carrie said. "I can't leave you down here."

She glanced back at the table. At the terrible things on top of it. Cal lowered his hand. He shook his head. Then he turned and melted into the darkness.

"Cal!"

Carrie swung the torch.

A large wardrobe stood at an angle away from the wall. Behind it was a door-shaped hole. The hole had once been boarded up with planks but they had been smashed apart, jagged edges still poking out at the sides. Cal had disappeared inside.

"Cal!" she screamed again.

He was gone. And she knew that this time, if she didn't go after him, he would be gone forever.

Noah's blue bear in one hand, the torch in the other, Carrie sprang towards the hole in the wall. And as she climbed through, she realised it wasn't a hole.

It was a tunnel, narrow and low-ceilinged.

She could hear Cal running now. Getting away from her.

Carrie took off after him.

45

EVERY ROOM of Grady Spencer's house was drenched in light. As a small child, there had been much to fear in the dark. As a man, he had taken that fear and used it for his own purpose. Now, in his twilight years, it was as if the young child he had once been had awoken inside him, bringing back all his night time terrors. For a while, with the boy here, those terrors had receded to the shadows. With the boy gone, they had slithered back out to taunt him.

Grady sat in his kitchen, a dark, sullen mood weighing him down. Caliban lay next to his feet, snoring gently. He was a good dog. A loyal creature. But he could never understand how it felt to be truly afraid. To be truly alone.

The journalist had taken some of that loneliness away for a few days. But the high Grady had felt from killing him had now come crashing down, washing over him like a great wave, filling his lungs. Soon, he would drown in darkness and loneliness. Unless he found someone new to keep him company.

He had thought the girl from next door, Natalie, might keep him entertained for a while. Perhaps even longer than the journalist. But she had been too wary. Too cynical to be trusting.

There was the other one, he supposed. The one down below. But he had little interest in him. That one belonged to the boy. But if the boy didn't come back . . .

Grady stared at his hands. They had once been powerful enough to snap bones. Now they were the hands of a decrepit old man. But they were still strong enough to throttle the life out of a body.

Standing up, Grady shuffled over to the kettle and filled it with water. He would have to get a new one. This one had been dented by the journalist.

Placing the kettle on the stove, he lit the burner. As he waited for the water to boil, his gaze roamed to the hallway. The sound of emptiness was like a dying breath.

"Come back," he mouthed, feeling the emptiness pierce his skin.

They had offered to take the boy to the farm. Away from Devil's Cove, so Grady would not be implicated in his abduction. The boy could grow and learn the ways of the farm, they'd said. Grady thought the farm and all its teachings were meaningless. He had told them so, too. And he had refused to let them take the boy.

But they had taken him, anyway.

Grady had been left alone for a long time. His life had become wretched and empty once more. Then the boy had come back of his own volition. He had chosen Grady over them.

But months later, the boy had left again. The farm had confused him. He'd no longer wanted to stay in his cage. Not the one upstairs at night, not the one down below.

The kettle began to whistle as the water began to boil. Caliban opened an eye. His ears twitched.

If the boy were here now, Grady would make him tea and bring it to his cage. Maybe he would let him drink it. Maybe he would scald him with it.

A punishment for not following his master's rules.

He could feel the hole opening inside him again, growing

deeper. Threatening to open so wide he would fall in and never get out.

"Come back," he said again.

And then Grady saw a curious thing. He saw the boy standing in the kitchen doorway, looking straight at him.

I've lost my mind, Grady thought. He shut his eyes, counted to three, and opened them again.

The boy was still there.

Across the kitchen, Caliban wagged his tail. Omitting an excited yap, he scampered to the boy, who crouched down to scratch between his ears.

Grady shook his head. The boy looked up at him, his strange dark eyes reflecting the old man's image.

Suddenly, Grady exploded with a high-pitched cackle.

"Well, well, well," he said, when he could catch his breath. "The wanderer returns!"

Cal gave the dog one last scratch and stood up.

Grady watched him, his heart bursting with joy. He had wished for the boy and the boy had returned. It was a miracle, pure and true.

But now he would have to teach the boy a lesson. So that he would never leave again.

46

IT WAS LATE. The house lay in darkness except for Jago's bedroom, where he stood in front of the window, staring down at the street while Nat lay on the bed, a glass of bourbon whiskey in her hand and a cigarette hanging from her lips. Neither of them had spoken for some time now.

Music filled the quiet. It was a band that Nat had recently discovered from the early nineties; Mazzy Star. They were a far cry from the angry punk music she usually listened to, but she liked the mystery and reverb of the slide guitar, and the singer's strange, ethereal voice. Somehow, it encapsulated what she thought midnight might sound like.

Nat turned and stared at Jago. She was relieved that their fight had been brief. Even though his words had been cruel, hurting her much deeper than she'd first anticipated, she was willing to forgive him. She knew what desperation felt like, how it could make you react in unpleasant ways. But she'd also made sure he knew that she was no pushover. Not anymore.

"Penny for them," she said, as Jago continued to stare out at the darkness.

He shook his head. "I should have called her back. I should have gone over there."

"I don't think Carrie would appreciate you showing up on her doorstep right now."

"But what did she mean? 'I know how to find your brother.'"

"Maybe Cal finally started talking. Maybe what he did to you woke him up."

"Then why didn't Carrie come get me? If she knows where to find Noah, I should be there when she does."

He turned. Nat grimaced at the sight of his swollen neck. She had cleaned the wound as best she could, soaking it with disinfectant that had brought tears to Jago's eyes. She'd urged him to see a doctor but he'd refused. She could see he was in pain. His movements were slow and stiff, his complexion pale. She had prescribed painkillers. He, alcohol. She wasn't sure it was the best combination.

Nat took a drag on her cigarette and blew a stream of smoke up to the ceiling.

"You know how volatile Cal is," she said. "I mean, Jesus, look what he's done to you. Maybe it's safer for everyone if you let Carrie do whatever it is she has to do. She wouldn't lie to you about your brother, Jago. I don't know her well, but well enough to know she's not a bad person. She wouldn't hurt your feelings just to protect herself."

"Maybe. But I can't just stay here doing nothing."

"That's exactly what you need to do. You have a hole in your neck. You should rest. And you should let me put a dressing on that. You don't want to get an infection." She looked away. "Besides, it's making me want to puke."

A smile rippled across Jago's lips. For the first time in two months, Nat saw his eyes glimmer with hope.

"Do as Carrie's asked you," she said. "Give her until tomorrow."

Jago's face grew serious again as he returned his gaze to the window. "What if tomorrow's too late?"

Finished with her cigarette, Nat dropped the stub inside an empty beer can. "It's so cool your mum lets you smoke indoors."

"She doesn't."

They were quiet for a long time, listening to the music. It had been a strange few days. Honey was still missing. Nat hadn't been able to bring herself to tell Rose what Jago had found up at the hotel. Far better to let her believe the cat had simply wandered off.

When Nat had wound up in Devil's Cove last year, she thought she'd been sent to live in the most boring place on earth. Noah's disappearance had changed all that. The last two weeks had made it even worse. Now, she craved the old Devil's Cove, where nothing ever happened and every day was the same.

Perhaps tomorrow she would get her wish.

Letting out a heavy sigh, Nat sat up. Her thoughts wandered back to Grady Spencer's house.

She could still smell the dust and despair on her clothes. And if she were being honest, she could still feel the fear that had gripped her at the top of Grady's basement stairs.

She hadn't told Jago about her visit to the old man's house. She hadn't had a chance at the seafront. But those uneasy feelings had followed her home and now they taunted her.

"What do you think about Grady Spencer?"

"I don't think much about Grady Spencer at all," Jago said, turning around. "How come?"

Nat told him about her encounter. As she spoke, she watched Jago's expression change from disinterest to deep concern. "Don't you think it's weird?" She reached over and grabbed the bottle of bourbon from the desk. "I mean, he lied to me. He said cats got in through his basement window. But I saw the basement window. It was under a grille in the ground."

Jago leaned out of the window, turning his head in the direction of Grady Spencer's house.

"I just thought he was wanting company. He's always alone and

I've never seen anyone visit. But then, at the top of the basement steps . . ."

"What?"

Nat shook her head, feeling increasingly troubled. "I don't know. It sounds stupid. I felt like he wanted to hurt me."

By the window, Jago was frantically rubbing his chin. "Maybe we've been looking in the wrong places all this time."

Nat raised an eyebrow. "You're not saying Grady Spencer had something to do with Noah's disappearance? Come on, he's an old man."

"You just said it yourself. He wanted to hurt you."

"But it doesn't make sense. What about Cal? Where does he fit into it?"

Something stirred inside Nat's mind. Maybe it did make sense. Most murderers were known to their victims. Often, they were friends or family. Sometimes even neighbours.

A chill gripped her. Was that what Grady Spencer had been planning this afternoon? Jago was on his feet and pacing the floor.

"Grady lives two doors down from us. He's always walking up and down with that stupid dog. Noah loves animals. He would have gone with him easily."

"What if I'm wrong?" Nat said, worried. She didn't want to be responsible for wrongly accusing an innocent man. But the more she thought about it, the more convinced she became that something wasn't right about Grady Spencer. And it was more than loneliness. She could still feel his eyes on her. His breath on the back of her neck. She set down her glass. Had he been trying to lure her into the basement? What would she have found down there?

"I should have seen it," Jago said, his movements crackling with energy. "He didn't even cross my mind."

"No one's going to suspect an old man. Not even an old bastard like Grady Spencer."

Jago stopped pacing. He stared at her with wide, dilated eyes.

"I'm going over there," he said.

"But Carrie—"

"Carrie could be wrong for all we know."

"*We* could be wrong." Nat jumped to her feet. "You can't just go and break into his house."

Jago was already grabbing his jacket. "I'll just look around outside."

"It's a bad idea."

"No, it isn't. It's the best idea I've had all day." He hurried to the door. "Are you coming?"

Nat's throat dried. She emptied the remnants of her glass and winced at the burn. The dread she'd felt in Grady Spencer's house hooked its claws in her skin. She couldn't go over there again. Even if Noah was still alive, trapped down there in the basement.

She shook her head. Every cell of her body was repelled by the thought of returning to Grady Spencer's.

But Jago didn't look disappointed. He looked alive.

"Stay here if you want."

"I can't. Rose wanted me home already."

He nodded as he pulled open the door.

"Jago, be careful."

He smiled. "Stay awake. I'll call you."

Then he was gone, leaving Nat standing in his bedroom, fear and excitement and dread spinning around her, making her dizzy.

"You better," she whispered. "Or I'll kill you myself."

47

The tunnel was endless, twisting and turning. One moment descending, the next growing steeper. Carrie's ankle throbbed as she stumbled forward. Shock and horror clawed at her heart. Terrible images flashed behind her eyes like strobe lighting. She tried to force them out. But it was impossible. They were burned into her memory, and they would remain there like scars until she died.

She'd lost track of how long she'd been following the tunnel. It could have been a minute. It could have been an hour. The lack of space disoriented her. The lack of oxygen made her dizzy. Cal had raced ahead. She'd ceased hearing his running footsteps a while ago.

But she pressed on. She had to find him. She had to understand.

Noah's stuffed blue bear swung limply from her left hand.

Noah. Poor Noah.

He hadn't deserved such a horrible fate, such a terrible final resting place. She would make sure the Pengellys had everything they needed to give him a beautiful farewell. It was the least she could do.

The tunnel was growing narrower, the ceiling lower. Carrie

stooped. Her fists scraped against rock. The ceiling dropped another two inches, raking against her scalp. She cried out in pain and fell to her knees. The torch flew from her hand and hit the ground, smashing the bulb and plunging her into darkness.

Claustrophobia took hold. A strangled shriek escaped her mouth. She squeezed Noah's blue bear against her chest.

Get a hold of yourself. If you don't, you're going to die down here.

Carrie sobbed. She sucked in stale air and dust, then expelled it in a series of coughs and splutters. Cal had come this way. Which meant there had to be an exit. She would have to find it in the dark.

Climbing to her feet, she left the broken torch on the ground and hobbled forward, slower this time, and using her hand as a guide.

She waited for her eyes to adjust to the dark. But there was nothing to adjust to. Only fathomless, infinite nothingness.

She pressed on, fingers brushing along the wall, Noah's bear clutched to her side. The ground started to rise again. Soon, it began to level out.

Carrie paused, catching her breath and taking the weight off her injured ankle. Then she was on the move once more, pushing through her terror, determined to catch up with her son.

The tunnel began to turn. She pressed her fingers against the wall and followed its trajectory.

She stopped still. There was light up ahead.

Almost crying, Carrie quickened her pace. She gritted her teeth as fresh pain shot through her ankle.

As the tunnel came to an end, she saw that the light was seeping through slats of a thick wooden door. Carrie lurched forward. She wrapped her fingers around the iron handle and pressed her ear to the wood. There was nothing. Only the thump of blood pumping through her veins.

She had no idea what might lie on the other side, waiting for her, but Cal had to have come through this way. Which meant she had to follow.

Carrie tugged on the door. It was old and stiff, the wood warped. Dropping Noah's bear on the ground, she took the handle between both hands and pulled. The door groaned as it grated against the jamb.

It swung open, flooding the tunnel with yellow light.

Carrie blinked, lifting a hand in front of her eyes. She waited a few moments for her vision to adjust. Then, with Noah's bear back safely in her arms, she exited the tunnel.

And stepped into another basement.

This one was L-shaped but not as cavernous. It was cleaner, the air drier. Shelves lined the walls, filled with boxes of things. A workbench sat at the centre. Above it, a naked bulb hung from a cord.

Carrie limped further into the space, her eyes swivelling side to side as she took in her surroundings.

An odour hung in the air. Cleaning products. Bleach. A trace of something else beneath it. Something that immediately transported her back to the horrors of the Mermaid Hotel.

What was this place?

It looked like the kind of basement found beneath a suburban home. Confusion clouding her mind, she looked over her shoulder, back at the door that led to the tunnel. She took another step forward, her eyes focused on the workbench.

Any remaining confusion was swept away.

It was no ordinary workbench, she realised. Because ordinary workbenches didn't have wrist and ankle restraints.

She came closer. The bleach smell grew stronger.

A stainless-steel trolley stood close by. Sparkling surgical instruments were laid out on top. She inched away from it, her back pressed against the shelves as she rounded the corner.

As she glimpsed to see what lay in wait on the other side, her limbs went numb. At the far end of the room, three large cages were stacked against the wall. Two of them were cast in shadows, but light spilled over the third.

An animal lay inside. At first, Carrie thought it was a large dog.

Then the animal moved and she saw it was no animal at all. Hands appeared, wrapping fingers around the iron bars.

Human hands.

It was Cal. Her son.

He glanced at her with sad eyes as she stared at him in horror. His gaze shifted to a point just above her shoulder.

Carrie smelled Grady Spencer before she laid eyes on him.

She spun on her feet. Pain tore through her ankle.

The old man stood over her, naked light painting his skin and illuminating his devilish sneer.

"Ah, Carrie, I was just coming to see you," he said. "You've saved me the walk."

Before she could react, Grady brought the paperweight crashing down on her head.

The basement flashed white. Then red.

Carrie fell to the ground.

48

SHE WOKE ON HER BACK. Pain ripped through her skull. She tried to raise a hand to soothe it but found she could not. A shadow loomed over her, cutting through the light. In an instant, she recalled what had happened.

"There you are," Grady Spencer said. "What a surprise to find you. I was going to stop by your house. The boy needs to learn a lesson, you see. He needs to learn his place is here, so he doesn't run off again. And he can't run back to you if you're gone."

Ignoring the pounding in her head, Carrie pulled at the restraints.

"You needn't bother with that," Grady said. "Everyone tries but everyone fails."

"You took him from me," Carrie gasped. She turned to see Cal watching her from between the bars. "You changed him."

"I didn't take nothing from no one, I didn't. He found me. Came wandering in through the same door as you. Only he was dripping wet and half naked. Came up from the beach, he did. Found his way here. He came to me when I was all alone. And now he's mine. He's been mine for years."

Grady Spencer lowered his face until it was inches from Carrie's. "You don't want him anyway. You replaced him. Don't even know why you're here."

Carrie swallowed, tasting blood. She pulled at the restraints.

"I'm here," she said, "because I love my son. Because you took him from me and I want him back."

Grady's face twisted with anger. He turned his attention to the instruments on the trolley.

"He's mine. My boy. My good doggy. Isn't that right?" He glanced over at Cal, who watched him closely.

Carrie slumped, conserving her dwindling energy. He had been here all along. She didn't know how but Cal had wandered like a fly into a spider's web.

He had been trapped here with Grady Spencer. A monster in the guise of a man. He had been here, just a few hundred metres from his home. Locked in a cage, starved, beaten, treated like an animal. A thing.

Carrie turned to her son.

"I'm sorry," she said, tears spilling onto the bench. "We should have looked harder. We should have found you."

Cal watched her silently, his head cocked.

A clatter directed Carrie's attention back to Grady Spencer, who was rifling through the instruments on the tray.

"I'm surprised you're not begging yet," he said. "That journalist cried like a baby. Pissed himself, too."

"And what about Noah?" Carrie hissed. She wrapped fingers around the restraint cords, searching for an escape. "Did he beg? Did he cry?"

The restraints were fool proof. She wasn't getting out.

"I never touched the Pengelly boy," Grady said, picking up a scalpel and twisting it in his fingers. "That little rat has nothing to do with me. You should ask your boy about him."

All the air rushed from the room. Carrie stared in horror at Cal. He stared right back.

"You're a liar," she stammered. "Cal wouldn't hurt a fly."

"Tell that to Margaret Telford's dog. By the time he was done, there was nothing left."

The room was spinning. Her vision wavering. "No, you're lying to me."

"Am I? Who do you think took the Pengelly boy from his garden? An old man like me with bad knees?" Grady smiled with pride. "The boy needed to start somewhere, didn't he?"

"No. I don't believe it."

Carrie shook her head. Nausea bubbled in her throat. Her son was not a killer. He was good and kind. He loved nature and animals and the colour blue. When he grew up, he was going to be a pirate, sailing the seven seas in search of buried treasure. He was not a monster, lurking in the dark. He was the light that cast it out.

Tears slipped from Carrie's eyes. "It's not true. It can't be true. I'll never believe it."

"People will always believe what they want to believe," Grady said. "They believed he'd be better off at the farm. But the boy came back to me. You believed your son was dead. And you replaced him. He believed you didn't want him anymore. And it was true. That's why he came back to me. Because I believe in him. Because I'm his master."

Carrie turned to Cal. Pain tore through her head. "It's not true. You know that, don't you? I love you, Cal. Your home is with me."

Grady snatched strands of Carrie's hair and pulled.

"*This* is the boy's home! He belongs to me! He does what I tell him. He hunts and he cuts, and he does it for me." His eyes grew dark. Saliva bubbled at the corners of his mouth. "He left me once because he was confused. But he came back to me. And now he'll never leave again."

Grady nodded at the cage. Carrie watched in horror as Cal pushed open the door and climbed out.

He stood for a moment, stretching his limbs.

From somewhere upstairs, Caliban began to bark. Grady Spencer grinned, exposing his teeth. He held out the scalpel.

"Now you'll see how well your boy has learned to cut," he said.

Cal came forward, his eyes fixed on the blade.

Carrie shook her head. She tore at the restraints.

Cal came closer, staring up at the old man. He plucked the scalpel from his fingers.

"Please, Cal." Carrie's body trembled violently. "Help me. Cut me loose."

Cal turned to face her. She stared into his eyes and saw a void.

"I'm your mother," she whispered.

"Do it, boy," Grady said, rubbing his hands together. "Show your father how well he's taught you."

"Please, Cal. Remember who you are. You're my son. I love you!"

Cal hesitated. His eyes moved from the blade to his mother's face.

Grady lashed out, cracking him across the top of the head. He struck him again.

"Do as you're told, boy," the old man said.

Cal straightened. He raised the scalpel.

"I'm your mother!" Carrie shrieked.

He advanced upon her.

49

JAGO STOOD IN THE STREET, watching Grady Spencer's house. All the lights were on, illuminating the dark, but curtains prevented him from seeing inside. When Nat had told him about her encounter, it was as if a lightning bolt had fired through the top of his skull, down to his feet.

In an instant, he'd known that Grady was responsible for Noah's disappearance. He had no evidence. No proof.

But he was sure.

He had known the old man for as long as he could remember. As far as he was aware, Grady had lived in this house for decades. He had never heard his mother mention friends or family, although he recalled seeing a visitor once; a tall, striking man in his forties, who'd pulled up in an old pickup truck. He remembered the man because, except for the postman, no one came to visit Grady Spencer's house.

Despite his solitude, the old man was a well-known face in the cove, if not a well-liked one. When Noah had disappeared, he had never been considered a suspect. Or if he had, it was only ever for a passing moment.

Who would suspect an elderly man of snatching a child from a backyard? Not the police. Not the inhabitants of Devil's Cove. Not even Jago.

He cursed himself as he opened the gate and jogged up the path. He stopped at the front door. Perhaps he should ring the buzzer, then rush the old man. There was that dog of his to contend with, but it was small and easily taken care of.

Jago's finger hovered over the buzzer. He hesitated.

Alternatively, he could look for an unlocked window and sneak inside. Then he would have the element of surprise on his side.

Following the path around the side of the house, he caught a glimpse of Nat walking up the street. She hadn't seen him. He stopped and watched her for a second, feeling a tenderness that surprised him. If she wasn't so completely obsessed with Sierra Davis, he might have taken a chance and asked her out. He pictured the horror on her face as she walked through Rose's garden and disappeared from view.

Moving quietly, Jago moved in between the clutter blocking his path, and rounded the corner. He caught his breath as he entered the backyard. Nat had described the maze of junk in vivid detail, but it was still an unnerving sight to behold.

The man must have kept every possession he'd ever owned. What a lonely life, Jago thought. Then, angry at himself for pitying the man who'd taken his brother, he turned his attention to the rear of the house.

There were lights on upstairs. The back door was windowless, the paintwork cracked and peeling. Jago reached out and tried the handle. It was locked. All the windows were closed. Somewhere inside, Grady's dog began to bark.

Nat had mentioned a basement window. Stepping back, he stared at the ground. Sure enough, he saw yellow light illuminating a grille in the ground. He crouched down and peered through the bars. The window was small and rectangular, not large enough for him to crawl through, even if he could get past the grille.

There was a light on down there. He could see the top of some shelves, a cement floor.

Jago lay down on his stomach and pressed his face against the grille. The wound in his neck flared with fresh pain.

He couldn't see anything else. The angle was all wrong.

He was going through the front door. He had no choice. Even if his instincts were wrong, even if he was arrested for breaking and entering, at least he would know of one more place where Noah wasn't to be found.

He was drunk enough, angry enough, and tired enough to break into every house in the cove if he had to. Maybe that was what needed to be done.

Jago got to his feet.

That was when he heard the scream.

He caught his breath. It had come from beneath him, vibrating through the grille and up his legs, making his teeth clatter.

An icy dread gripped him as he listened, but all he heard now was the rustle of leaves as a breeze blew through the branches of Briar Wood.

He hadn't imagined it. The screams had been real.

Adrenaline fired through him. Reaching for the back door, he grabbed the handle and slammed his shoulder into the wood. The door wouldn't budge. He whirled around, found an old car battery near his feet, and heaved it into his arms.

There was a window by the door. He ran at it.

The car battery struck the glass. The window imploded. Glass rained down. Covering his fist with his sleeve, Jago knocked out the remaining loose shards and hoisted himself through.

He was in a cluttered kitchen. Towers of books and newspapers filled the floor. There was a smell. Like air from an ancient tomb.

Spotting a block of knives, Jago removed the largest blade and ran into the hall.

He turned in time to see Caliban shooting towards him,

yapping and snarling and flashing his teeth. He opened his jaws and lunged for Jago's ankle.

Jago dodged. He swung his foot, sending the dog tumbling and rolling along the floor. Caliban yelped. He scrambled onto his paws and growled. But he did not attack again.

The layout of the house was identical to Jago's. The basement door was on his right. He threw it open. His fingers gripping the knife handle, he charged down the steps.

There was a door at the bottom. He threw his shoulder into it.

Jago charged into the basement.

And slid to a halt.

In the centre of the room, Carrie Killigrew was strapped to a bench. Cal leaned over her, a bloody scalpel in his hand.

Next to them, Grady Spencer stood, grinning from ear to ear, watching the scene with rabid excitement.

All three turned as Jago entered.

His eyes darted from face to face. He ran forward, skirting around the bench, heading straight for Cal.

He slammed into him, knocking him into the shelves behind. Boxes crashed to the ground. The scalpel flew from Cal's hand. Stunned, he tried to get to his feet.

Jago brought his knee up, slamming it into his temple. Cal's head struck the shelf. He went down. His eyelids fluttered. His body grew still.

Jago swooped down and picked up the scalpel. He turned on Grady. "Where's my brother?"

The old man stared at him, open-mouthed. He erupted with laughter.

"The cavalry has arrived!" he said, slapping his thigh.

On the bench, Carrie groaned. Blood matted her hair. A dark wet stain was spreading on the arm of her shirt. Jago moved to her, discarding the scalpel but keeping the knife trained on the old man.

"Where's Noah?" he said, loosening the strap around Carrie's left wrist.

"Jago," she groaned. "We need to go."

"I'm not leaving without my brother." He freed her other arm while Grady watched, a twisted smile on his lips. Jago waved the knife. "Tell me where he is."

The old man threw his hands into the air. His smile widened. "I've already told *her*. It's nothing to do with me."

"Jago, please." Carrie pushed herself up, wincing as she began to unbuckle the restraints on her ankles.

A deep panic was rising from the depths of Jago's stomach. Sweat broke out on his brow. His eyes darted around the room then flew back to Grady Spencer.

"Tell me or I'll kill you," he said. The knife trembled in his hand.

The old man continued to laugh.

Carrie freed one ankle then the other.

Jago turned and saw the cages, cloaked by shadows. His eyes moved back to Cal, who remained unmoving on the ground, then scanned the shelves.

"Please, Jago," Carrie said, her voice strangled with fear.

Jago caught his breath. Noah's bear was sitting on a shelf, its one eye twinkling.

He saw the blood a second later.

"Noah…"

A strange calm washed over him. Every stab of pain, every morsel of grief and fear he had endured the last two months fell away.

There was nothing inside him. Everything was gone.

He was empty. Dead.

Jago stared at the bear. The bear smiled at him.

At the same time, the smile faded from Grady Spencer's mouth. His eyes grew wide and uncertain. He shook his head and pointed at the cages.

Before he could speak, Jago stepped forward, brought the knife up, and slit the old man's throat.

He turned back to the shelf and grabbed the bear, cradling it to his chest as Grady collapsed to the floor, where he choked and gurgled, his blood spreading out in a deep, black pool.

From a million miles away, Jago felt a gentle hand on his shoulder. He heard Carrie urging him to leave.

Pressing the bear to his chest, he turned to go with her.

A tiny, slurred voice stopped him in his tracks.

"Jago?"

Slowly, he turned. Beside him, Carrie drew in a shocked gasp. They both looked towards the cages. From the darkness of the centre cage, a small, trembling hand reached between the bars. Then fell limp.

Jago rushed forward. Behind him, Carrie stared with wide eyes. Reaching the cage, Jago peered into the shadows.

"Noah?"

He could just make out a small, unmoving shape in the darkness. A padlock secured the cage door. Jago pulled at it then frantically looked around.

Behind him, Carrie stooped over Grady's dying body and rifled through his pockets. Finding a bunch of keys, she hurried over and handed them to Jago. He rifled through the keys, slipping one into the lock, then trying another. The third key snapped to the left. The cage door swung open.

Holding his breath, Jago reached into the shadows.

And pulled out his brother.

He was painfully thin and caked in dirt. Dark shadows circled vacant eyes. He was drifting in and out of consciousness.

But Noah Pengelly was alive.

Tears streamed down Jago's face.

"Hello, little buddy," he said. "How are you doing?"

Noah's haunted eyes opened. He looked up at Jago.

"I want to go home." His voice was small and trembling.

Jago pressed his brother to his chest. More tears spilled down his cheeks.

"We can do that," he laughed. "Why not? Let's go home."

He stood, Noah's legs and arms wrapped around his body, his cheek pressed against his own.

Beside him, Carrie reached out and stroked Noah's face. But she did not smile. Her face was blank. Her eyes haunted by ghosts.

"Come on," Jago said. "I need to get him out of here."

They turned to leave.

And saw Cal blocking their way.

50

CARRIE STARED AT HER SON. She no longer recognised him. Blood trickled down the side of his head. One of his eyes had closed over. The skin around it was bruised and swollen. The other was fixed on her. Sweat poured from his brow. His chest heaved up and down. In his hand, he held a large knife with a serrated edge.

"Cal . . ." she breathed.

Beside her Jago clutched Noah to his chest.

Her son was in there somewhere, beneath the feral exterior. Grady Spencer had tried to destroy him. To tear him down so he could build him up into something terrible. Something resembling himself. But there was goodness still in there.

There had to be.

He had hesitated before cutting her. And he hadn't gone for her throat, just her arm. Cal was still in there somewhere, drowning in darkness. If only she could reach him.

"Cal, baby," Carrie said, raising her hands, palms out. "It's over now. You're safe. Put the knife down and come to me."

She opened her arms up, inviting him in. Cal remained unmoving, his gaze shifting between Carrie and the Pengelly boys.

"Come on, now. Put it down. No one's going to hurt you. You're safe."

But Cal did not put the knife down.

"You've done a good thing," Carrie said. "You led me here so we could save Noah. That makes you a hero, Cal. Do you realise that?"

Jago opened his mouth to protest. One look from Carrie made him shut it again.

She took a small step forward. Cal immediately tensed. He pointed the knife at her.

"Do you remember when you were a little boy and you found a bird in the back garden? It had flown into the window and broken its wing. You picked it up and you laid it inside a box, on a bed of grass. And you took care of it. You brought it worms to eat. You fed it drops of water from an old baby's bottle. And when it died, you buried it yourself. You cried, but you told me you knew the bird was happy now because it was no longer in pain." Carrie was crying without realising it. "You don't want to hurt anyone, Cal."

She stared at her son, her heart breaking, over and over. He was that bird now, his mind a broken wing. But he didn't need to die to be free of pain.

She could take it away. She could heal him.

Carrie took another step closer.

"Please Cal," she said. "I love you. I've always loved you. Let the boys go."

Cal lowered the knife an inch. His gaze shifted to Jago, then to Noah, who stared back at him with dull, drooping eyes.

"Let them go. I'll stay here with you. It'll be just the two of us. We can talk."

Cal glanced down at Grady Spencer's cooling body lying in a dark expanse of blood.

His shoulders sagged. His head lowered.

Carrie felt anger and envy rampage through her body. *He's not your father! He's not the one who loves you, who birthed you. Who spent the last seven years reliving the day you disappeared, over and over.*

She swallowed her anger down and nodded at Jago.

"Go," she said.

Jago's grip tightened around his brother. He stared at her uncertainly.

"Go now."

Jago inched forward.

Cal's head snapped up. He raised the knife. His lips parted and exposed his teeth.

"Keep going," Carrie urged. She stepped forward, putting herself between the Pengelly boys and her son. "They're leaving now, Cal. We can, too. We can go home, just the two of us. Melissa's at her grandparents. We'll have the house to ourselves. We can get you cleaned up then make some hot chocolate. And we can sit and talk, just like we used to."

Jago moved closer to the door. Cal turned, pointing the knife at him.

Carrie moved closer. "Look at me, Cal. Keep your eyes on me."

Cal leaned forward and swiped the knife through the air—a warning that if Jago took another step forward, it would be his last.

Noah began to cry in his brother's arms.

Carrie took another step towards her son.

"Let them go," she said, raising her voice. "Come home with me. You never have to see this place again."

"Carrie . . ." Jago's voice was trembling.

"Go. Now."

"But—"

"I mean it!"

Clutching his brother to his chest, Jago swallowed and trained his eyes on the basement door. He moved forward.

Cal raised the knife above his head.

He parted his teeth and emitted a terrible, hissing shriek.

Jago broke into a run.

Cal lunged, bringing the knife down.

Carrie ploughed into him, lifting him into the air. They hit the ground together and rolled.

Jago didn't look back. With Noah wailing in his arms, he wrenched open the red door and flew up the basement steps.

The air had been knocked from Carrie's lungs.

Beneath her, Cal bucked and kicked. He opened his jaws and snapped at her, narrowly missing her neck. A low growl gurgled in his throat.

The knife was still in his hand. Carrie grabbed his wrist and smashed it against the ground. The knife clattered away.

Cal howled in pain.

"I've got you," Carrie breathed. "I'm right here."

She pushed herself up, pressing down on his wrists, watching him squirm and thrash beneath her.

And then, like a candle being snuffed out, the fight left him.

The pain and fury that was twisting his face melted away. A tear slipped from his eye. Cal grew very still.

Spent and exhausted, Carrie waited, holding him down until she was sure the anger was gone. She waited another minute. Then, very slowly, she released him. She sat back, pulling her knees up to her chest. Cal was motionless for the longest time, gazing into the lifeless eyes of the man who'd kept him prisoner for seven years. Who'd tried to take his humanity away. Who had tried to mould him in his own image.

"Cal?" Carrie watched her son watching the dead man.

Darkness returned to his eyes. Slowly, Cal sat up.

The knife lay just a metre away.

"Cal? Baby?"

Cal got to his feet. He glanced down at Carrie. There was nothing there. All his humanity was gone. She had lost him.

He reached for the knife.

Carrie pushed herself away on her hands. Her back struck the shelves. Cal stared at the blade that was now back in his hand. He stared at Grady's body, at his mother.

Carrie tried to pull herself up.

He loomed over her, this boy who had once been her son.

She stared up at him and it was like staring into space. She held her breath and shut her eyes. She waited for the pain to come. For her blood to flow.

For her son to end her life.

But he didn't.

Carrie opened her eyes in time to see him run from the basement and into the tunnel. The old door slammed behind him.

Then he was gone. Lost to her.

Carrie sat against the shelves for the longest time, staring at Grady Spencer's corpse.

She wanted to bring him back to life so that she could watch him die, over and over again. She wanted to reverse time, back to that Saturday morning when Cal had whined and whined until she had relented and agreed to take him to the beach.

She could do none of these things.

Instead, with every inch of her body aching, Carrie pushed herself up against the shelves and onto her feet.

She looked back at the old, wooden door that led to the tunnel, that led to Cal.

Then, finding the last of her strength, she hobbled from the basement and climbed the steps of Grady Spencer's house of death.

The front door was open, letting in the night time breeze. Caliban was nowhere to be seen.

She dragged herself forward, barely registering the towers of newspapers, magazines and old boxes that littered the hall.

She reached the door. She stepped through it.

Outside, the street was alive with chatter. Carrie stumbled along the garden path and reached the gate. The road was full of people, neighbours who had come out in force. She saw Rose and Nat standing side by side, arms wrapped around each other.

All eyes were on the trio, who stood in the middle of the road, entangled in laughter and tears and a never-ending embrace.

Tess Pengelly wept uncontrollably as she planted kisses on her boys' faces. Noah winced and looked confused. Jago laughed and ruffled his hair.

No one noticed Carrie leaning on Grady Spencer's garden gate. But she watched them all.

She tried to smile. And found she couldn't.

51

THE HOSPITAL WAS BUZZING with noise and activity. Carrie sat up in bed, feeling grateful for the private room she'd been given. She would be here overnight, a precaution against the concussion Grady Spencer had given her. The rest of her wounds were cleaned and dressed. Her ankle was badly sprained but would recover with rest.

There were parts of her, however, that could not be healed.

She stared through the open door at the uniformed police officer stationed outside her room. Another officer had been sent to Joy and Gary Killigrew's house. Dylan had been contacted via radio. By sheer coincidence, the fishing trawler was returning home early. A storm was coming. One that had made the crew nervous.

Noah Pengelly had also been admitted to the hospital, where he would no doubt remain at least for a few days.

Carrie should have felt joy and relief to know the boy was alive. That she had played a part in saving his life.

But she felt nothing.

Her son was gone. Vanished from her life again. Only this time, it had been his choice.

A fresh wave of nausea washed over her. She leaned back on the pillows and closed her eyes. She must have drifted off for a short while because when she opened them again, Detective Turner was sitting in the chair beside the bed.

Another detective, a woman she hadn't seen before, stood talking to the uniformed officer outside.

"How are you doing?" Turner asked. He leaned forward, his face lined with concern.

Carrie glanced away. She shook her head and instantly regretted it. When the room righted itself again, she turned to face him.

"Have you found Cal?"

"I'm afraid not."

"What will happen if you catch him?"

"I'm not sure. I suppose it will depend on what else they find at Grady Spencer's. CSI is there right now. There's another unit on the way to the hotel. They could be there for days."

"What do you mean it depends on what else they find?"

The detective paused, a troubled look on his face. "Human remains have been found at the house, Carrie. Some old. Some more recent. We have to consider the fact that Cal may be implicated in murder."

Carrie shook her head wildly. "Grady said Noah was supposed to be Cal's first . . . He'd been keeping him alive in case Cal came back. So that Cal could . . ."

She turned away. *So that Cal could kill him. And Grady could rejoice in Cal's transformation into a cold-blooded psychopath.*

Carrie looked at Turner. "Have you checked the tunnel? That's where he went. That's how he . . ."

"We have a handful of officers searching it now." He leaned closer. "It looks like the tunnel splits in two. One branch leads from Spencer's house to the hotel, the other from the house down to a cave near the beach, just past that arch of rock. What did you say it was called?"

"The Devil's Gate."

Carrie felt the hairs on her arms spring up. As a child, she'd heard the stories about old smugglers' tunnels hidden beneath the streets of Porth an Jowl. As much as they sounded like something straight out of *Treasure Island*, plenty of tunnels had been located around the coast of Cornwall, leading from sea caves to old inns, shops, and abodes, where plundered cargo would be stowed away, waiting to be sold on. Carrie had thought all those tunnels had been sealed up.

Seven years ago, on the beach, while she'd been preoccupied, Cal had gone in search of hidden treasures. He'd found hell instead.

Detective Turner glanced over his shoulder. "DS Mills would like to talk to you, if you're up to it. We need to take a statement."

Carrie followed his gaze. "What about Melissa?"

"There's an officer right inside. Your daughter is safe."

"I want her here with me."

"I'm sure that can be arranged if you think it's necessary."

Melissa's drawing flashed in Carrie's mind. "It is. How's Noah?"

"Traumatised. Undernourished. But he's going to be fine. Thanks to you."

Something passed over his face. A look of frustration, maybe. Or disappointment. Carrie could understand why, but she was in no mood to be lectured about taking the law into her own hands.

Ignoring her throbbing ankle, she brought her knees up to her chest. Her boy was gone. Lost to the sea. Lost to Grady Spencer.

She thought about the skull she'd found hidden beneath Noah's stuffed bear. Had there been others before Cal? Missing children who had refused to bend to Grady's sick ways.

She pushed horrible images from her mind.

Something else sprang into her thoughts. Something Grady had said.

"'They believed he'd be better off at the farm. But the boy came back to me.'"

Turner stared at her, confused.

"That's what Grady Spencer told me. I don't understand what it means."

"The farm?" Detective Turner mused. He shook his head. Out in the corridor, the female detective raised her eyebrows. "I believe DS Mills would like to talk to you now, if you're ready."

On the bedside cabinet, Carrie's mobile phone began to buzz. From somewhere beneath the numb haze, she felt her heart leap.

"I need five minutes."

Turner nodded. He stared at her with an expression that fell between pity and respect.

"Take care of yourself, Carrie," he said, standing. "For what it's worth, I'm sorry."

Carrie watched him walk away. She picked up the phone.

Dylan's panicked voice filled her ear.

As she soothed and assured him that his wife and daughter were safe, thoughts of her son filled her mind. He was out there somewhere. Frightened. Confused. As lost as she was without him.

She could no longer feel that invisible cord connecting them. It had disappeared when Cal had escaped into the tunnel, severed by the closing door.

He was alone now.

But Carrie was not. And knowing she was not alone would get her through the coming weeks and months. It would be the one thing to stop her from falling into a dark and infinite abyss.

"I love you, Dylan," she said into the phone, interrupting him.

There was a moment of static silence.

"I love you right back," he replied. "And I'll be home soon."

Carrie hung up. The quiet of the room bore down on her. She felt the abyss calling to her like a Siren, luring her towards the edge.

I am not alone, she thought.

I am not alone.

52

DAWN WAS BREAKING as Cal emerged from the trees and into a cornfield. Above him, the sky was painted in swathes of purple and tangerine. He stopped still, his breath snatched away. He'd spent so long in the darkness of Grady Spencer's basement that he could navigate the shadows as if he were walking through daylight. Every sunrise was precious to him. A magical, miraculous sight to behold. He stood for a long time, his mouth open, molten fire reflected in his eyes. Then his mother's face put out the lights, and darkness returned to him.

He got moving again, taking long strides between the rows of towering corn, until he cleared the field.

The farmhouse looked abandoned. Paint peeled off the window frames. Guttering hung from the roof. The rear garden was a barren stretch of rocks and weeds. Circling the house, he strode past a water tank and an old, disused harvester, which had rusted over time and been reclaimed by nature.

It was early. They would all be asleep. He wondered if they would welcome him with open arms or if they would turn their backs, just like he had done to them. It had been a mistake to leave the farm and return to Grady Spencer. His master had been angry. He had beaten Cal daily. It was his lesson, Grady had said. A lesson to learn how rejection felt.

Weeks later, when he'd finally been granted freedom from the cage, Cal had gone wandering, exploring the hotel while Grady napped, or sneaking outside into Briar Wood. One evening, he'd returned with Noah.

Grady had mistakenly thought Cal had chosen the boy to be his first kill. But Cal had been lonely. He'd needed a friend to play with. And Noah had reminded him so much of Jago.

Like the front of the farmhouse, the windows at the back were boarded up. A cat, flea-bitten and malnourished, sidled up to Cal and rubbed against his calves. Cal bent down and gave the animal an affectionate scratch. The cat purred and spun a full circle.

Grady had handed Cal a large kitchen knife. "This is a rite of passage," he'd said. "The boy becomes a man."

And Cal had almost done it. He'd pressed the knife to Noah's throat until a thin red line had appeared in his skin. Part of him, the part that had become like Grady, had wanted to press harder. Just like when he'd practiced on those animals.

But he couldn't do it. Noah was good and kind. He did not deserve to die. Cal should have taken him to the farm, where he would have been safe from the evils of the world. Where he could learn about the new dawn that was coming.

Cal had refused to kill Noah. Grady had said he wasn't ready. That he was a disappointment.

He'd brought the knife to him again two weeks later. When Cal had failed to use it once more, Grady had beaten him until the room went dark.

Then, when Grady had returned a third time with the knife, and had held Noah upside down like a chicken on a butcher's hook, Cal had become afraid.

A voice had whispered in his mind: *Kill him.*

He'd run from the basement, leaving Noah alone with Grady

Spencer. He'd run through the tunnel, down and down, until he'd reached the sea. And he'd stood there for the longest time, swaying in the wind, wondering what kind of a boy he was becoming.

Once he had cared for an injured bird that he knew would die. He had given it comfort, held it in his hands until its time came. Now, he'd put a knife to a little boy's throat and had wanted to open him up.

Standing at the mouth of the cave, Cal had listened to the sea calling him. He had let it take him. It should have swept him far out, where pirates sailed the seven seas in search of buried treasure.

Instead the sea had rejected him, spitting him out onto the beach. Because the sea had known exactly what kind of a boy he was.

Margaret Telford shouldn't have saved him. That was why he'd punished her. He hadn't wanted to be saved.

At his ankles, the cat let out a long, whiny mewl. He would bring it scraps of food, if he were welcomed back. If not, he and the cat would go hungry together.

Pacing up to the old red door, Cal's hand hovered over the handle. He hesitated. Then knocked.

He waited. The cat lost interest and sauntered away.

Finally, he heard footsteps shuffling inside. Locks were drawn back. The door opened. A woman, tall and round, with a lined face and a ruddy complexion, stared out at him. Her expression was stern, her eyes hardened.

"Well," she said. "Here's a face I didn't expect to see again."

Cal lowered his head and stared at the ground.

"Grown tired of you, has he?"

Cal shook his head.

"Found himself a new toy?" The woman ran a hand through her short, red hair. "What is it, then? Grew tired of being treated worse than an animal, did you?"

Shame burned Cal's cheeks. Grady's dead eyes stared at him from the shadows.

"Spit it out, boy. Or does the cat still have your tongue?"

Cal looked up. Tears brimmed in his eyes. The woman's face softened. She grew worried. "Something's happened."

He nodded.

"Something bad?"

He nodded again.

"Best you come in, boy, and talk to Jacob. No one followed you, did they?" The woman hovered for a moment, glancing over Cal's shoulder at the farmland beyond. "Come on now. Don't be shy. This was your home for a time. It can be again."

Cal remained on the doorstep, peering into the farmhouse with nervous eyes. He should never have returned to Grady's house. But his mother didn't want him. He knew it, no matter how much she tried to convince him that she did. All she cared about was her new family and finding Noah.

Now that he was calmer, he was glad she *had* found Noah. And surprised that Grady had kept him alive.

There could only be one reason for that. He'd been keeping him for Cal. Waiting to give him back the knife, so the boy could become a man. Made in his master's image, empty and alone.

Stepping forward, the woman hooked an arm around Cal's shoulder and pulled him towards the house.

"The Dawn Children welcome you back," she said. "Back into the fold with open arms. Now, in you go."

His heart racing, Cal stepped inside.

The woman closed the door.

"I'll put some tea on, warm you up," she said. "Then I'll wake Jacob. And we'll get to the bottom of your troubles."

Cal nodded.

I am not alone, he thought.

I am not alone.

DESPERATION POINT
DEVIL'S COVE TRILOGY BOOK 2

**It began with *The Cove*. Now the suspense continues in the second
book of the Devil's Cove trilogy.**

Devil's Cove used to be a safe place to live. Until a serial killer was caught
hiding behind a familiar face.

As the Cornish community reels in shock, missing teen Cal Anderson has
been implicated in the murders. Desperate for answers, his mother Carrie
is determined to track him down.

But so is someone else...

Crime writer Aaron Black has arrived in town. His career is in ruins and
he's determined to save it by writing a bestseller about the killings. But he
needs Cal, and he'll do anything to find him - even if it means
endangering lives.

Because there's more to the horrifying truth than anyone can imagine.
And for Carrie and her family, the real nightmare is only just beginning.

OUT NOW

ACKNOWLEDGEMENTS

Writing a book is never done alone. Thank you to Natasha Orme, for your stellar editorial work and insight; to Sarah Grey, OT, for your invaluable help with researching hospital procedures and patient aftercare; Andrea Lydon, former CSI, for your amazing insight into all things forensic; Philip Bates and DI Gail Windsor for guiding me through police procedures and the challenges specific to policing Devon & Cornwall; to Alan Burton for translating Devil's Cove into Cornish—*yeghes da!;* to Sarah Hosken for being the best unofficial research assistant; to my family and friends for their continued support, especially Kate Ellis, Alasdair Gray, Dutch Hearn, Casey Hintz-McDonnell, Victor Martinez Cecilia; to my advanced reader team, whose enthusiasm knows no bounds!; to Mr Smith, my absolute favourite.

ABOUT THE AUTHOR

Malcolm Richards crafts stories to keep you guessing from the edge of your seat. He is the author of several crime thrillers and mysteries, including the PI Blake Hollow series, the award-nominated Devil's Cove trilogy, and the Emily Swanson series. Many of his books are set in Cornwall, where he was born and raised.

Before becoming a full-time writer, he worked for several years in the special education sector, teaching and supporting children with complex needs. After living in London for two decades, he now lives in the Somerset countryside with his partner and a cat named Sukey.

Author website: www.malcolmrichardsauthor.com